CRUEL DECEPTION BOOK 1

DEG
of
INNOCENCE

INTERNATIONAL BESTSELLING AUTHOR

VIA MARI

COPYRIGHT

Degrees os Innocence contains content suitable for adults 18+.

Published by Book World Ink

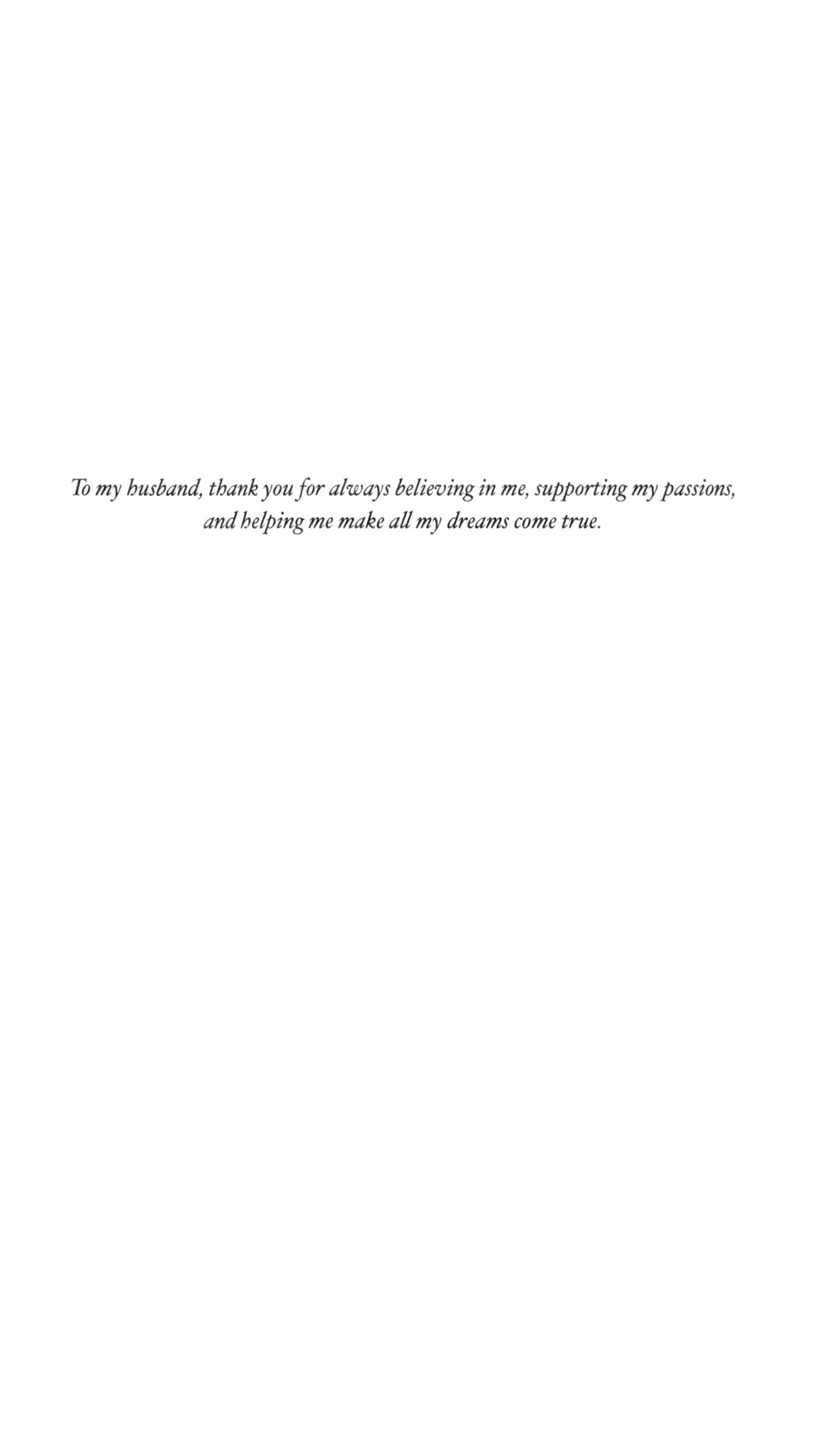

To my husband, thank you for always believing in me, supporting my passions, and helping me make all my dreams come true.

ONE

The weather is warm, with a slight breeze and I imagine the stars will be even brighter as the night continues to encroach. The resort is luxurious, and I can't help but admire the architecture and atmosphere the designer has created with tall taupe-colored pillars, natural stones and glass that allows for expansive views of nature's landscape.

I opt for outdoor dining and take the path leading to the other side of the resort. It's early yet, and I settle onto a barstool next to a couple who are laughing softly and seem to be enjoying each other's company. The young bartender is friendly and chatty as she takes my order, recommending an island specialty called an Aruba Ariba. The drink arrives in an elegant looking glass, adorned by an exotic melon-colored tropical flower. I take a sip and murmur my appreciation to the bartender of its sweetness, although it's slightly stronger than expected. The tiny lights on the distant horizon are mesmerizing. It's hard to tell from this far away if they belong to vessels or something else.

I'm pulled back from my thoughts as the drink in my hand sloshes onto my dress, and the seat beneath me starts to sway. I grab hold of the bar, steadying myself, managing to stand upright just as the man next to me falls to the ground, taking my barstool with him. His wife has turned white and appears in a state of shock. I turn to scan the bar area, looking for help and realize the four of us are the only ones around.

I fall down by the gentleman's side to see if he's just had too much to drink, but he is unresponsive. I yell to the bartender, "Call 9-1-1!" *I wonder if Aruba has 9-1-1...* "Please, get a paramedic right away!" I try to remember my CPR training... Check the breathing. *Is he breathing? The man is not breathing. Oh, shit!* "Get a paramedic down here, please," I hear myself yell. *Okay, just be calm.* I need to start chest compressions. *Oh, God, the man is large, will I be strong enough? Where should the heel of my hand go? Yes... here, I remember.* I need to compress at least two inches each time to deliver enough oxygen. I begin to push on the man's chest, rearranging myself on my hands and knees to use the weight of my body to compress, starting to count as I go. *Dammit, how many compressions? I think it's thirty...* yes. I remember... it's thirty and the last training I went to eliminated rescue breaths. I continue compressing and count out loud. I reach thirty and move to his head to check for breathing. He's still not breathing. Oh, God, please don't let him die! I begin compressions again. "Damn," I exclaim...still nothing. I can feel the burning in my arms. I keep going, pushing deep enough to compress his chest each time praying the paramedics get here soon. I push my body back to alleviate the cramping in my arms. I am aware of sounds behind me, and a male voice yelling. I reach fifteen and keep counting. I continue to count... twenty-two, twenty-three and twenty-four. Then someone is kneeling across from me, and I look up... twenty-five and twenty-six. I'm looking into the face of a man with startling green eyes.

He interrupts my counting. "When you reach thirty, I will take over, and you can watch for his breathing. Switch now!" he commands.

I push myself back and quickly move to the man's head. He is still unresponsive. I am aware of the stranger's intent gaze... he continues compressions, counting aloud with each, until finally we hear the emergency staff coming up the stairs, and a wave of pure relief rushes over me as they affix the AED and after what seems like forever manage to get a pulse. There is a flurry of activity as he is hooked up to monitors and oxygen and the IV is started. He stirs and groans softly and I look over at his wife, emotional myself, as I see the tears of relief pouring down her face as she kisses his hand. She moves out of the way as the paramedics prepare to transport him, walking over to me and embracing me in her arms. "I can't thank you enough," she says between sobs.

I hug her back feeling exhausted, and so grateful that her husband did not die. "I'm just so glad he is alive. Please go be with him," I respond before she is swept away with the paramedics who are quickly pushing the gurney down the ramp to an awaiting ambulance. The thought that this man almost died hits me and I am unable to control the flood of tears that slip down my face. I self-consciously wipe them away as I feel a strong hand on my shoulder.

"Are you okay?" he asks softly, turning me to face him. His eyes are expressive and filled with concern.

"Yes, I'm just so glad that he is alive. I think I'm just a little shaky, that's all. Thank you for taking over. I don't know how much longer I would have lasted. I was scared no one was coming."

"There's no need to thank me. Let's find a table and make sure you're all right," he says, placing a hand on the small of my back and guiding me through the bar area under the natural stone alcoves that lead into a more formal dining area overlooking the sea.

The hostess leads us to a quiet table close to the ocean, and he pulls back the chair for me. "Would you like a glass of wine?" he asks me as the waitress arrives.

"Yes, please," I answer, listening as he orders for the two of us. I realize he's asking me another question and look up. "I'm sorry," I say, realizing I did not hear what he asked.

"I asked your name, but it's clear you may be in a little bit of shock, your hands are trembling," he says.

"I'm sorry, my name is Katarina, but most people call me Kate," I respond.

"It's nice to meet you, Katarina. Most people call me Chase."

I feel the slight warmth of a blush spread across my face as I listen to my given name rolling off this man's tongue. He appears American, but he speaks the language so formally. I find myself taking in his features. Thick sandy brown hair cut short, but not too short. The man's jawline is broad and angular, appearing set as he appraises me. The wine arrives, and I take a sip, enjoying the light, crisp taste before swallowing, realizing he is still looking at me and that I'm beginning to blush again under his scrutiny.

"Katarina, are you okay?" he asks, appearing sincerely concerned. "That man was fortunate you were there. If it weren't for your efforts, he would no longer be alive," he states with a shake of his head.

"I'm fine, but grateful you arrived when you did."

"I was on the other side of the restaurant when I heard someone had collapsed, and a young woman was performing CPR."

"I had just arrived and was enjoying the view when it happened. There wasn't anyone around but the bartender and his wife," I explain.

"So brave," he says pausing for a beat. His deep green eyes are intent and controlled. "Have you eaten this evening, Katarina?" he asks.

"No, I was going to have a drink by the ocean before ordering," I say.

"Good. I haven't either and I think you'll find the food excellent here," he says, handing me a menu and affording me time to peruse.

"What would you like for dinner?" he asks after looking through the menu.

"Anything is fine, thanks," I say, realizing immediately that I haven't even looked at the menu. His eyebrows lift. I don't know what has gotten into me, but I can't seem to take my eyes off him and feel a slow blush growing across my face. "The long day and all the excitement must have gotten to me," I hear myself explaining.

"I see," he says, still holding my gaze. "Do you care for seafood? If so, I'll order bay scallops, an island salad, and Bolo de banana. The meal is done well at this resort."

"Yes, thank you, it sounds lovely." The waiter brings two more glasses of wine, and I realize I have finished my first glass. As I reach over to pick up the newly delivered glass, his hand rests on top of mine, and I'm sure I visibly flinch as I feel the current his touch creates.

"Maybe you should have water, instead, Katarina." I'm slightly confused by his words, but then it dawns on me; my drink splashed all over the front of my dress, and I must be a sweaty mess from the compressions.

I look down and can make out the telltale stains, which now blend into the floral colors of my dress. I wonder if I smell like alcohol and realize he probably thinks I have been drinking this evening. "You're smiling, Katarina," he says breaking through my reverie.

I wish he would stop saying my name like that. The way he pronounces it, rolling it around his tongue and the feel of his hand on mine is unnerving. He finally removes it to pour a glass of water from the pitcher and places it in front of me. He apparently feels some sense of responsibility to make sure I'm okay and not in a state of shock or drunk.

"Chase, I haven't been drinking tonight. I ordered a cocktail just before the man collapsed and it spilled all over me when he fell. I just realized I must look a mess and probably need to eat. I spent the day on the beach and skipped lunch. I was just getting ready to order something when this happened," I explain.

He looks slightly perplexed and almost apologetic. "I'm sure the day has taken a tremendous toll," he says as our food arrives. The scent of butter and garlic waft through the air as the waiter places the seared bay scallops surrounded by a circle of dark red salad, in front of each of us.

"I hope you like Treviso. It's a warm island salad. They grill the leaves in the wood stoves," he says.

"I haven't had it before," I admit before trying a bite. "It's almost like radicchio, but different, almost smoky, and the balsamic and goat cheese are the perfect complements. I take it you've stayed here before."

He nods. "Yes, the resort is a favorite of mine and the food is always well prepared."

I reach to take a sip of wine and watch to see if this is going to meet with further resistance, but other than a slight twitch of his mouth, he refrains, enlightening me with the history of the resort while we eat. The waiter clears the table and lets Chase know he will be back with dessert shortly.

"My favorite part of the meal," he explains with a grin.

The waiter returns and it's easy to see why it's a favorite. The bananas have been grilled, are slightly browned and caramelized, served with a topping of brown sugar and sherry, and adorned with raisins.

"This is so good," I say, taking small bites and marveling in the sweetness of the grilled bananas.

He enlightens me with the history of plantains and the many uses as we finish our dessert, but I'm sure he's anxious to carry on with his evening plans. Almost as confirmation, when the waiter clears our table, he offers to show me around the resort and walk me to my suite.

"Thank you for the offer, but I'm sure you have much better things to do than escort me around. I feel much better, and I do need to get some work done. Will they bring the check?" I ask.

I can see the side of his jaw twitch. "I visit the resort often. They'll put the meal on my tab, Katarina," he says.

"Thank you for stepping in when you did and for such an excellent dinner. I hope you can relax and enjoy the rest of your vacation now," I say, standing up to leave, but feeling somewhat shaky. I grasp the edge of the table for support, but not before he notices. He is by my side immediately, placing one arm on my elbow and another on my opposite shoulder.

"I think the evening's events, coupled with the fact you went so long without food has taken its toll. I'll walk you back to your room."

"I'm okay," I reply, feeling silly and more than a little embarrassed. "I don't want to be a bother, and I can *certainly* walk myself back to my room," I add.

"If you continue to resist, I will pick you up and carry you to your room. Now, lean on me and I will make sure you get back to your room safely." I resist a flippant comment about his highhandedness but am grateful for the support even though the arm draped around my shoulder is making it hard to concentrate on anything else. "Which suite are you in?" he asks as we move into the main resort area.

"I'm in room 2902," I say, looking up just in time to catch the glimpse of surprise that registers across his features.

"You're in room 2902?" he asks.

I wonder if he thought he heard the number wrong. "Yes, a group of us are staying for a weeklong event that starts Monday. I came in a couple of days early to relax a little and get a head start on preparations."

He gazes down at me, his jaw pushed to an angle. "You're near the top of the Mayan Towers," he says, guiding me toward the elevator with a firm hand on my shoulder. As we reach floor twenty-nine, the elevator stops, and he guides me towards my suite. He's very tall, maybe six feet one or two, and the dress pants and shirt he has on do nothing to disguise his lean muscular frame. I feel his gaze on me and try to focus my attention.

"Do you have your key card?" he inquires. I nod and reach into my purse. "Hand it to me, Katarina," he murmurs. I wonder if he's impatient to deposit me in my room and enjoy his evening. I fumble for my card, finally retrieving it from the bottom of my purse. He takes it from me, effortlessly sliding it into the slot before guiding me in and asking me if I'm okay.

"I'm fine, really. I was just a little shaky, but appreciate you walking me back. I don't want to keep you from your evening, besides I have a lot of work to do."

"I'm glad you're feeling better. I'll give you a call in the morning and check to see how you are. What is your phone number?" he asks.

I quickly contemplate what reason I have for not giving this perfect stranger my telephone number, but am brought back into the moment by the sound of his voice.

"I can always come back and check on you," he says, sensing my hesitation, his eyes alight with mischief.

I smile at my silliness. The man is standing in my suite. I give him my phone number, and he quickly enters it into his contacts.

My eyes are nearly level with his chest, and I can almost make out its rise and fall underneath his dress shirt. I have a hard time listening to his words. The scent of amber and spice waft to my nostrils as I breathe his cologne in.

His fingers lift my chin to meet his gaze. "I'll call you tomorrow to make sure you are okay. Get some rest," he says before leaving.

I can't help wonder if I am in a little state of shock. My legs still feel shaky, my heart is racing, and I can't seem to regulate my breathing. A hot bath in the oversized whirlpool sounds like a good idea. I turn on the water and strip out of my soiled sundress. The marble ledge boasts of an assortment of fragranced bath oils. I pick one of the Kashmir lavender scents known for its relaxing properties and am soon rewarded with a sweet floral scent that wafts through the air as the tub foams up. I sink into its depths reveling in the sheer luxury of the soft, silky water as it bubbles around me. I can't help but think back to the evening, of the man, moments from dying and the man who helped me save his life. *If Chase hadn't joined me would I have been able to keep going?* I try to get the picture of the man out of my head, thinking instead of Chase and how he took over, intent, controlled and commanding and to the gentle way he said my name. The water is beginning to turn cooler and I am much calmer and relaxed when I finally get out of the bath and slip into my robe.

TWO

I fire up my Mac and curl into the oversized reading chair, but before I have finished signing on the swooshing sound of an incoming text alerts me to a message from my best friend, Jenny. She owns Torzial, the consulting firm I work for, but has become my best friend over the years.

Message: I hope you are relaxing!

Reply*:* Until a guy collapsed... Ended up giving CPR- I'm still decompressing.

JENNY'S RING tone is almost immediate, and I hit the button for FaceTime. "What the hell happened, Kate? You're supposed to be relaxing."

"I was having a drink and trying to do just that. All of a sudden the guy next to me collapsed. There was no one around, so I had to start CPR until Chase arrived. I didn't even think I remembered how to do it. Thank goodness it came back to me."

"I can't even imagine. Is the guy okay?"

"As far as I know he is. We were able to keep him alive until the paramedics arrived, and they were able to get a pulse. They hooked him up to oxygen and were taking him to the hospital the last time we saw him," I say.

"Unreal. Who's Chase, the doctor?" Jenny asks.

"No, he's just a guy who's staying at the resort. He came into the bar and took over compressions. Good thing, too, my arms were just about to give out. He took pity on me afterward. Bought me dinner and walked me back to my room." She is my dearest friend, offering me my first job at Torzial after high school and allowing me flexibility in hours as I worked my way through college. It feels comforting to talk for a while longer before reassuring her that I am okay.

I sign into my Outlook account, scanning the multitude of emails which have accumulated since I left Chicago, before settling in to read about the progress which has been made on the land contract for the medical facility. I send a response to the attorney and am just starting to peruse another when an incoming message catches my attention.

I HAVE to read it twice. I can't believe the owner of Prestian Corp is emailing me, personally.

TO: KMeilers@TorzialConsulting.org

From: CHPrestian@PrestianCorp.org

GOOD EVENING,

I don't think your contract includes working all hours of the night. While I appreciate your dedication, you should be relaxing for the long week ahead.

C. **H. Prestian**

Chief Executive Officer, Owner

Prestian Corporation

TO: CHPrestian@PrestianCorp.org
From: KMeilers@TorzialConsulting.org

DEAR MR. PRESTIAN,

I appreciate your firm allowing me to arrive ahead of the team. The resort is beautiful, and I'm sure they will enjoy the luxurious setting. I do have a little more online work to ensure the week is a success.

Thanks,
Kate
Kate Meilers
Project Consultant
Torzial Consulting Firm

TO: KMeilers@TorzialConsulting.org
From: CHPrestian@PrestianCorp.org

YOU ARE at one of the most exotic resorts in the world. Enjoy the weekend. Otherwise, I will feel inclined to renegotiate our contract to ensure you are not working at all hours of the night.

C. **H. Prestian**
Chief Executive Officer, Owner
Prestian Corporation

WHAT THE HELL? The guy owns the entire company. It's not like I can just ignore his email. I ponder how to respond, as I craft my message.

TO: CHPrestian@PrestianCorp.org
From: KMeilers@TorzialConsulting.org

I WILL BE SIGNING off shortly. However I do need to reply to certain emails to receive what I need for the event on Monday. Unfortunately, you have been courtesy copied on these so will see the responses.

Thanks,
Kate

TO: KMeilers@TorzialConsulting.org
From: CHPrestian@PrestianCorp.org

ONLY THE **NECESSARY** WORK THEN.

C. **H. Prestian**
Chief Executive Officer, Owner
Prestian Corporation

HE SEEMS like a complete control freak… and the arrogance! "I will renegotiate your contract if you don't do what I say…" Blah, blah, blah… I shake my head, responding to the critical emails and decide to forego the others for a good night's sleep.

The resort is still relatively quiet in the morning, and I order room service to take advantage of the view from my balcony. I am in the middle of breakfast reviewing a medical journal when an email from Mark arrives. He is the project coordinator for Martel & Sons, the architectural firm who will be designing the medical facility. It appears as though he is backing out on his agreement to send representatives and I shake my head in frustration as I send a response.

To: MPowers@Martel&Sons.org

From: KMeilers@TorzialConsulting.org

CC: CHPrestian@PrestianCorp.org, JWarling@TorzialConsulting.org, BCarrington@PrestianCorp.org

DEAR MR. POWERS,

I have reviewed your request to have Martel representatives excused next week. The group will be developing the patient experience, and it is imperative the design team understands this work. The efficiencies gained by having them present will far outweigh the initial cost of time and resources. Please let me know who will be representing this project on Monday, or if I need to arrange for alternative design representation.

Thanks,

Kate

Kate Meilers

Project Consultant

Torzial Consulting Firm

TO: KMeilers@TorzialConsulting.org

From: CHPrestian@PrestianCorp.org

Let me know if assistance is needed in the matter. It is Saturday. Why are you working?

C. H. Prestian

Chief Executive Officer, Owner

Prestian Corporation

. . .

IT'S GOING to be a long weekend if he's intending to stalk my every exchange. I peruse the other emails while trying to decide how to respond to his message.

TO: KMeilers@TorzialConsulting.org
From: MPowers@Martel&Sons.org
CC: CHPrestian@PrestianCorp.org,
JWarling@TorzialConsulting.org,
BCarrington@PrestianCorp.org

DEAR MISS MEILERS,

Thank you for the note, but the department is short staffed. We have created several options and feel confident one will meet your needs. Each is a state-of-the-art design and maximizes efficiency, which we understand is the goal of this particular project.

Mark

Mark Powers, Project Coordinator
Martel & Son's Design

I put thought into responding as professionally as possible, but inside I am fuming. Why did Prestian Corporation hire this company if they don't understand that design of the building should be driven by the needs of the patients?

TO: MPowers@Martel&Sons.org
From: KMeilers@TorzialConsulting.org
CC: CHPrestian@PrestianCorp.org,
JWarling@TorzialConsulting.org,
BCarrington@PrestianCorp.org

MARK,

The goal is to develop a new patient-centered health care model and create a facility to support it. The delivery of care will be completely different than how we provide it today, therefore, will require an entirely new design. Please let me know who will be representing this project on Monday, or if I need to arrange for alternative design representation.

Thanks,

Kate

KATE MEILERS

Project Consultant

Torzial Consulting Firm

TO: KMeilers@TorzialConsulting.org

From: CHPrestian@PrestianCorp.org

VERY NICE RESPONSE... However, it is Saturday and you are still working.

C. **H. Prestian**

Chief Executive Officer, Owner

Prestian Corporation

TO: CHPrestian@PrestianCorp.org

From: KMeilers@TorzialConsulting.org

DEAR MR. PRESTIAN,

It appears Martel & Sons would like us to select from preset designs instead of letting the process drive design. It's more than a little concerning.

See you Monday.

Thanks,

Kate

KATE MEILERS

Project Consultant

Torzial Consulting Firm

TO: KMeilers@TorzialConsulting.org

From: CHPrestian@PrestianCorp.org

YOUR CONCERNS ARE VALID. Let me know if you need assistance in procuring resources for the event. BTW-You are still working!

C. H. Prestian

Chief Executive Officer, Owner

Prestian Corporation

I DECIDE NOT to respond to his last email and am just a couple hours into an analysis of projected growth when my cell phone rings. The number is not familiar, but the voice is unmistakable. "Hello, Katarina. I wanted to give you a call and find out how you were today."

"I'm feeling much better, Chase. I think you were right, I just went a little too long without eating," I reply.

"That's good to hear. Do you have plans for the afternoon?" he asks.

I'm sure he is just being polite, and I have no intention of becoming someone's chore for the day.

"I do, actually. In fact, I'm working on an analysis for a project and won't be finished for some time," I say.

"That's unfortunate. You are on a beautiful island. Surely your work can wait?"

"I wish it were the case, but I need to finish it," I say although I'm trying to decide why it can't wait for a little while.

"I'm very glad that you are feeling better. Hopefully your work won't take you long, as it would be a shame to work all day. However, we both know what happens when you go a prolonged time without eating so if I don't see you downstairs before six, I will stop by and personally escort you to dinner," he says before disconnecting.

I look at my phone, shaking my head in disbelief. He clearly must think I can't take care of myself at all after last night, I surmise.

The rest of the day flies by, and I feel a sense of accomplishment and excitement when I save the last of the documents to the project's shared account. It is getting late, and I am hungry, having only nibbled on a bagel left over from breakfast since then. I am just getting ready to wrap up for the day when Mom's call comes in.

"Hi Sweetie, just thought I would give you a ring and see how you were fairing with everything," she says.

"I'm okay, Mom," I say, sighing and mentally preparing myself for the well-intended inquisition to come.

"Has Matt called you at all?" my mom asks.

"No, I haven't talked to him since the night he proposed a couple weeks ago."

"Katie, maybe you should call him. You were the closest of friends for years. You just need to talk to each other."

I groan inwardly knowing she's only concerned about me. "Mom, I'm not going to call him and I don't expect him to get ahold of me. He was really hurt when I turned down his marriage proposal. The note asking me to move out was the last contact I've had with him and I'm trying to respect his wishes," I say, hoping to alleviate her concern.

"Well, I still think you should give him a call. You had no idea he had feelings for you like that. Try to explain it to him, at least salvage the friendship," she suggests.

"Mom, he never once gave me any indication in the years we lived together that his feelings were anything but platonic. In fact, I always thought he may be, well, you know, interested in guys. He never brought anyone home or talked about his relationships and then one day he asks me to marry him in front of a room full of people?

"I'm not blaming you, Sweetie, just suggesting that you talk to each other."

"I'll think about it, Mom."

"How are things going in Aruba?" she asks, finally changing the subject.

"Everything is going great. The preparations are coming along nicely for the event on Monday, and I'm hoping things will go well," I say. We chat for a few more minutes before disconnecting and I am just getting ready to close my laptop when an incoming message from Mark pops up in my inbox.

FROM: MPowers@Martel&Sons.org

To: KMeilers@TorzialConsulting.org

CC: CHPrestian@PrestianCorp.org, JWarling@TorzialConsulting.org, BCarrington@PrestianCorp.org

MISS MEILERS,

I HAVE BEEN able to procure two representatives for the event. They will be arriving on Sunday night and staying in the Mayan Towers. Please let me know if you require anything, before the meeting.

Mark

MARK POWERS, **Project Coordinator**

Martel and Sons Design

TO: KMeilers@TorzialConsulting.org
From: CHPrestian@PrestianCorp.org

IT APPEARS they will be participating. Now can you stop working? If not, I will need to make good on my earlier threat.

C. **H. Prestian**
Chief Executive Officer, Owner
Prestian Corporation

I WONDER if he is always such a controlling asshole. I decide not to respond to his email, besides, it's a beautiful evening. The resort lights are starting to turn on as dusk arrives, and I can hear the faint sound of music in the distance. I quickly search my closet and choose a strappy sundress. It's a simple little number, and it feels delightful to let myself be free of constraining undergarments. The blue color matches my eyes and is an excellent complement to my hair. I brush through the long coppery mane and admit defeat. It has a mind of its own, unruly as always, and curling at will. I apply a little face powder and lip gloss and I'm ready to go.

I can hear the music before I reach the bar. This time, it is full of people listening to a local reggae band. I take a sip of the strawberry daiquiri and lose myself in the soft and sultry tones of the music while watching the moving lights in the distance. I jump slightly at the feel of a hand on my shoulder and glance up to see Chase looking down at me.

"Good evening, Katarina. I'm glad you were able to put your work away for a short time," he says. The twinkle in his eye and quirk of his lips makes it hard to tell if he's mocking me or sincere.

"I finished that a little while ago."

"It must have been quite an extensive analysis," he says.

"It was. I'm preparing for a weeklong healthcare planning session," I say, not sure why I feel the need to explain myself.

"That seems much more interesting than exploring the islands," he says and his eyes are still alight with amusement.

I can feel the warmth on my cheeks. "It was very sweet of you to offer. I didn't want to be a bother, and I never left my computer all day. I did take advantage of the fantastic weather and views from the balcony of my room, though."

"It would hardly have been a bother, Katarina. The planning session is here on the island?" he asks, joining me at the table.

"Yes, the company that hired me is flying a design team in from the States. The island is breathtaking. I'm sure the group will love the surroundings this week," I say.

"I couldn't agree more. How is your drink?" he asks.

"It's good. Although, I was going to order the wine we had yesterday, but couldn't remember the name."

"Well, that can be easily remedied. The bartender is at the other end right now. I'll walk down," he says, seeking out the attention of the server. I have a few moments to observe him unnoticed as he waits for our drinks. He is leaning casually against the bar in tan khakis, boat shoes and a polo that does nothing to conceal the shape of his small waist and broad shoulders.

I push what's left of the daiquiri aside and take a sip of water before he returns with the wine. It is light and crisp like I remembered, with a mild sweet fruitiness. I let the flavor resonate before swallowing, enjoying the rich finish that I recalled from the night before. I'm aware he's watching me intently, and I can feel the same warmth as yesterday rise to my cheeks.

"You're blushing, Katarina. What are you thinking about?" he asks.

"It's been an unusual couple of days. I still can't believe we ended up performing CPR," I say, trying to regain my composure.

"I contacted the hospital earlier, and while they couldn't give out any information, I was able to leave a message for Mrs. Trennor to call me back. The couple is from Texas and on vacation for the week. She told me her husband required three stents to open arteries to his heart. It sounds like he is recovering nicely, though," he says.

"That's wonderful news, Chase," I say.

"I thought so too, but you still haven't answered my question. We were talking about your blush," he says.

"I'm still a little embarrassed that not only did you have to take over CPR, but had to see me back to my room because I couldn't even manage that."

He looks at me with mild amusement. "Katarina, rest assured ... it was the highlight of my evening."

I'm finding it hard to shift my eyes from his gaze. Maybe it's just the wine, but everything about this man is appealing and playing havoc with my senses. The band is playing a slow, steady number and Chase stands up.

"Katarina, come and dance with me," he says, gently guiding me with one hand at the small of my back to the dance floor. The song playing is a musical number combining guitar, piano and drum in a much different way than most genres. It is sultry and romantic, and I find myself playing the piano keys in my head as the song progresses. I'm acutely aware of his hand still on the small of my back while his other hand finds mine, effortlessly guiding me to the sensual beat. He is an active and competent dancer, drawing me close and pressing my face into his muscular chest. I can smell the fresh scent of soap through his clothing and feel the beat of his heart as we move.

I'm keenly aware that my own heart is racing, and I wonder if he can tell the effect he is having on me. Our eyes lock, and he holds mine captured under the intensity of his gaze. His hand leaves mine, gently pushing the curl hanging near my eyes out of my face, pulling me closer as we continue drifting across the floor. He keeps his arm firmly around my shoulders as one song ends and the next begins.

When the set ends, he has our drinks replenished and tells me about the band that is playing and some of the other island entertainment, before leading me back onto the dance floor. I lose myself in the rhythmic music, enjoying the slow song selections and the feel of his body close to mine. In between sets he orders a meal of keri keri, a boiled and flaked fish which has been highly seasoned and accompanies an island salad. The meal is enjoyable and light, and as soon as the waitress has cleared our table, we are back on the dance floor. As they begin to wrap up for the night, I am acutely aware that I miss the feel of his arms around me and sense the warmth rise to my cheeks.

"Katarina, you have a lovely blush. I'll walk you back to your suite. It's getting late," he says.

I feel a keen sense of disappointment that the night is over as we make our way back to the Mayan Tower elevators. "Chase, do you know what the blinking lights over the ocean are? I thought they were vessels coming to shore earlier, but they're still out there."

"They are coming from the lighthouse. You really should see some of the historical sites while you're here. I'll pick you up tomorrow morning and show you around the island."

"I have to admit it would be great to see some of the sights while I'm here. I have a few things to complete before Monday, but I can finish relatively quickly tonight and still have time to go out tomorrow," I say.

The elevator stops and with a hand on the small of my back he guides me towards my suite. This time, I have my key card out and quickly insert it into the door to gain access.

"I enjoyed the evening very much, Katarina. I'll pick you up at ten tomorrow morning. I'm looking forward to showing you around the island," he says, brushing a wisp of hair off of my cheek, before leaving me to return to the elevator.

THREE

I've missed a couple of messages and a call from Jenny. I text her that I was out for the night and will call her tomorrow, still thinking about the evening. She'll never believe that I was out dancing with someone until all hours of the night. I can hear her now. *Who are you and what'd you do with my friend?* I laugh at the thought and slip into my nightgown, curl up into bed, and begin reviewing emails to make sure things are ready for Monday. I reread Prestian's note from earlier and try to decide whether I should send a polite response or not reply at all. He *is* the head of the company that has employed me. "It appears they will be participating. Now can you stop working? If not, I will need to make good on my earlier threat." I resist the temptation to email a sarcastic comment back and opt instead for a brief note letting him know that I am finished working for the evening. I close my Mac and slide into the luxurious linens and find myself dreaming of dancing with a man with dark penetrating green eyes and a steady heartbeat.

I wake to the sound of the alarm in the morning with a sense of excitement and anticipation of the day. I make some coffee in the kitchenette and decide to work for a while before Chase arrives. I pull up the project charter sent to me by Brian, chief operating officer at Prestian Corp. He's very thorough, and I've enjoyed working with him on preparation material in the last few weeks. I update the charter to include patient experience data, metrics and a summary of my analysis before sending it back to Brian and his team.

TO: KMeilers@TorzialConsulting.org
From: CHPrestian@PrestianCorp.org

THE CHARTER APPEARS WELL PUT TOGETHER, and the additions add a significant amount of depth. I'll take a look at it a little later in the day and add the known risks from a cultural and political perspective, along with the mitigation strategies. There will be significant pushback to the changes in the delivery of healthcare that have been proposed. In fact, it may become very unpleasant until we push through the status quo and necessary changes.

P.S. IT IS SUNDAY. Why are you working?

C. **H. Prestian**
Chief Executive Officer, Owner
Prestian Corporation

TO: CHPrestian@PrestianCorp.org
From: KMeilers@TorzialConsulting.org

DEAR MR. PRESTIAN,

Thank you for the kind note. I look forward to reviewing the risks and mitigation strategies. Your company is paying me to work, and there is much more to complete to bring this facility together. It has the potential to be one of the most prestigious and most efficient hospital and clinic systems ever designed.

KATE,

KATE MEILERS
Project Consultant
Torzial Consulting Firm

TO: KMeilers@TorzialConsulting.org
From: CHPrestian@PrestianCorp.org

THIS FACILITY WILL BE one of the most prestigious and most efficient building ever designed without you working twenty-four hours a day. Stop working or I shall begin drafting a new contract.

C. **H. Prestian**
Chief Executive Officer, Owner
Prestian Corporation

TO: CHPrestian@PrestianCorp.org
From: KMeilers@TorzialConsulting.org

DEAR MR. PRESTIAN,

There is no need to draft a new contract. I will be done working shortly. I just need to finish a few things before signing off.

Kate,

. . .

KATE MEILERS
Project Consultant
Torzial Consulting Firm

TO: KMeilers@TorzialConsulting.org
From: CHPrestian@PrestianCorp.org

WHAT MORE IS there to do?

C. **H. Prestian**
Chief Executive Officer, Owner
Prestian Corporation

UGH! Is this guy always so insufferable? Honestly, he can't be serious! I still need to organize all of the exercises we'll use during the event before tomorrow not to mention everything else.

TO: CHPrestian@PrestianCorp.org
From: KMeilers@TorzialConsulting.org

DEAR MR. PRESTIAN,

I still have preparation for Monday, among a multitude of other items. Please do NOT begin contract renegotiations when you see me online later!!

Kate,

. . .

KATE MEILERS
Project Consultant
Torzial Consulting Firm

TO: KMeilers@TorzialConsulting.org
From: CHPrestian@PrestianCorp.org

ARE YOU ALWAYS THIS TENACIOUS? If so, this is going to be a very long project!!

C. **H. Prestian**
Chief Executive Officer, Owner
Prestian Corporation

ME, tenacious? This guy has got to be the most overbearing—Ahh—***asshole*** comes to mind again. I chuckle to myself while glancing at the time on my computer. Shit, it's almost ten. I close the Mac and scurry for clothes, sliding into a long skirt, matching cami and sandals. As I head to the bathroom, I pull a large comb through my hair and decide to pull it back for the day, before carefully applying eyeliner and a little gloss for my lips.

FOUR

I open the door to find Chase dressed in khaki shorts and a casual tan polo. I can't help but admire the sturdy athletic build. I wonder what he does for exercise and quickly avert my eyes from his shoulders and chest. His eyes are alight with amusement. He can't possibly know what I'm thinking... at least, I hope not.

"Good morning, Chase."

"Katarina, you look beautiful today," he says.

"Thank you," I respond, feeling the rising blush on my cheeks.

"Are you ready?" he asks, eyes still not leaving mine. I nod, and it's not long before I feel his hand on the small of my back, guiding me toward the Mayan Tower elevators. The resort is heavily lined with beautiful palm trees, which are swaying in the gentle breeze coming off the ocean.

"We're taking the Jeep out, so I think you'll be happy you've tied your hair back," he says.

The valet pulls the Jeep into the loading area, and Chase helps me step into the passenger side before climbing into the driver's seat and navigating his way through the island traffic.

"Aruba is on the continental shelf of South America. It's one of three islands that comprise the sovereign island nations within the Kingdom of the Netherlands. We are actually only about twenty miles north of the coast of Venezuela," Chase explains as he slows to show me some of the desert landscape.

"Really... I had no idea we were that close," I reply, wishing I had researched the area a little more before arriving.

We approach the coast, and he pulls the Jeep to a stop in front of a large dock. A tall older gentleman with graying hair and worn jeans greets us as we approach.

"Welcome back, my friend," he says with a broad grin.

Chase extends his hand. "Mikael, it's nice to see you again."

Chase introduces Mikael as one of his friends and owner of the commercial charter we are taking. He chats with him for a few moments and lets him know we are interested in learning about the lighthouse. "Katarina has been admiring the lights from the resort," he explains as Mikael reaches out to give my hand a warm shake.

"Welcome to the island, miss. I hope that you will find the tour and history most interesting," he says.

Chase pulls me close as he leads me up the ramp and onto the deck of the large boat already crowded with tourists. My insides are tingly and deliciously warm being this close to him, and I breathe in the fresh clean scent of his skin. I can feel myself blushing at the proximity.

"You can't seem to control your blush, can you?" he asks softly so only I can hear.

I shake my head slightly embarrassed that he noticed and wishing my body would stop giving me away at his slightest touch. As the catamaran moves out to sea, the color of the seawater seems to transition from a light turquoise to dark emerald green.

"You can see an outline of the lighthouse in the distance if you look closely. It's just on the northwestern tip of the island in an area known as Hudishibani and won't take long to reach," he says as we get farther out. The water is relatively calm, and Chase regales me with the history of the island and lighthouse until we arrive. As the boat anchors, he takes my hand, guiding me down the ramp and over the rocky paths filled with cacti and desert terrain.

"You know so much about the island. How long have you been coming here?"

"My dad brought me to the island as a graduation gift when I finished my master's degree about ten years ago. My mom had passed away earlier in the year, and it was good for the two of us to get away. We spent a couple of weeks just exploring the islands, and I've been visiting regularly almost any chance I get."

"It's no wonder you enjoy it here so much with those kinds of memories. Does your dad ever come back with you?"

"He has a couple of times," he says, helping me over the uneven path and stones, keeping a firm grip on my hand. As we round the corner, he pauses, allowing me to take in the rolling white sand dunes. The beaches are peppered with various shaped cacti adorned with yellow, red, melon, and pink blooms, aloe plants, and all around are massive rock formations, as far as the eye can see, making it a perfect backdrop to the lighthouse in the distance. He is a wonderful tour guide, and the day goes by quickly as he shares stories of the early settlers and even the modern day struggles the islanders still endure. When we are done exploring, we make our way back to the catamaran just as the other tourists are arriving. They have set out afternoon cocktails and appetizers for our enjoyment on the way back to the mainland, so we take a drink and a small plate with us back to our table on the boat. He has slid in beside me instead of across from me and takes my hand in his. Just the small gesture brings the familiar warmth to my cheeks. He's gently rubbing his finger over my skin and appears deep in thought. When he realizes I'm watching him, he puts his arm around me. "Good?" he asks. I nod my affirmation, and his arm tightens around me in response.

It does not take long to get to shore, and before we head down the ramp, he stops to talk with Mikael who seems to be in his element chatting with many of the other tourists. "Mikael, as always, it's been a pleasure," he says to the older man, shaking his hand before we leave. "There is a rather quaint restaurant between here and the resort. They serve the best Keshi Yena on the island. We'll stop there for dinner," he says as we get into the Jeep.

"That's an interesting name," I say.

"It's an island mix of chicken and vegetables," he explains, amused at my raised eyebrows.

"Well, after all the fresh air dinner sounds wonderful. It wouldn't do for me to have to have you help me back to my room again," I say.

"Indeed," he says, and I can see his lip quirking from my view of him as he drives.

The restaurant is a two-story structure set off the highway and already appears full. The hostess greets us and smiles warmly at Chase. "When did you get back, Mr.—"

"Please, he interrupts, you've known me long enough, it's Chase," he says to the hostess.

"When did you get back to the island, Chase," she says warmly.

"I arrived Friday morning. The weather has been great," he says to her.

"Would you like to dine inside or out?" she asks.

"Inside, I'd like to show Katarina the craftsmanship that went into the restaurant, and we've been outside most of the day."

"Please follow me," she says, leading us into the restaurant and towards a private dining area. The table is secluded and overlooks the water with a breathtaking view of the blue-green sea and whitecaps rolling in and crashing against the rocks along the coast.

"Chase, it's beautiful. No wonder you love it here," I say.

He smiles, and I wonder if he can tell the effect it has on me. "Katarina, you have the most beautiful blue eyes, all the colors of the sea," he murmurs. I can't conceal the blush his words create.

"I don't mean to embarrass you, but I can see and feel your body's response to mine. Do you feel it, Katarina?" he whispers.

I try to avert my gaze, but his green eyes are smoldering, holding mine captive. My throat is dry, and I hear the rasp in my voice as I respond. "Yes, I've never experienced anything like this before." His appreciative smile is comforting, and I recognize the quirk of his lip before my blush rises all the way to my cheeks.

"You're blushing again, Katarina. I'd like nothing better than to make you blush over and over again," he says.

The waitress stops to take our order, and Chase begins speaking to her in what I believe is Dutch. I'm relieved that he orders for both of us since nothing on the menu is familiar to me and I certainly don't know the language. "I think you will enjoy the Keshi Yena. It's an Aruban dish and the restaurant still uses the cheese shell filled with seasoned chicken, vegetables, and the raisins which give the dish its unique flavor," he explains after the waitress has poured our wine and left.

"We have many hidden treasures such as this in and around the island. I'm glad you seem to have such an appreciation for their beauty."

"You were speaking in Dutch?" I ask.

"Yes, in most areas of the island English is common because tourism is prominent. However, there is still a great appreciation for the culture and native language," he explains.

He takes my hand from across the table "You're quiet. What are you thinking?"

"That I am attracted to a man I've known less than forty-eight hours. I don't know anything about you, except your name, you frequent the island, you're a little overbearing, extremely handsome, and that your eyes smolder and jaw sets when you get annoyed. I don't date much, and it's all a little overwhelming if I'm honest."

He squeezes my hand in response and his bright eyes never leave mine. "It would disappoint me greatly if you felt different, Katarina," he says, suddenly smiling. "So you think I'm a little overbearing?" he asks.

I can't help but laugh and shake my head in affirmation.

"Um, yes. Especially when you told me you were going to pick me up and take me to my room," I say, laughing at the memory of his comment.

"Katarina, I'll let you in on a little secret. I am extremely overbearing if that's the word you like," he admits, grinning.

Our food arrives, and the aroma is strong and smoky. I try a small bite and find the marinated chicken, seasonings, and fruit as delicious as he promised. "Mmm, so good," I say, murmuring my appreciation for the taste.

He's watching me intently, and his eyes seem to darken right in front of me. "I'm glad you like the dish, Katarina. Your appreciation for the tastes you like, in wine and food, is almost sensual. You can't possibly know what that does to me," he says.

I can feel my skin warm under his gaze and compliment. "Do you always say whatever is on your mind?" I ask, smiling.

"Usually, am I embarrassing you?"

"Maybe a little, but I quite like it," I reply, realizing that it's the truth and that I feel comfortable in his company.

"Good. Now tell me a little about you and this project that required you to work so much this weekend," he says.

"Well, I live in Chicago, and I'm a Lean consultant. We're currently working on the design of a new healthcare facility in the city. I'm going to be holding a weeklong event here on the island to improve the existing care model before we begin designing the medical complex. I asked for a place the team could convene for a week thinking that Prestian Corp, the company that hired me, would supply a large conference room in one of the buildings they own in Chicago. Instead, they provided the conference room here at the Ridalgo. They are flying everyone in and have rooms reserved for the entire team. In fact, the caregivers should have arrived on the island today. Unfortunately, I still have a little prep work to do tonight and still need to set the conference room up for the event tomorrow. I'll skip my run tonight and go for a nice long one after I get done tomorrow," I say as we finish eating.

"It sounds like a very worthwhile project and a busy week. I suppose I should get you back to the resort relatively early then," he says, pulling my chair out for me.

When we reach the resort the valet takes the Jeep, and Chase guides me through the lobby to the Mayan Tower elevator. This time, I have the key card in the front of my purse, and as I reach for it, he pulls me in closer, lifting my chin so that I'm looking directly into his eyes.

"A man could drown in your eyes, Katarina." He gently pushes the long curl that has escaped from my hair clip out of my eyes, and then reaches behind me, unlocking the clip. My hair spills out of the barrette and down onto my shoulders and breasts, as he brushes it out of my face.

"I have wanted to do that all day... and this..." he murmurs as his lips find mine, kissing me with a firm gentleness, exploring my mouth and tongue with his, slowly building the urgency and desire between us. One of his hands cradles my face, while the other resting on the small of my back pulls me closer. His desire for me is evident as he holds me and I can hear the soft murmur, which escapes my throat. He moans at the sound of it, kissing my lips deeply and sensually. He pulls back slightly, looking down at me. "Katarina, you are so beautiful and desirable. Hand me your key card," he says, taking it from my hand and sliding it into the reader. The green light comes on, and he pushes the door open.

"Are you going to come in?"

He reaches down and puts a finger to my lips. "I won't be able to leave if I come into your room. You're not safe with me tonight." His words excite me, but I feel disappointed that he's leaving, and he must see it in my expression. He smiles at me. "Katarina, you know I want to come in and what I want to do with you. It's taking all the resolve I have to keep from ravishing you right here and now," he says.

"Chase," I reach up and pull his face down closer to mine, so his lips touch my own. "I wish we had more time tonight," I say against his lips.

"I want you to promise me that you'll remember how you feel at this exact moment tomorrow," he says.

"I'm not likely to forget," I reply hoarsely. He captures my lips, and his tongue invades my mouth, stirring my desire. The warmth spreads throughout my body, and I can feel myself moistening under his touch. "Chase, are you sure you don't want to come in?"

"Katarina, I don't want our first time together to be rushed, and you need to finish working. Now go before I change my mind, take you into the bedroom and do terrible and shocking things to you," he says. I look up, and his eyes are smoldering with desire. I feel like a schoolgirl and try to hide my smile.

"When you're finished working at the conference center text me," he says.

"I will. It's just on the other side of the resort," I explain.

"It's safe enough, or you wouldn't be going on your own."

I look up to see if he's joking, but he appears dead serious. "When you leave the resort for your run tomorrow night, take the coastal area to the left. You'll have a beautiful view, but if you reach the Spindles Resort start heading back. We'll go to dinner afterward. Don't forget to text me tonight when you return," he says, bending to kiss me softly on the lips.

FIVE

I strip out of my clothes and head for the shower. Every nerve ending in my body is alive, and the multiple-level showerheads feel amazingly sensual. I can't help but think of his kiss ... my nipples are hard and extended as I soap myself, and I find myself brushing my fingers against the sensitive skin. I continue to wash, enjoying the slow and sensual soapy experience, thinking about his hardness pressed into me. My hand moves towards the area in between my thighs, and my fingers brush against my clit, which is warm with desire. I wonder what his touch would feel like and quickly finish washing before rinsing off and applying the coconut scented moisturizer onto my body. I throw the large white resort robe on, wrap my hair in a towel, and fire up the Mac just as I hear the familiar beep of a new message on my phone.

MESSAGE: I am still thinking about our kiss.

Reply: I was still thinking about it too, during my long, hot, and soapy shower.

Message: Are you teasing me, Katarina?

Reply: Not at all...It's true.

Message: I **do** know where your room is.

. . .

I SMILE at his last message and get back to assessing the data for the project. It provides a pretty compelling case for changing the current model of care in the city of Chicago. I send an email to the team hoping they will have an opportunity to review it before the event. I am just getting ready to leave for the conference room when an incoming message catches my attention.

TO: KMeilers@TorzialConsulting.org
From: CHPrestian@PrestianCorp.org

IT IS SUNDAY EVENING. Why are you still working?

C. **H. Prestian**
Chief Executive Officer, Owner
Prestian Corporation

TO: CHPrestian@PrestianCorp.org
From: KMeilers@TorzialConsulting.org

DEAR MR. PRESTIAN,

I have finished working on the time studies and data analysis. I just need to go through some of my emails and then I will be signing off.

Thanks,
Kate

KATE MEILERS

Project Consultant
Torzial Consulting Firm

TO: KMeilers@TorzialConsulting.org
From: CHPrestian@PrestianCorp.org

I HAVE SEEN nothing on the email that requires your response this evening. There's always tomorrow.

C. **H. Prestian**
Chief Executive Officer, Owner
Prestian Corporation

TO: CHPrestian@PrestianCorp.org
From: KMeilers@TorzialConsulting.org

DEAR MR. PRESTIAN,

I am planning to skim through them and respond to anything that I don't want outstanding since I will be facilitating and have limited access to email tomorrow. As a reminder, we have you scheduled at 8:00 a.m. to kick off the event. Your assistant told me you would be arriving to the island late tonight and will need to leave for the states shortly after the presentation tomorrow. In fact, she asked me to cut the presentation in half so you can be back stateside for another meeting. I think the shortened version will suffice, but your leadership and presentation of the material will be critical in helping the design teams understand the importance of the change.

Thank you for agreeing to do this.

Kate,

Kate Meilers
Project Consultant
Torzial Consulting Firm

TO: KMeilers@TorzialConsulting.org
From: CHPrestian@PrestianCorp.org

PLEASE SEND me a copy and adjust my presentation on the agenda to reflect an hour. There has been a change of plans to the stateside meetings, and I will give the full presentation.

C. **H. Prestian**
Chief Executive Officer, Owner
Prestian Corporation

TO: CHPrestian@PrestianCorp.org
From: KMeilers@TorzialConsulting.org

Dear Mr. Prestian,

Attached is a copy of the presentation. Please review and let me know if you have questions, or if modifications or changes are desired.

Thank you for taking the time to do this.

Kate,
Kate Meilers
Project Consultant
Torzial Consulting Firm

SIX

The directions to the conference center are well marked, and I'm pleased to see the room has lots of wall space and is equipped with an overhead projector and screen. I quickly set up the exercise boards and call to confirm the food and beverage plan. The resort will bring in bagels, pastries, muffins and fruit each morning, along with fresh coffee, flavored syrups, and assorted creams. Lunch will be provided each day, along with a variety of nuts, cheese, and a fruit platter for the afternoon breaks. The chairs and tables are already set up in horseshoe fashion so everyone can see the overhead screens from their seat. I set up the supply table and look around. I think I'm as prepared as I'm going to be. It's getting late by the time I get back to my room, change into my robe for the evening and pull out my cell to text Chase.

MESSAGE: Home and safely behind the wheel of my Mac.

Reply: Good. How much more work do you have?

Message: Just email. I need to get that cleaned up before the week starts.

Reply: Just what has to get done then get some sleep! You will need it for tomorrow.

Message: Promises, promises. As I recall, I was turned down flat... What's a girl to do??

Reply: Sleep, before you provoke me into your bed tonight!

Message: I really can't be held responsible... after being tormented all day.

Reply: You have no idea what it is to be tormented, yet. I plan to cause you many excruciatingly pleasurable nights. Work now, then bed!!

Message: I am going...

He's so hot, and I know I'm playing with fire... but I can't resist. I sign onto email and see that Brian has had an opportunity to review the data.

KATE,

Thank you for the data analysis. I've shared it with the medical group and want you to be aware they have concerns with the number of exam rooms being discussed. While they understand the goal is to increase efficiency and decrease space requirements, they feel limiting rooms would reduce productivity.

They currently use a model allowing each provider one office, and three exam rooms.

Sincerely,

Brian Carrington
Prestian Corporation
Chief Operating Officer

BRIAN,

Thanks for your note. When I did the initial analysis, it showed an ability to decrease square footage costs by load leveling rooms. Each provider will still be able to utilize three exam rooms, but they would be shared spaces and driven by schedules. The savings would be more than 2.3 million dollars based on the current number of providers and process. Once the future state work is complete, we'll know better the time and resources, including exam space, required for each patient encounter.

THANK you for making me aware.

Kate,

Kate Meilers

Project Consultant

Torzial Consulting Firm

TO: KMeilers@TorzialConsulting.org

From: CHPrestian@PrestianCorp.org

2.3 MILLION IS a lot of savings. I'm looking forward to seeing how the operations side and the methodologies you teach align.

C. H. Prestian

Chief Executive Officer, Owner

Prestian Corporation

TO: CHPrestian@PrestianCorp.org

From: KMeilers@TorzialConsulting.org

YES, it is. It's a matter of scheduling and load leveling to maximize existing space, coupled with a little change management.

Kate

KATE MEILERS

Project Consultant

Torzial Consulting Firm

TO: KMeilers@TorzialConsulting.org
From: CHPrestian@PrestianCorp.org

I'D LIKE to discuss this, among other things, after the event. I hope you are not working too late. Otherwise, I can still renegotiate this contract, and do not believe for one second that I will not.

C. **H. Prestian**
Chief Executive Officer, Owner
Prestian Corporation

TO: CHPrestian@PrestianCorp.org
From: KMeilers@TorzialConsulting.org

WE CAN DISCUSS this at any time convenient for you. I have several pressing emails to respond to and then will be signing off. No need to RENEGOTIATE.

KATE

KATE MEILERS
Project Consultant
Torzial Consulting Firm

TO: KMeilers@TorzialConsulting.org

From: CHPrestian@PrestianCorp.org

I DO BELIEVE all capitalized letters is a form of yelling when on email. Did you just yell at me?

C. **H. Prestian**
Chief Executive Officer, Owner
Prestian Corporation

TO: CHPrestian@PrestianCorp.org
From: KMeilers@TorzialConsulting.org

NO OF COURSE NOT. I just meant to be emphatic. I will be signing off shortly.

KATE

KATE MEILERS
Project Consultant
Torzial Consulting Firm

TO: KMeilers@TorzialConsulting.org
From: CHPrestian@PrestianCorp.org

I SEE there are quite a few emails that you may feel compelled to address this evening. Please do not. We'll deal with this tomorrow. Go offline!

C. **H. Prestian**
Chief Executive Officer, Owner
Prestian Corporation

TO: CHPrestian@PrestianCorp.org
From: KMeilers@TorzialConsulting.org

YES, I am just reading several others and see Mark has quite a bit to say about the studies. If you feel it best to deal with this collaboratively tomorrow, then I will not respond.
Kate

KATE MEILERS
Project Consultant
Torzial Consulting Firm

SWOOSH...I look at my cell and see it's an incoming message from Chase.

Message: Still pouting?

I don't know what has gotten into me lately, but I am clearly attracted to this man and can't help but smile at our game.

Reply: Still pouting... quite tormented and frustrated!

Message: Careful Baby or I will feel the need to come and put you out of your misery! Not joking!

Reply: Promises, promises... I am going to crawl into bed and try to sleep, although the ache between my legs is almost too much to bear...

Message: If you continue down this path I will be knocking on your door in a few moments. Do not tempt me. I want our first night together to be perfect and unrushed.

Reply: Okay, good night then. Still pouting.

Message: Good night, Baby. Sleep well, and remember what I told you about tomorrow.

Reply: I don't know why tomorrow is going to be any different than today. I still need to work a little each night. I won't argue, though...

Message: Sweet dreams.

The alarm on my phone pulls me out of a fitful sleep. I don't feel rested at all after tossing and turning all night thinking about dark, smoldering green eyes, sandy hair, and a tall, muscular and tanned body pressing urgently against me. I shower and look through my closet, finally deciding on a black and gray jumper that I can pair with flats since I will be on my feet most of the day. I get dressed, throw on a little makeup, and allow my hair to air dry while I review the list of team members. I think we have the right balance of administrators and people that perform the jobs. I decide to have breakfast before I get to the conference room, hoping the food will settle my nerves a little. I order an omelet with Egg Beaters, fresh peppers, onions and mushrooms along with an English muffin and coffee.

When I reach the conference center, I pull up the presentation and spend time conversing with each team member as they arrive. It's drawing near eight and everyone in attendance has gotten breakfast and is seated except Mr. Prestian.

"Welcome everyone. Thank you for freeing your schedules up and making the trip. I'm excited about the opportunity we've been given for developing a comprehensive healthcare delivery model in the Chicago area."

I stop short as Chase walks into the conference room dressed in a dark suit. I'm sure the absolute confusion I feel is apparent. *What is he doing here?* He walks across the space and takes the microphone from my hand.

"Miss Meilers, I see you already have the presentation up. Ladies and Gentlemen, as you know, the facility we are about to create and design is the biggest community venture ever undertaken in the city of Chicago. It's going to be the first of its size that will use Lean methodologies, before design. Lean is the concept of eliminating waste and streamlining processes to increase quality and efficiency. The focus on quality and service to our patients will ultimately drive effectiveness and cost, as a result. I am owner and chief executive officer of Prestian Corporation, and it's my privilege to fund the collaboration between private and community clinics, community hospitals and what have historically been referred to as our community service programs. Miss Meilers has been gracious enough to allow me time on the agenda to discuss the importance of this project and outline the process we intend to use in developing this new healthcare delivery model and state-of-the-art facility. We will spend the week identifying areas of opportunities and developing a new model to improve care, and it will mean a significant change to all involved."

He moves through the slides effortlessly, and I think I may be in a state of shock.

How is he the same man? Why didn't he tell me? The reality hits me. I'm contractually obligated to work for this man, and in a relationship with him. I can't seem to take my eyes off him, but he's not even looking at me. In fact, he's looking at everyone in the room, except me. I don't understand and feel confused, hurt and embarrassed. I have to stay composed. Luckily, he's only here for the hour and then will be heading back to the States which must be why he avoided having any more contact with me yesterday. As he nears the end of his presentation, I look up to catch him focused on my face.

"I have been extremely impressed with facility outcomes using this approach and look forward to working with the team this week as we develop a patient-centered approach to healthcare in Chicago," he states.

He is staying all week? Surely I heard that wrong.

"Miss Meilers, thank you for allowing me to present. I will hand it back over to you now," he says, smiling at me as he heads to the empty seat.

I review logistics of restroom locations, breaks, lunches, and then move into the morning's agenda, feeling self-conscious and less than composed.

"Team, I'd like to start this morning with an icebreaker. Please share with the group where you work, your current position in the company, and what you expect to get out of this weeklong retreat. I will start, and then we can move to the left. I am Kate Meilers, and am employed by Torzial Consulting firm as a consultant for special projects. At the end of the week, I expect we will have mapped out new and improved processes for patients requiring any multitude of healthcare services and be in a position to design a state-of-the-art facility to support that."

I'm always interested in what people believe they will get out of the week and listen intently as the team goes around the room, ending with Chase.

"I've already introduced myself, so I'll just add that I expect by the end of the week we will have a future delivery model identified, but then will start the journey through cultural barriers and political resistance as we do the right thing for patients in our community."

The rest of the morning goes as planned. Break approaches and I head for the door. I can feel him, rather than see him, behind me. I keep moving... I just need some distance, and the bathrooms are right around the corner. As I approach the door, he grabs my arm.

"Katarina please, stop!" He turns me around to face him and looks down at me with an intensity I've not seen before. "I'll explain everything tonight. It probably doesn't make any sense right now, and I understand that."

"No, I don't think you do. You're not the one that has been lied to and thoroughly embarrassed here," I retort. I have to stay composed if I am going to get through this day. "I need to use the restroom before the break ends, so if you would kindly let go of me, I would appreciate it."

He lets go of my arm, and I have to avoid his eyes, or I know the tears will come. I am so angry, hurt and confused right now. I head to the bathroom for a short reprieve before the meeting starts.

As the team reconvenes I train them on the fundamentals of Lean principles to ensure they have an understanding of the waste and inefficiencies we will be looking to identify and reduce. The group is participative and engaged, laughing at some of my examples of waste and asking questions along the way. Chase seems to be enjoying the morning, laughing with Brian, his chief operating officer, on the other side of the table. He looks up as if he knows I'm looking at him. His eyes are hooded and controlled, and I look away quickly. I just need to get through the day without thinking about him.

By the end of the day, the team completes the emergency room department flows including hospitalizations and follow-up appointments, which will allow us to work on primary care and referral flows in the morning.

We start a quick exercise going around the room to gauge the team's experience for the day before convening. Mark from Martel is clearly not happy. "I think it's wasteful to have a design team here all day. We aren't the ones taking care of the patients, and we've got two people sitting here all day when we could be getting work done stateside," he says.

"Mark, I appreciate your thoughts. Should I document that not all team members feel the benefit in the process?" I ask.

"You can put it on the board however you want, but I'm not sure that's what I said."

"Mark, I want to capture your thoughts accurately, so please help put those feelings into words and I will list them for you."

I can sense Chase's anger and feel the vibration of my phone as I wait for Mark to respond.

I look down at the incoming message.

Message: Don't waste your breath. We'll hire a different company.

"Just leave it on the board, it doesn't matter what it says to be quite honest with you," Mark says, clearly frustrated. The day went so well except for the last few moments with Mark. I decide to chalk it up to his lack of understanding of the process and think about how to deal with him later. Chase is already gone when the team finally disperses. I don't know what I expected, but feel disappointed he didn't stay to talk to me. I pack up my computer and personal belongings and walk to the other side of the resort, trying to keep my emotions in check. I have managed to maintain composure all day, but now I need a nice long run. I change into running gear, spray on sunblock, throw my hair into a pony and head downstairs and out onto the beach. I finally meet someone that I am seriously attracted to, and it turns out I work for him. I have never allowed myself to get involved with anyone at work. I feel myself blush as I remember the messages from the night before and how I practically begged him to come to my suite. Why didn't he tell me? He was texting me as one person and emailing me as another. I feel the start of tears of anger and sheer embarrassment. How could he play with my feelings like that? He knew how he was affecting me. I wipe the tears from my face and try to remember what he said to me yesterday. "*Katarina, I want you to promise me that you will remember how you feel about me at this exact moment tomorrow, okay?*"

I know, but that was yesterday, and you were an entirely different person. I try to relax and soon lose myself to the beat of the music and tranquility of the sea. My halfway song by Gotye comes on, and I turn back towards the resort just as a couple is getting lifted into the air to parasail.

SEVEN

I feel calmer as I get into the shower and let the warm water from the dual showerheads massage my skin. After about ten minutes, I feel even more relaxed and wrap my hair in a towel to pull some of the moisture out of it while contemplating what to wear. The evening is warm, and I opt for a flowery sundress, lacy panties, and sandals. I'm conscious the dress does not allow for a bra. I brush my face with powder, add some lip gloss, and let my hair down. What a mess. I put some product in it to try and tame the wayward curls and begin straightening it for the evening.

I hear the knock as I finish and open the door to find Chase dressed in khakis and a sports shirt.

"Come in. I wasn't sure if you were planning to stop by or not. I was just getting ready to go out for dinner," I say.

His eyes deepen, and his jaw instantly sets in a way that shows his displeasure. "You thought I wouldn't come after what I told you last night?" he asks.

"Chase, I don't know what the hell to think! We've been together almost every moment for the last few days. Why didn't you tell me who you are?"

"Katarina, I said I will explain this to you tonight."

"I'm confused and feel mad and hurt right now. It changes everything for me," I stammer.

"Katarina, let's get something to eat and I will explain why. After that, you can decide if you are still mad at me. Is that fair?" he asks.

He guides me toward the elevator and into the waiting SUV, opening my door before getting into the vehicle on the driver's side. The silence is uncomfortable, and I'm relieved the restaurant is not far away. The hostess escorts us to the back of the restaurant, through the patio and out to a veranda overlooking the sea. It's completely secluded, and I wonder if Chase called ahead to ask for the private dining area. "I've never seen you this quiet," he says after the waitress takes our wine order.

"I just don't know what to say to you right now, Chase."

"I can see that, Katarina, and I'll try to explain." The wine arrives and he thanks the waitress. "When I walked into the bar you were desperately working to save that man's life with no regard for your safety. I don't often see those traits in people. I was mesmerized. I tried to rationalize the attraction with experiencing something traumatic, but I could feel it with the slightest brush of your hand, Katarina. The truth is I wanted to get to know you better. You surprised the hell out of me when you told me your room number. It's actually part of a block of suites leased for the retreat this week. You're staying in the room directly below mine. There aren't many people on the team this week, and it wasn't hard to put things together. Katarina, I could feel how your body responded to mine, and it was clear that you did not recognize me. You can't know what that means to me. I didn't tell you, selfishly hoping I had found someone attracted to me and not my money. I most often see the greedy and manipulative side of people, doing things to further their careers, or improve their bottom line. The time we spent together was like nothing I've ever experienced, and I know you felt the attraction, too. It almost drove me mad, but I didn't want to sleep with you until you knew the truth. Otherwise, there is nothing that would have kept me from you. I wanted to tell you last night, but I didn't want to scare you away, and I was pretty sure that once you started the event, you wouldn't leave. I'm sorry. I should have told you sooner," he says.

I am unable to hold back the warm tears that are flowing down my face. "Chase, how can you think like that? I would never get involved with someone for their money. I almost begged you into my bed several times, and now I find out I work for you. Do you know how out of character that is for me? There's a reason I have not dated for such a long time, and I vowed ***never*** to get into a relationship with someone I work with... ever. Now, I find out not only will I be working with you, but I work *for* you and probably for the next couple of years."

He circles the table to put an arm around me. "Look at me... I've never felt an attraction like this to anyone, and I know you feel the same. I can feel it in how your body responds to mine. We were meant to be together, and this is only going to end one way, Katarina," he says hoarsely. He wipes the tears from my face and bends to kiss me, capturing my lips and pushing them apart as his tongue explores deeper, engaging mine. He pauses and his steely green eyes hold mine captured. "Do you feel how attracted we are to each other?" he asks.

I can only nod as he wipes a few stray tears away from my eyes and pushes the hair out of my face.

"I don't think I'm able to be in a relationship with a person who employs me," I manage to whisper. He pulls me close, crushing me into his chest, and I can feel the beat of his heart pounding in my ears. He lifts my chin gently, "Katarina, look at me. I have absolutely no intention of giving you up."

"You don't understand how I feel, Chase. I just can't," I say, shaking my head.

I think my body is on autopilot as I manage to excuse myself from the table and wind my way out of the restaurant into the warm tropical breeze. I can see the tower from our resort in the distance. I take off my sandals and move slowly onto the beach, but then find myself in an all-out run trying to leave behind all the pain of the day. It feels good to find my pace and run as the tears continue to flow. As I follow the shore around the rocks, a firm hand grasps my shoulder almost causing me to lose my balance. I falter as I'm spun around to find Chase glaring at me, his eyes deep, dark and angry as he regards me.

"What the hell do you think you are doing?" he says, trying to catch his breath.

"Let go of me," I manage to pant. "I told you, I can't be in a relationship with you," I sob.

"What makes you think you have any control over this?" he asks, glaring at me. "Do you believe you are in control of your life and not someone of a higher power? People do not experience this kind of attraction every day, and I already told you, this is only going to end one way. If I need to fire your ass and renegotiate the Torzial contract, so be it. I know how you feel about me, Katarina," he says, folding me into his arms and capturing my lips with the urgency of his kiss.

My hands find the back of his neck instinctively, pulling him closer, completely overcome by the depth of my desire for him.

"Katarina, please don't cry, Baby. We'll figure this out together," he says, gently wiping the remaining tears with his hand.

"When did you decide to stay?" I ask, sobbing.

"I felt you tremble under my touch and knew I couldn't leave," he says, gently stroking my cheek. "Are you hungry?" he asks.

"No, and I don't want to go back inside," I respond.

"Let's get you back to the resort," he says, leading me back to the SUV. The silence on the return drive is unnerving, allowing all the self-doubt, insecurities and memories of failed relationships to wash over me like a tidal wave. I try in earnest to quell my simmering anxiety as we reach the entrance and Chase guides me toward the elevator. He pushes the button to my floor and places his arm around my shoulders, lightly rubbing my arm with his thumb. The gentle caress soothes me, calming my nerves and my body slowly begins to relax against the strength of his own.

As we reach my door, he takes the key card from me and closes the door behind us. He pulls me close, mouth seeking mine while his hand moves to my neck, caressing me, sending warm waves of desire through my body. My arms lock around his neck, pulling him closer, needing to feel his body next to mine. His hands move to the back of my neck, and he slowly begins to undo the tie around my neck, but holds my dress in place as he kisses me.

"Do you want this, Katarina?"

I can only nod, all fears and doubt ignored, as he slowly pushes the ties aside. I hear his sharp intake of breath as my breasts are exposed to him. His eyes deepen with arousal as he pulls the dress past my waist allowing it to slide to the floor. He pushes my panties past my hips and lets them fall, his eyes exploring the length of my body, hungrily taking in every inch. He brushes his hand gently across my face. "Katarina, this is how I imagined you when I first saw you blush, standing before me naked and vulnerable, blushing up at me," he says. He bends down, scoops me into his arms, carries me into the bedroom, deposits me on the bed and removes his clothes to lie beside me.

"You are so beautiful," he murmurs. He caresses my breasts slowly, first with his hands and then with his mouth. He begins gently, and as my nipples respond he increases the suction, sucking and gently teasing each nipple with his tongue and lips.

My hands hover over his abdomen lingering at his navel, then trailing the path of hair just below it before finding the hardness of his desire. He groans as I stroke him, and I savor the way he pulses under my touch. "Chase, I'm not protected," I whisper. "I stopped at the store yesterday, though, so I do have something."

He kisses me gently. "You knew you wanted this, didn't you, Baby?"

"I've wanted this for days. I've never felt like this... ever."

He smiles at me, bending down to retrieve and show me the condom from his pants. "We were meant to be together, Baby. There was always only one way this was going to end," he says, continuing his assault on my nipples until my breasts are aching with desire and my legs are quivering. He moves farther down my body, caressing my waist and belly with his warm tongue, exploring until the desire between my legs is almost excruciating. He slowly parts my legs with his hands and his tongue discovers the fine hair between my thighs. I moan audibly as his tongue begins to gently caress my clit. The slow, persistent rhythm almost drives me over the edge immediately, but he skillfully prolongs his ministrations allowing the desire to build until I lose control, gasping and trembling around him. He continues softly sucking, prolonging my climax until I am completely spent and then deftly unseals and rolls the condom into place. He is watching me intently as he lifts me to the top of his body, slowly lowering me inch by inch onto his rock hard cock.

"Katarina, you are so tight around me," he groans.

I can feel every inch moving inside of me, slowly stretching me to accommodate his girth. He brings me all the way down, agonizingly slow, never taking his eyes from mine as he slides me along his length. His hands are around my hips, lifting me up and down effortlessly, guiding me over the top of him very deep and slow. I begin to build again to the feel of the rhythm and fullness inside of me as he starts to increase our pace, pulling me down harder and faster around his cock.

"I want to feel you tremble around my cock... cum for me, Baby... cum," he urges, and I begin to crumble around him, again, as his body finds its release, deep inside of me. I collapse on his chest, and he holds me close, both of us relishing in the aftermath of our passion. I can hear his heartbeat pounding fast and furious against my face, and I gently run my fingers through the patch of hair on his chest and then across one of his hardened nipples. His eyes are smoky, and he has that quirky slanted smile that I'm getting used to.

"Baby, you're not the slightest bit safe doing what you're doing," he says, kissing me and urging my lips apart. I can taste the aftermath of our lovemaking and my desire on his lips, and blush at the memory.

"Katarina, I love the way you blush. Are you embarrassed?" he asks.

"A little. I've never experienced anything like that before."

He looks down at me tenderly. "Baby, I've never experienced this type of attraction either," he says, gently brushing the hair from my face.

I shake my head. "No, I mean I've never experienced what just happened," I explain.

"What do you mean, Katarina?" he asks softly.

I'm sure my face is bright red by now. "I've never experienced what you just did to me or what happened to my body when you did it," I answer quietly.

"You mean you've never experienced someone bringing you to orgasm with their mouth?" he asks.

"Chase, no one has ever done that to me, and no one has ever brought me to an orgasm before," I mutter, now completely embarrassed.

His eyes hold mine captive, looking at me incredulously. "I don't know if I fully understand what you're saying," he says, slowly trying to absorb what I mean.

"I've only been with two other people. The first time was a painful mistake, and I didn't want to try again for a very long time. The second relationship just did not make me feel like this... and I guess... well, I just thought something was wrong with me."

"How long has it been since you were with someone?" he asks.

"A little over three years. It was just never a good experience for me, and I've been focused on work," I explain. He shakes his head in pure disbelief, pulling me closer and kissing me gently.

"That's why you're not using protection," he says.

I nod. "I just didn't want to take something I didn't need."

He nods in understanding and caresses my face. "It would probably also explain the extreme tightness. You must be sore, Baby."

"I'm not that sore," I reply.

He smiles at me. "So does that also explain the shower comment you messaged to me the other night?" he asks softly. I nod, as I desperately try to avoid blushing. Those deep eyes are locked on mine, his eyes glazing over with passion. "Katarina, you know what that does to me? All I could think about the other night was you in the shower with soap all over your body, touching yourself," he murmurs.

His mouth descends on mine, urging my lips open, caressing my nipples with his fingers, bringing that now familiar ache back to the pit of my stomach and between my thighs. I moan softly as his fingers roll the delicate nipple back and forth with slow, deliberate, steady and firm strokes. My hands find their way to his hair, the back of his neck, and down his muscular shoulders. His lips find the sensitive area of my neck, kissing and sucking the skin, all the while continuing his pleasurable assault on my nipples. His lips devour mine with growing urgency and push them apart with his tongue. My hand travels the path of hair on his chest to his belly and below, finding him aroused again and pulsing. As I take him in my hands and slowly stroke him, he moans in response. He uses one free hand to find the sensitive area between my legs, exploring and caressing me. I let out a gasp as he finds just the right spot, applying pressure with long firm strokes that set the world between my thighs on fire. He slowly puts a finger and then two inside of me.

"Katarina, you are dripping, Baby," he says as he continues his slow and provocative assault on my senses. His cock is throbbing under the stroking of my hand, and his desire is evident as it leaks from the tip of his arousal. He reaches down for another condom and slowly rolls it on before penetrating me with long firm strokes that reach deep inside of me. I rise to meet him, over and over.... until I feel myself building again, and hear myself moaning with pleasure. He increases our momentum and with deep, long and urgent thrusts brings us to the edge again, wrapping his strong arms around my trembling body as I try to catch my breath.

I pull his face to mine, kissing his lips. "I've never felt anything like this in my entire life. You make every part of my body feel alive and on fire when you touch me," I confess.

He caresses my hair as I lay on his chest listening to his heartbeat. "You're exhausted and have a very long day tomorrow," he says, kissing my forehead gently. He picks me up and takes me to the shower. The water spills over us, and he gently kisses me, long and passionately, eventually setting me down, so my feet connect with the floor, before letting me go. He warms the body wash in his hands before spreading it on the loofah and soaping my body while the lukewarm water cascades over us.

"I better let you finish up. Otherwise, I won't be responsible for your lack of sleep tomorrow," he says after a short while. I begin applying a conditioner to my hair but find it impossible to look away as he begins soaping his body. We finish our shower, and he hands me a towel while finding one for himself, quickly drying off and wrapping it around his waist while I snuggle into the luxurious resort robe and wrap my hair in a towel.

"Let's put you to bed, Baby," he says, startling me as he scoops me back into his arms and carries me to the king-size bed. He lays me down gently, kissing me softly on the lips as he pulls the down comforter over me. I am so exhausted I can't keep my eyes open and snuggle deeper into my comforter. The last things I remember are his lips capturing mine in a sensuous and promising kiss and the smell of soap on his freshly-showered skin.

EIGHT

I wake to an unusual ringtone and reach over to answer the landline on the nightstand.

"Hello, this is your courtesy call," says a woman with a slight accent.

"Thank you," I reply, still waking up and a little disoriented. The clock registers six a.m. I climb out of bed realizing I'm still in my robe and that I seem to have lost the towel from my hair at some point. I hurry into the bathroom to get ready for the day when I hear the familiar swoosh.

Message: I hope you received your wake-up call. I'll pick you up for breakfast.

Reply: I did. How did you know I was starving?

Message: You didn't eat last night... I was with you when you were expending your energy.

I smile and barely have time to get ready and slip into a red and black dress with matching heels before he knocks on the door.

He arrives freshly shaved wearing a very nice fitting charcoal business suit. His eyes take in the fitted dress and heels appreciatively. He closes the door and pulls me into his arms, kissing me deeply. "Good morning," he says huskily as he pulls my body closer. "You look beautiful today, Katarina. It's going to be impossible for me to concentrate on what you're saying today, instead of what's under your skirt."

I feel myself begin to color. "I want to see what's under your dress," he says, pulling the sides of it up past my thighs and slowly exposing my panties. He catches his breath audibly as his fingers run over the red lace and black trim that conceals the soft auburn hair between my thighs. I moan softly as his lips find mine, and his fingers brush over the sensitive spot between my legs.

"I'll be thinking about that all day," he says, running his hand gently over my cheek. He kisses me softly on the lips and pulls my dress into place before we leave for the restaurant. I'm conscious that his touch and the anticipation of what's to come later have left me moist. I like the feel of his hand on my back as we walk through the large outdoor halls to the restaurant, but I am filled with dread as I recognize one of the physicians from the team on the far side of the restaurant. The hostess seats us right away, and I feel relieved that he has not appeared to notice us as Chase reviews the menu and asks me what I would like for breakfast.

"Coffee, and I think just a croissant and fruit would be nice," I say before he orders for the two of us when the waitress arrives.

"Chase, I don't want to ruin an amazing night, but I need to know how you're planning to handle the situation?" I say, watching him warily and trying to gauge his reaction.

"What situation are you referring to?" he asks.

I can't tell from his expression if he's amused or smirking at me. "You know, I work for you, and now, well...with everything that happened last night. I just want to have a game plan, so no one knows we're involved at work, that's all."

"Are you embarrassed by what we've shared, Katarina?" he asks, his eyes searching mine.

"I'm not embarrassed, Chase, but I need to determine how I'm going to separate my attraction for you and the fact that you employ me. I'm trying to be honest with you. I don't want to give up what we have, but I've worked extremely hard to get where I am in my career. I don't want to throw it away because people think I'm sleeping with the boss.

His eyes are dark, and his jaw appears firmly set. "What people think is more important than how you feel?" he asks, his eyes glinting and hard to read.

"No, but there are things in my past that make it difficult for me to have a relationship with someone I work with. I just need time to work through this."

"Katarina, I'm not sure what you're asking. It's going to bc impossible to keep our relationship away from the media once we're in the States."

"I haven't thought about everything, Chase. At least for now, can we keep our relationship on a professional level when we're in public? It shouldn't be that hard since yesterday you treated me like you didn't even know who I was. As I recall, it was Miss Meilers this and Miss Meilers that. A little more time should not be that hard, right?"

He does not answer, and we finish our breakfast in relative silence. The tension is palpable, and I feel a twinge of regret, but everything is happening too fast.

"We should head to the conference room if we don't want to be late. I will be careful not to give our relationship away today, but we're far from finished discussing this. When you're comfortable I'd like to hear why you have such an aversion to having a relationship with someone that you work with," he says, pulling my seat back for me as we finish our meal.

We walk through the archways towards the convention center, and I'm painfully aware his hand is not on the small of my back. As we enter the convention area, he turns to me and says, "Thank you for providing me with an overview this morning, Miss Meilers."

I glance around and see members of the Prestian Corp team nearby. "You're most welcome, Mr. Prestian," I respond, as we enter the conference room.

I lead the team through the morning's exercises and when we reach a good point to break I dismiss the team for fifteen minutes. As I head toward the restroom, I hear the familiar swoosh of my phone.

Message: Just wondering... how wet are your panties?

Reply: I don't know. I am not wearing any...

Message: If you're not careful you will find yourself bent over in the bathroom.

Reply: Maybe that's what I'm looking for?

Message: You give off some pretty mixed messages. How do you think the press would react to me bending you over in a public bathroom?

Reply: Ah, good point. You wouldn't dare...

Message: I have no issues with what the press thinks about my life. I would dare!

Reply: You started this. My panties were terribly wet... I was forced to take them off.

Message: Baby, you should be punished for tormenting me.

Reply: Punished?

Message: YES!

Reply: I need to get back into the event!!

As I return to the conference room, Chase is typing on his phone and drinking a cup of coffee. He looks up as I enter and lingeringly appraises me from top to bottom. His eyes darken with carnal appreciation. I can feel myself moisten, and my cheeks warm under his gaze. He smiles, and there's that sexy little quirk that I like so much.

The afternoon session is productive and at the end of the day, current state processes have been completed before Chase leaves for a conference call. I prepare the room for the next day and go back to my room to change into running clothes. As I lace my shoes, I hear the swoosh of my iPhone alerting me to an incoming message.

Message: Dinner tonight?

Reply: Sounds great. I'm just getting ready for a run.

Message: Are you leaving shortly? If so, I'll pick you up at 6:30.

Reply: Yes, in about 5 minutes. 6:30 p.m. sounds good.

I select shuffle on my iTunes playlist and head toward the same beach path as yesterday, passing the guy that was looking for metal the day before— his hat screams, *TOURIST*—and makes me smile to myself as I pass him.

The day's tensions begin to ease away as I head down the coast. The island is breathtaking, and I can see why Chase loves the island and the people here so much. My thoughts drift to our conversation this morning and I contemplate how to tell him why being in a relationship with someone I work with scares me so much. I cringe recalling the look on his face and question in his eyes, knowing I intentionally let him think my career was more important than any feelings I may have for him, but unable to get the memories of my mom's heartbreak out of my head.

Gotye comes on about thirty minutes into my run, and I take my cue to turn back. The resort comes into sight, and I see Mr. Tourist talking on his cell. The tiki bar seems more crowded than normal, and I decide to stop and see what's going on. I claim one of the empty stools, and it's not long before the bartender asks for my order.

"An ice cold beer I think. What would you recommend?"

"Amstel Bright or the Balashi," he says.

"I'll take whatever you pour."

He smiles, displaying a bright white set of teeth and a large grin. "One Balashi coming right up, Miss."

"So, why is there such a big crowd tonight?"

"We're having a barbecue for everyone staying at the Ridalgo. It's pretty early, yet. I'm sure it will get even busier later."

The beer is ice cold and tastes great. I decide to text Chase to see if he's interested in joining me.

Message: Done with my run and at the tiki bar. Interested in a drink before I head up to shower? Barbecue on the beach for dinner?

Reply: I'm right behind you!

I can't help but admire the tall, muscular frame approaching in shorts, sandals and a sports shirt, so unlike the executive by day. He asks the bartender for a Balashi. "Excellent choice, sir," he says as he hands Chase the beer.

"What am I supposed to do with you?" he asks, once the bartender is out of earshot. "One minute you want me to act like I don't know you and the next to take you to a barbecue where anyone from the resort may be. You do send some completely mixed messages, Katarina," he says clearly amused.

"I saw a crowd, was thirsty, so I stopped to see what was going on. The bartender told me about the barbecue, so I texted you... I didn't think about it being a public place."

"We can have dinner on the beach or go to a restaurant that is a little more secluded, whichever you prefer," he says, gauging my reaction. He leans closer to me and his eyes are alight with mischief. "So, where did you put your panties when you took them off?" he asks quietly.

"So you did like that?"

"You have no idea how much I liked that. I've been thinking about it all day. You are very uninhibited for someone who has encountered so little. It's going to give me great pleasure watching how you react to different experiences and sensations," he says quietly, so only I can hear.

"I'm a little intrigued about what you meant by *punishment,* this afternoon," I whisper. His eyes are dark, and his arousal is evident as he looks at me.

"Bring your drink and let's walk back and get ready for dinner." He swipes the key card as we enter my room, and we're barely past the door before his lips descend upon mine, pulling my body against his own. "You have been driving me crazy," he says against my lips. "I've been watching your tight little ass walk around in that dress all day. I thought I might have to bring you upstairs when you texted me that you weren't wearing any panties. Then if that's not enough, I find you talking to that bartender wearing practically nothing," he says.

I look up at him and smile enjoying the banter immensely. "Did that bother you?"

He pulls me closer, and his arousal is rock hard, pushing into my body with unbridled passion as he holds me close. "What do you think, Katarina?"

I'm flushed with excitement as he draws my arms into the air, pulling my sports bra up and over my chest, caressing my nipples, which harden immediately under his expert touch. He pulls my shorts and panties down to my ankles, kneeling to unlace my shoes before pulling them off one by one. He leads me into the bathroom and turns on the shower before discarding his clothing. I am mesmerized by the sight of his lean cut muscles and have a hard time looking away as he guides me into the shower.

He turns me to face the wall, so the warm water coming from the dual showerheads is pulsing over my body. "Put your hands on the wall and spread your legs for me," he whispers in my ear. I put my hands against the cool walls of the shower and feel the soapy loofah begin to glide gently over my skin while his lips find the sensitive and freshly washed skin of my neck. His tongue softly pushes into my ear sending tingling sensations all the way to the delicate spot between my thighs. He slowly caresses and rolls my aroused nipples, continuing to rub the loofah over the sensitive skin below my belly and then between my thighs. The soapiness slips between my legs as he kisses the skin along my neck, causing me to push back in response.

"Katarina, stay still. Otherwise, I'll have to restrain you," he says into my ear.

What? Why does that make me so hot?

His finger glides against my sensitive clit, slowly, touching her, caressing. One finger enters me, then another. "Katarina, I want you to be wet and aching with anticipation this evening." He pushes in a little deeper as I moan and then extracts his fingers, never stopping his assault on my neck, which has me writhing with excitement.

I am disappointed at the loss of his fingers and turn around to put my arms around his neck. He pulls me close. "Baby, I want your body to be right on the edge, aching with desire and anticipation of what's to come tonight," he says, capturing my lips with his own and pulling me tightly against him so I can feel how aroused he is, too.

"If you are not prepared to have our relationship announced by the media, then we should go somewhere besides the barbecue for dinner," he says, repeating his question from earlier.

"I've never been to a beach barbecue, and it sounds like fun."

"You're certain, Katarina? We've been in public places together for the last couple of days and the rumors can spread quickly," he says before rinsing his hair under the shower.

"I'm sure, Chase. I'm still trying to work through it, but I want us to go together."

He captures my lips in a deep lingering kiss that takes my breath away. "A barbecue on the beach it is, Baby."

"I think that should serve to get me out of this torturous punishment," I say, watching his eyes light up.

"Torturous, huh?" he says, smiling widely. "I like that... but not even your beautiful little pout is going to get you out of this tonight. I want your body to ache with desire the same way I did, especially after you told me about your panties. Patience and anticipation, Katarina," he says, kissing my lips gently.

I'm going to get dressed and have a beer on the balcony while you get ready," he says, getting out of the shower and handing me a large towel.

I rifle through the closet settling on a long multicolored skirt with a matching strappy camisole top, slip into a pair of flat thong sandals and put on a pair of large hoop earrings. I choose not to straighten my hair, but instead let it hang in natural curly waves, and apply a little moisturizer, powder, and lip gloss before going in search of Chase.

He's on the balcony talking on his cell phone with an Amstel Bright in his hand. "Just make sure it's finalized by tomorrow and full-time around the clock," he says before ending the call. "You look lovely this evening, Katarina," he compliments.

"Thank you. I see you raided the minibar. Can I try a sip? The bartender recommended both the Balashi and the Amstel Bright, but gave me the Balashi when I asked him to choose."

"Yes, take a sip but then let's head downstairs before I want to punish you even more for talking so much with this bartender," he says.

"Overbearing and possessive?" I ask, lifting my eyes.

"You have no idea, Katarina," he says, before taking possession of my lips and parting them with his tongue. "Let's go to dinner before I change my mind about teaching you the pleasures of anticipation and take you to bed for the night," he says, guiding me toward the door.

I feel thrilled with the game and even surprisingly of his possessiveness. The beach is crowded, and tables have been set up with pathways lit by flaming Tiki torches. We find a somewhat secluded table and a waiter with a large wide smile arrives to take our order. "Did you like the Balashi or the Amstel?" Chase asks me before ordering.

"I liked both, but I'll have the Amstel, please," I say.

He orders two Amstel Brights, and we listen to the sound of the local band coming from a little farther down on the beach. The waiter returns to our table with two ice cold beers and Chase talks to him about an upcoming festival before he takes our order for dinner.

"I'm surprised we haven't seen anyone from work," I say.

"Are you concerned about that?"

"I'm trying not to be, but maybe just a little," I say as the waiter returns with our meal.

He places an aluminum packet in front of each of us, cautioning us to open the steaming meal carefully. As we do, the aroma of unique spices escapes. The slow-cooked meat is covered with a sweet smelling red sauce paired with rice and vegetables.

"I'm glad we decided to come to the beach tonight instead of a restaurant. The meat is excellent. Maybe we should call it an early night, though," I suggest when we finish our meal.

"Katarina are you anxious for bed?" he asks mischievously.

He's obviously enjoying my torment. *Two can play at this game*, I think. "I guess we can stay out a little longer, but I might have to find a place to take off my panties," I say, whispering to avoid being overheard.

"Indeed," he says, smiling at my attempt to goad him.

"Let's walk for a bit and enjoy some of the local bands," he suggests, putting his arm around my shoulders as we venture toward the music where a large crowd has gathered. The dance floor is created with surrounding torches, and strings of white lights are hanging from a large gazebo. The beat is slow and sultry, and many couples are dancing. Chase takes my hand. "Dance with me?" he asks.

He holds me close to his chest, and I can feel the beat of his heart as he swirls me around and his powerful thighs guide me to the rhythm of the music. As we turn, I catch a glimpse of Mark staring at us from his spot at the bar. Chase hears my sharp intake of breath. "What's the matter, Katarina?" he asks.

"Mark is here...he's just staring at us."

He looks down at me, and I'm sure he can see the uncertainty in my eyes as I try to avert my gaze. "Katarina, look at me. I want you to think about something. We are two adults, doing nothing wrong. It is only your fear of how people will judge us that can be used against you. Do not let him see it bothers you that he has seen us together," he says, comforting me by rubbing his hand along the top of my shoulders.

"It just caught me off guard, that's all," I say, trying to convince myself to relax.

"When we get off the dance floor we'll acknowledge we've seen him and ask how his evening is going. Try not to let him see that it bothers you," he instructs. As the song ends, Chase leads me toward Mark as though spotting him for the first time.

"Mark, glad to see you're out enjoying the local entertainment tonight. It's a great night for an island barbecue. I haven't been to one in a couple of years," Chase says.

"Yes, it is. Are you enjoying the entertainment this evening, Kate?" he asks.

"The bands are impressive, and the weather has been perfect this evening. It's easy to see why people love the island so much," I reply, trying not to appear frazzled and attempting to get a handle on my nerves.

"Did you have dinner, yet?" Chase asks Mark.

"No, I ended up shooting the breeze with a couple of guys on vacation, and we've had a few drinks. Would you like one?" he asks.

"We were just about to head back to the Ridalgo, but maybe another time," Chase replies.

"I think he's had a few too many of the island drinks already tonight," he says as we get far enough away not to be overheard.

"Yes, he looked as though he had been there for a while, didn't he?"

As we enter the elevators, he fobs the elevator security pad and pushes in the pass code for the 30th floor, leaning over to kiss me gently.

"Are you worried about Mark?" he asks.

"Maybe a little if I'm honest. He just seems so disgruntled about the whole process. How did his company get selected for the design?" I ask.

"They've done a few other designs, and unfortunately, the two contracts were comingled. It's something we can undo if we need to, though. You look a million miles away, Katarina. What are you thinking about?" he asks.

I can't help the blush that rises to my cheeks. "Right now I'm having difficulty thinking about anything except you and what we're going to do when we get upstairs," I say.

He kisses my lips gently before the elevators open onto his floor and says goodnight to two men standing outside of his suite before opening the door.

"How many suites are on this floor, Chase? There can't be that many with as large as this is."

"It's the only one on this floor, Katarina," he says, hugging me from behind and kissing my neck gently. He continues trailing kisses along the side of my neck, capturing the sensitive skin between his lips while his hands move slowly over my hips, pulling me back into the hardness of his body. "Do you feel what you do to me, Katarina?" he asks as his lips travel to my ears and back down to my neck, causing me to moan softly. "I've been looking forward to what I started earlier all night," he says, leading me through the expansive suite and into the bathroom. He pulls two condoms out of his pants and places them in one of the recessed shelves in the stone shower.

I can't help but smile at the gesture. "I see I am in for a double treat, today? Maybe I should misbehave more often," I say, enjoying the look of amusement play over his features.

"I love your playfulness, now let's get you out of these clothes," he says as he begins to undress me, slowly pulling the camisole over my head and tugging gently on the elastic waist of my skirt, allowing it to float to the floor before he slides my panties over my hips, freeing me from them before undressing himself. He helps me into the warmth of the shower and his lips are urgent, parting mine beneath them. My hands find his hair, pulling him to me as his fingers find my nipples, slowly caressing my breasts until they are erect, exploring before he turns me around to face the shower and spreads my legs with one move of his powerful thighs. "Now stay very still," he murmurs as he slides the loofah between my thighs, washing me, repeatedly circling over the highly aroused area between my legs before sliding beneath me. His tongue travels sensually towards the tender flesh of my lower belly, lingering, filling me with anticipation and I hear my own intake of breath as his tongue finds its way between my parted thighs to gently caresses my clit. My hips writhe against him and he grasps my bottom, holding me still as his tongue continues its onslaught. I am unable to move and he keeps me poised on the brink for some time, before guiding my hips with his hands and bringing me trembling over the edge. I gasp at the command he has over my body and the way it responds to his touch. He explores me, intimately, as he moves behind me... sliding first one finger and then two fingers into me. "Baby, you're so wet and tight," he says, slowly stretching me. Satisfied, he dons a condom from the shelf, entering me slowly, allowing me to adjust to his thickness before exploring deeper.

I push back, reveling in the depth of his cock as he roots deep inside of me. He skillfully increases his rhythm, slowly, pushing deep inside of me as I feel myself rising in need with him. He grasps my hips... pulling me closer toward him, pushing deeper and rubbing against the sensitive spot inside of me. "I want you to feel all of me," he says, grasping my hips and pulling me onto him, allowing himself to penetrate deep inside of me and then slide against the most sensitive part of my body. I feel myself building again and try to hold back. "Baby, cum for me," he urges, causing me to shatter around him as he finds his own release, trembling against me. My legs are weak underneath me and he holds me tightly, kissing the back of my neck with warm lips as we catch our breath together.

NINE

"Let's get showered up, it's getting late and we have an early morning."

I reach for the shampoo and realize they are all the brands I use and that he's purchased them for me. "You bought me shampoo, conditioner, and a loofah?" I ask.

"I just wanted you to have a few familiar items," he says as we finish showering and dry off. He holds a robe open for me to slip into and wraps the tie around me that has the company name stitched into it. "I really love this. I've never heard of the Cashmere Boutique, but it feels like silk against my skin," I say.

"I like you in it," he says, handing me a towel to wrap my hair as he grabs another to dry himself. "There's a toothbrush for you on the sink," he says as I try to suppress a yawn.

"I should probably get dressed and head back," I say, realizing that it's after midnight and I need to be up early and have no clothes other than what I was wearing.

He gives me a long and lingering kiss before taking my hand and guiding me into his bedroom. "Stay with me tonight, Katarina. I want to feel your body against mine and you're so tired you'll be asleep within a matter of minutes," he says, laying me on the king-size bed before getting in and folding me into his arms.

"I am so tired I can barely keep my eyes open," I say, not wanting to leave the warmth of his arms as he curls me into an embrace. I wake in the night with his arms wrapped around me, and my face still lying on his chest. I listen to the steady beating of his heart and think about the night we spent together. My body responds to his so easily and my climax is effortless under his touch. In fact, I try to hold back and can't. I always thought I was one of those frigid women you read about. I slowly trace the patterns of chest hair in circles and then gradually, my fingers find their way down the path to the hair on his belly. He is so muscular and sexy, and I have never been so attracted to anybody in my life. My fingers play along the path of hair just over his lower belly, caressing and exploring when I hear his breathing begin to change. I look into his open green eyes, watching me, holding me closer, and bending to kiss me gently. My fingers continue their exploration, teasing and moving lower, urged on by the quickening of his breathing. I take his already hardened cock with my hands, exploring how it feels, slowly caressing and applying pressure as he responds to a throbbing urgency. My other hand softly cups his scrotum as I continue my exploration. His breathing becomes deeper, stronger and faster, and I can feel the sound of his heartbeat quicken simultaneously. I slowly slide down the length of him and take the tip of him into my mouth, savoring in the way he feels, caressing the tip of his erection with my tongue, urged on by another sharp intake of breath. I take him in deeper, sliding my lips around the shaft and gently suck as I come back up. I can feel his deepening desire as I continue the pattern and his hips rise to meet me. "Oh, Baby," he moans. I slowly increase my rhythm, little by little, caressing the swollen area beneath his shaft as I continue to suckle him with my lips and tongue. I can feel him throbbing and continue, increasing the rhythm and suction until he lets go and I feel him release in my mouth. "Oh, Baby," he moans as he trembles with the last of his release. I swallow and continue sucking until I know he has exhausted himself completely, and only then, I slowly pull back, licking his shaft as I do. He reaches down and pulls me back up to his chest, kissing my face as it rests against his chest. "That was beyond amazing, Katarina," he whispers hoarsely. I lay against his chest for a short while listening to his heart beat as it returns to normal and we fall back asleep.

I wake to the sound of an unfamiliar beeping and realize it's the alarm clock on the nightstand and it's already six a.m. I'm still somewhat wrapped in my robe and scoot into the bathroom to rinse off, brush my teeth and slip into the clothes from the day before. I walk into the living room and Chase is on the balcony, working on his Mac and drinking a cup of coffee. "Good morning," I say, smiling at him a little sheepishly as I pour myself a cup from the carafe before joining him.

"The views are incredible from here. Is this where you always stay when you come to the island?" I ask.

"Most often. I own the Ridalgo resort," he says.

"You own it?" I ask stunned.

"I own a lot of property, Katarina. I purchased the resort from the family when Señor Ridalgo passed away. He was a friend of my father's and I couldn't bring myself to change the name of the resort he and his family worked so hard to create. It's one of the few properties I own that doesn't bear the Prestian name," he explains.

"It's beautiful, Chase. I'm just a little shocked that you own the entire thing," I say, wondering how much a resort like this must actually cost. It's the most impressive resort on the island. "Señor Ridalgo had good taste in architectures. Every setting is created to maximize views of nature, even the interior spaces with the sky lights and glass elevators," I say.

"Yes, he was definitely a man with a vision," Chase says.

I finish my coffee and look at the time realizing I only have a short while to get ready before we are expected in the conference center. "I really should get back to my room and get ready for the day," I say.

"I'll walk you down." As we get into the elevator, he takes my hand. "I really enjoyed last night, Katarina," he says, turning me around to face him, pulling me close and gently kissing me before the elevator arrives at my floor.

"I'll meet you in the conference room," I say, and reach up to give him a kiss good-bye before pulling the door behind me. I dress quickly in a skirt, blouse, and heels, carefully selecting a sexy pair of panties that were part of Jenny's selections on our recent shopping spree. I manage to fix my hair and arrive in the conference center with ten minutes to spare. Chase is busy working on his Mac while others are either getting breakfast or networking with each other. I have time to pour a quick cup of coffee before we begin the day.

The team starts to identify issues within the current healthcare model and the morning flies by. I give the team a fifteen-minute break and grab my phone as I head toward the bathroom. Swoosh...

Message: Nice job holding this group together! Inquiring minds want to know if you are wearing panties today.

I smile. He's so fun to be around.

Reply: Wouldn't you like to know!

Message: Such sass! Be careful, Katarina. I might feel the need to punish you.

Reply: That plan might end up backfiring, as I recall it ended pretty well for me!!!!

Message: Yes, we might have to look at alternative punishments for you.

I can feel my face flush even before I walk into the room and try to avert my gaze from his direction, but I can sense his eyes moving over my body, lingering and penetrating.

The group listens to several live video sessions from clinics who are trying to improve the way primary care is delivered and to a hospital team in Houston responsible for developing a new care model that is starting to see significant outcomes. It's a long afternoon of sitting and I take a much-needed walk during the short afternoon break.

Swoosh...

Message: You look tired!

Reply: A little... I'll catch a second wind. I just need a quick walk.

I look up and nod to the guy standing by the corridor window. He looks familiar, but I can't quite place him.

Message: I need to video into a conference directly after the event. Dinner after that?

Reply: Sounds good.

Message: You're going to be late.

Reply: Just around the corner.

I walk in just as he looks up and see his bright smile. I melt inside. I really like him, a lot. He's hot, amazing in bed and so fun to be around.

The last item on the agenda is a video of patients who provide us with heartrending stories of gaps in care and service failures. The team is given a real glimpse of the general care from the patient's perspective before we wrap up for the night. Chase has already left, presumably to sign onto his conference call, so I head back to the room to change into running gear.

Message: Dinner in town tonight?

Reply: Sounds good. Do I have time to get a run in?

Message: Sure. Text me when you're back and ready.

Reply: Okay

The Aruban sun is hot and I am drenched in sweat as I finish my run and head into my room. I've barely gotten out of the shower when there is a knock on the door. I pull on my robe and wrap my hair in a towel to answer. When I open the door Chase is talking to someone on his cell and motions he will be one moment. I gesture for him to come in just as he's disconnecting with the person on the phone.

"It'll take me a little bit to get ready. Would you like a drink?" I ask.

"No, Katarina, unfortunately, I'm going to be detained this evening. Brian and I are working on a project overseas and we need to finalize some contract details. Given the time difference and all the stakeholders involved, we're going to need to redline the contract and turn it around tonight. I was looking forward to spending the evening with you," he says, pulling me into his arms.

I am surprised at how disappointed I am and try hard not to let it show. "I completely understand. I can get caught up on some other work tonight."

"Do you need anything from me in the next couple of days?" he asks before kissing my lips lightly.

"No, you've done an excellent job of participating and challenging the status quo, and it's helped keep the focus on the patients."

He pulls his cell phone out scowling at the message. "Excuse me for a moment, Katarina," he says clearly irritated. "Sid, this is Chase.

What's happening? No, absolutely not. Why don't you take the team over and get prepared for the long haul? I don't think given their current position the negotiations will be as quick as we'd hoped. Let me know once you arrive and are settled in."

"Is everything okay?"

"Hopefully soon, Baby. Don't stay up too late working," he says, kissing me good night before departing.

I finish drying my hair and call in an order for room service before settling in at the dining room table to work on the project. After a short while the telephone on the bedside table rings and I walk into the room to answer it.

"Hello, as part of our commitment to customer service I am calling to confirm that you've ordered room service and to verify your meal choices," the man on the other end of the phone says.

"Yes, of course. I ordered the blackened tilapia salad with lime vinaigrette dressing, on the side," I say.

"Thank you for taking the time to verify this. Would you care to add anything else to your order this evening?"

"No, I believe that will be all, but thank you for checking," I say.

"It should be delivered within the next ten minutes then," he says before we disconnect and I return to the work at hand, totally engrossed until a knock on the door pulls me away from my thoughts.

I open the door and two men wheel a stainless steel cart into my room and place a dome shaped plate on the dining room table, along with a silver bucket of ice cradling a bottle of wine. I recognize the bottle. "I don't think I ordered wine," I say to the waiter.

"It is compliments of the house for participating in our customer service efforts," he says, pouring it into a glass that has been placed on the table.

"How did your team know I like this wine?"

"It's our job to know what you've ordered and we tailor our service accordingly," he says.

"That certainly was not necessary, but thank you," I say, as they wheel the silver tray out of the room and close the door. The wine is delicious and an excellent accompaniment to the salad that is loaded with crisp romaine, blackened tilapia, cucumber, red onions and sweet ripe tomatoes. It takes a couple hours to finish the facility details and I decide to have another glass of wine as I review some of the material related to our project. After another hour passes, my mind wanders to what Chase is doing.

I curl into bed realizing that I still know so little about him and what he does for a living. Contract negotiations at all hours of the night and it didn't seem as though they were going well. I try to take my mind off of him and skim an article that addresses the issues surrounding so many of the critically ill. They are staggering: affordability of medication, access to care at the time they need it, transportation, communication breakdowns between different care groups and the list goes on. I am just finishing up an analysis of emergency room data and volumes when I hear a message come through.

Message: Still working?

Reply: Just finalizing a little data in case questions arise tomorrow.

Message: I'm sure you have everything you need. You should rest!

Reply: Bossy and overbearing?!?

Message: Indeed.

Reply: Are you done working now?

Message: Unfortunately, we will be here for some time. Sleep well.

IN THE MORNING, I feel less than rested having thought about the importance of the event decisions throughout the night. I jump into the shower letting the water invigorate and wake me up, slowly resigning myself to getting out and wrapping up in one of the oversized towels while I decide what to wear.

Swoosh...

Message: Good morning... I have a conference call this morning so will meet you there. Also, have another one during lunch and at the end of the day.

Reply: Anyone ever tell you that you work too much?

Message: Actually, no.

Reply: We'll have to discuss this behavior. I may need to punish you for this!

Message: Indeed?

He is the last to walk in, dressed in a dark suit that fits his sculpted body to perfection. I quickly avert my gaze and begin the meeting, but I can feel his eyes lingering on my body. I turn slowly to look at him, and he smiles, a large heart-melting smile meant just for me. It takes an effort to return my attention to the focus of the day and the other people in the room. The team, aside from Mark, seems engaged in the brainstorming exercise and we have a board full of ideas for improvements before we break for lunch. Chase has already left for his noon conference, so I mingle with the team over lunch.

I hear the familiar swoosh and smile.

Message: I'm impressed with the morning's outcomes.

Reply: Thanks!

James, the office manager for one of the physician practices, engages me in a conversation about access to the clinics and the ongoing recruitment efforts. We are standing in the middle of the room when I feel eyes on me from behind. I turn in Chase's direction as he walks in and takes a seat. Swoosh...

I try to keep my mind on the conversation at hand, until James takes a seat with his colleagues at a nearby table.

Message: Does the man have no sense of personal space?

Reply: Mr. Overbearing and possessive is back!

Message: He is indeed!

Reply: It makes me really hot...

Message: Careful, Baby...

The afternoon agenda is full but we are able to get through it successfully. We categorize and prioritize the areas that will require redesigned workflows in order to improve the care we deliver to patients in the Chicago area.

Chase leaves shortly before the others and I know it's to get signed onto his meeting. I organize the exercise boards for the next day and head toward the restroom. The environmental services staff has already begun their nightly cleaning and the restrooms are closed, so I go into the lounge area. Mark is talking on his cell and having a cocktail. He doesn't seem to notice as I walk past him to the restroom.

Swoosh...

Message: I'm almost finished with the call. Done working?

Reply: Yes...

I'm excited Chase appears free for the evening and am thinking about that as I return from the restroom.

Message: I'll pick you up in half an hour. Are you going to wear panties?

I decide to be social before responding and as I approach Mark's table, I stop dead in my tracks as I overhear him. ***"Should've seen the bitch today, she clearly has Prestian by the balls. Fucking him hard, too.*** Yeah, he actually seems to be sold on that Lean shit," he says.

He is alone and talking on a cell phone. I look around quickly to see if I can get out of the room without walking directly past him. I continue toward the exit, fighting for composure and trying to keep the tears at bay. As I get to the exit, I walk faster and faster, heading toward my suite. I change into running clothes, grab my phone and earplugs, and head back to the elevator. I hit the shuffle button on my phone, throw it into my shorts pocket, and head toward the beach as the elevators open. I feel the warm tears begin to trickle down my face. His cruel words come back to me, **"The bitch, she's fucking him hard, too."** *Why didn't I listen to my instincts? I knew getting involved in a relationship with someone I work with was a bad idea. How many nights did I lay awake listening to my mom cry after Steve left her?* Mark was talking to someone... probably someone at his company, so it'll be known all over Martel Design before we get stateside. *How am I supposed to walk into that room tomorrow? How can I even look at that crude man? Who else from the team knows?* I feel the hot tears of embarrassment flow down my face and wipe them with the back of my hand. I have to clear my head and think about how to handle this.

If Chase finds out, he'll fire him, and if he does, word will spread that Martel lost the contract because he made an inappropriate comment about me. I'll be the talk of the industry. It's obvious I can't tell Chase about Mark, and will have to deal with it myself. Maybe I just need to pretend I either didn't hear him or that it didn't bother me. The tears start to subside as I continue my run, working through my emotions and trying to determine what to do.

My cooldown song comes on and I realize that I am about an

hour from the resort instead of a half hour. I look around my surroundings and do not recognize anything in the area. The small buildings are crowded together creating little alleys and obscuring the views of the coast. I finally see a land marker I recognize and turn back in the direction of the large rock formations in the distance. As I do, I stop dead in my tracks as three men dressed in dirty khakis and bandannas move in front of me. I take a step backward, as the men come closer and then turn, panic inciting a full-out run, but I am not fast enough. My hair is caught, and I am slammed into the ground face first. I feel the intense connection of my temple with rock and then the weight of a knee pushing into my ribs and back as he shoves me, roughly, face down. He has the back of my hair pulled in a tight grip, holding me pinned. His hands move farther down the expanse of my shorts, rummaging in my pockets and the grasp on my hair tightens painfully. I hear shouts and the hold on my hair immediately loosens.

I look up and see three men in the near distance. They are quick to give chase to the men who have left me in the sand and begun to run in the other direction. They begin to overpower my attackers and I grimace at the delivery of forceful blows to the aggressors as they bring them to the ground. One of the men reaches down to retrieve the hat that has fallen into the sand during the scuffle. He brushes it off against his pant legs before placing it on his head. It is the tourist and he is talking on his cell phone as he walks toward me.

"She's safe Chase, but she did get attacked," he says, reaching out a hand to assist me up. "No, we were right behind her. If we had been a couple minutes ahead, we could have prevented the entire thing. I'll feel a hell of a lot better when we get a routine and details in place. You're not far. Just round the high rock on your right, and take a quick left by the first blue shack," he says before disconnecting.

I see Chase round the corner, and I walk instinctively to him, hiding my face in his chest before he scoops me into his powerful arms. He carries me through the alleys to a beach cart and places me into the back seat of the cart before sliding in next to me and stripping his shirt off to gently wipe the tears, sand and blood from my face. He turns to the man who has followed us. "Jay, have the guys find out what their intent was before the police arrive and have a resort doctor meet us in my room," he says.

"Already on it, Jay says, texting a message to someone from his phone before getting into the driver's seat. Chase pulls me close and gently strokes my hair as I lean against his chest. I dab my lips and am surprised to see blood on my hands. He wipes it onto his stained t-shirt and pulls me closer, kissing my hair. Jay pulls the cart around to the back of the resort. We are stopped at the gates, but the guards quickly wave us through once they see Chase and Jay in the cart. As we arrive at the entrance, he climbs out of the cart and leans over to pick me up. I start to protest, but he's not listening. "You're not walking anywhere until you get checked over," he says, scooping me into his arms. He effortlessly carries me through the back halls and toward an unfamiliar elevator and doesn't put me down until we are inside his suite.

He kisses my forehead. "I should have given you some clearer direction on where to stay. Are you in a lot of pain?" he says.

"Mostly my head and lips... I think I hit my head on a rock when he slammed me down. Do all of those men work for you? I know the one you call Jay."

"What do you mean you know Jay, Katarina?"

"I've seen him a couple of times when I was running on the beach and then in the hall earlier today."

"Katarina, the three men are part of my security team, that's why he looks familiar to you. They've been assigned to watch you since Sunday," he explains.

"You've had people following me?" I ask confused.

"Not exactly, Katarina. Keeping you safe. When you feel better, we'll talk more about security. Right now, let's get you into bed."

"I just want a bath," I say, wanting to rinse the sand and blood off of me, but not sure if I can stand up for the length of a shower. It is impossible to keep my emotions in check and the steady stream of tears on my cheeks rush uncontrolled down my face. "I don't even know why I am crying," I sob, trying unsuccessfully to stem the flood of emotion.

"Baby, it's perfectly normal after an attack like this. "I'll have Jay stop by your room and pick up a few of your belongings," he assures, handing me a glass of water and Advil. "Drink slowly and take these," he says, walking through the bedroom to start the whirlpool tub. I follow him into the bathroom as he is emptying the contents of a small container in the water. I pull my sports bra over my head self-consciously and his jaw clenches as I grimace at the pain in my side. His eyes turn to hard steel as he brushes the hair out of my eyes and gently kisses my forehead, helping me out of the rest of my clothes, holding onto me as I get into the chamomile-scented whirlpool. He undresses, sliding in behind me, and pulls me back against his strong, comforting chest using the soapy loofah to rub my neck and shoulders, gently massaging some of my stress away. "Do you want to wash your hair in here or the shower?" he asks.

"I think I'll just stay in here," I respond. I slide down his body until my head is all the way in the water and almost on his lap. I look up realizing I'm pressing against his manhood and he gazes down at me with amusement.

His lips are turned up with a quirky smile. "Wash your hair, Katarina, before I decide not to be such a gentleman," he says. He tenderly massages the shampoo into my hair and I rinse it out before he helps me out of the whirlpool. I slide into my robe and flip over to wrap my hair in the towel, but I'm caught off balance as I come up and Chase catches me, steadying me and manages to keep me upright. His eyes are dark and expressionless as he helps me into his bed before he steps out of the room.

"What's taking so long, Jay? Never mind, she's just arrived," I hear him say as he opens the door and lets someone into the suite. "Thanks for coming. She got attacked by a group in the district area and hit her head and face when they threw her to the ground. I'm also concerned about the pain in her ribs when she moves," he explains.

"Chase, your assistant told me her name is Kate. Is that right?" a female voice asks.

"Yes, her name is Kate. Follow me," he says briskly, ushering her into his bedroom. He introduces me to a well-dressed middle-aged woman with caring eyes and a warm smile as Dr. Mederea. Her sleek dark hair is parted in the middle and curls in to frame her face, falling just below chin level.

"Dr. Mederea has been the chief physician on staff at the resort for some years. As the largest resort on the island, we offer medical services to both our employees and patrons," Chase says.

"Thank you for coming to see me," I say, more than a little embarrassed at all the fuss and wishing everyone would leave me alone so I could just go to sleep.

"I'm happy to check on you, Kate. I have a few questions and I'll examine your ribs while we talk if you don't mind," she says.

"No, I don't mind," I reply as she discreetly parts my robe keeping me turned towards her as her fingers move over the bruised area of my ribs.

"Do you recall if you lost consciousness when you hit your head?" she asks.

"No, I didn't lose consciousness. It just stunned and scared me."

"Does your head hurt now?" she asks.

"Yes, a little bit. Chase gave me some Advil when we got back and it seems better now.

"Yes, I know. His assistant contacted me to find out if it would be okay. About how long ago did you take it?" she asks me.

"About forty-five minutes ago."

"Have you had any nausea or episodes of dizziness?" she asks.

Chase answers for me. "Yes, she did," he replies, silencing my look of indignation with a glance. "She flipped her hair down to wrap it in a towel and on the way up lost her balance. It's never made her dizzy before."

"Let's check some of your range of motion," she says, instructing me to raise my arms and move them in circles, and then again behind my back. "Your ribs are not broken, but you are going to be sore and bruised for a while. You'll want to continue Advil and alternate with Tylenol to get ahead of the discomfort today. I'll leave instructions for alternating, but the real concern is that you most likely have a mild concussion, Kate. I'm going to suggest bed rest for a couple of days," she says.

"Dr. Mederea, I am in the middle of an event with a team that was flown in from the States. There is absolutely no way I can take a day off right now. I need to go to work tomorrow," I explain.

"Kate, I am offering you my professional advice based on your symptoms. Head injuries are nothing to take lightly. You need to let your brain rest and heal. That is my advice," she says.

"I don't mean to sound rude, but..."

Chase cuts in, speaking directly to Dr. Mederea. "I'll see that she doesn't overexert herself. How long would you recommend?" he inquires, ignoring my glare.

"I'll leave you with a list of symptoms to watch for and as long as none present she can return to work on Monday. A little bed rest until you feel better and then you can go out and enjoy the island, but no running, jumping, or contact sports," she advises before leaving.

"Chase, I will feel better by tomorrow," I say, frustrated by the turn of events but so incredibly tired.

"No work tomorrow, doctor's orders," he says. "Now get into bed and rest. Your eyes are so heavy you can barely keep them open," he says, kissing me on the forehead.

"I'm really sorry for all this mess. I had no idea I had ventured that far," I say, sliding into bed as he pulls the comforter over me. He gently pushes the hair out of my eyes. "There is absolutely nothing for you to be sorry about. The team members will be contacted to find out if they want to stay in Aruba until Monday or fly home tonight and back in on Sunday night. My guess is most will stay and enjoy the island for the weekend. She gave you good advice: rest, no alarms, computers or televisions," he says, kissing me gently.

"I should go back to my own room. You must have better things to do than watch me lie around," I say.

"I want you where I can keep an eye on you. Now stop worrying about everything and go to sleep," he says.

"Don't you have to go back to the States?"

"I can work quite comfortably from here. I have an online meeting and then I'll be back to check on you," he says.

TEN

I wake up and try to acclimate. The clock on the nightstand registers three thirty a.m. and I go in search of Chase. He's stretched out on the couch with the Mac on his lap. "I woke up and you weren't there," I say. He puts the Mac on the coffee table and pulls me into his arms.

"How are you feeling?"

"I'm okay. You just don't expect something like that to happen. I went too far and by the time I remembered your warning, it was too late," I say.

"Shh.... Baby," he whispers, holding me close as I nuzzle into his chest. The steady sound of his heartbeat and the hand gently stroking my hair is calming. I feel my body start to relax as he keeps me held close and protected until I drift off to sleep.

When I wake up, I find myself all alone on the couch and him on the balcony working. "It's almost ten thirty. You must have needed sleep," he says.

"I probably slept so long because you kept waking me up," I say, recalling the multiple attempts to rouse me in the night.

"Doctor's orders," he says, smiling. "I just called to have breakfast delivered and was going to come wake you. Feeling more rested?" he asks.

"Much better. What happened to the men who attacked me? Did the police take them into custody?"

"Yes, Jay learned they are part of a criminal ring that targets unsuspecting tourists. They all have priors and after yesterday, I don't anticipate they will be back on the streets anytime soon. Jay filed the official report, but they'll need your written and signed statement. I can drive you over to the police station a little later in the day," he explains.

"That's good," I say, feeling relieved that they will no longer be able to ply on other tourists. "Just out of curiosity, you really had a whole team of security guards following me every day?"

"Do you really feel up to talking about this right now?" he asks.

"I do... I'm not sure if I should be mad at your assumption it would be okay with me, but on the other hand, I'm so thankful that you did. I don't know what would have happened if Jay and the team had not shown up."

His face doesn't give away his emotions. "Katarina, I hadn't planned to discuss this with you today, but you're going to need a lot more in the way of security in the future," he says, excusing himself to let room service in. They place a large tray in the middle of our balcony table. I'm famished and help myself to scrambled eggs, fresh fruit and a croissant while Chase pours the coffee.

"Why do I need more security?" I ask.

He sighs. "Jay had the three men checked out and while we don't believe you were attacked because of your relationship with me, there are others who would prey on you to get me to change my position on certain things. It's completely possible this was a random mugging, but I am not taking any chances where you are concerned. Jay and the team are still investigating the situation."

He reaches across the table and takes my hands in his. "Katarina, if you are in a relationship with me you're going to need full-time security, and it's probably going to feel like an invasion of your privacy."

"Full-time?" I ask, trying to fathom what that really might mean.

"Yes, around the clock, Baby. After a while, you'll get used to it and barely know they are around. In addition, you'll also need to live in an apartment that provides an adequate level of security."

"Chase, honestly, I can probably live with having a little security after yesterday and I don't mind renting an apartment with security, as long as I can afford it. It's actually good timing since I was planning to look at vacancies when I get back to Chicago."

He strokes the inside of my palm with his forefinger. "I think we should talk about this in more depth when you're feeling better."

"I'm feeling much better, just needed to catch up on my sleep," I say, between bites. "I'll look at apartments that have security options when we get back to Chicago. Since working is out of the question today, I may walk down to the beach area and get a little sun."

"Great idea. I have a few conference calls scheduled, but I'll make sure Jay knows where you are going," he says.

I narrow my eyes at him. "I'm only going to the beach, but thank you, and for taking care of me last night," I say.

"You don't have to thank me, Katarina. There are some bottles of water in the refrigerator that you can take with you. It's almost eleven thirty and the hottest part of the day will be in the next few hours, so you'll also want a good sunblock. The cabanas are very nice and offer a good amount of shade this time of day."

"You sound like a sunscreen commercial. Don't worry, I'll stay in the shade," I reassure, giving him a kiss before getting up to leave.

I rummage in my overnight bag and see that I won't have to stop by my room. Whoever packed for me thought to include a swimsuit? I spritz sunblock on my skin before slipping into my suit, pulling on the matching cover-up, and heading into the kitchen to throw a couple of large bottles of water into my bag. Jay follows me from a distance until we get to the beach and I'm happy that he doesn't tag along too close. The Ridalgo has its own private beach and the expanse of coastal property is impressive. I slip off my sandals and cover-up before sliding into the luxurious comfort of a double-sized cabana offering a perfect view of the turquoise Caribbean. The warm breeze and pounding of the surf are relaxing and it's not long before I find myself drifting off.

"Excuse me, Miss," a voice says, rousing me from a light slumber after an hour or so. I sit up and a man with a colorful island shirt is holding out a creamy looking drink. "Compliments of the resort, it's one of the island specialties and non-alcoholic," he says with a broad smile, handing me the glass.

"Thank you very much," I say sleepily, taking it from him as he moves on. The Ridalgo sure knows how to pamper its patrons. The drink smells a little like piña colada and as I start to take a sip, Jay calls to me while approaching my lounge chair. "Kate, hold up a second. What did the bartender say to you?"

"He was just handing out complimentary beverages and told me it was non-alcoholic," I explain, confused at his inquiry.

"Kate, the drink did not come from the resort," he says, taking it gently from my hands. I look around and do not see the bartender anywhere. Jay hits a contact on his cell. "Sheldon, don't lose him. No, he told her it was complimentary. I'll see Kate back to the room and get it tested," he says into the phone.

"What is going on, Jay?" I ask, self-consciously putting my cover-up on and gathering my bag.

"I'm sorry, Kate. We've had even closer eyes on you since the incident yesterday. The man is not an employee at Ridalgo. I don't mean to scare you, but we think the drink may be laced with something."

The apologetic look on his face tells me that he is quite serious. "Jay here," he says answering his cell, leaving me time to absorb what he's just said. "No, she didn't ingest any. Sheldon is tracking him right now. I'm taking it to Dr. Mederea. They'll be able to test it in the clinic lab. I'll contact the police once we know what we're dealing with. I was going to say I would have her up to the suite shortly, but I see you and Matt are already here," he says, disconnecting the line as Chase and Matt come into view walking briskly along the beach toward us.

Chase puts his arm protectively around me. "I want to know everything there is to know about this man and the men from yesterday. Find out if there's a connection. Any common friend, businesses, groups online, anything— no matter how small," he says through gritted teeth to Jay.

"We're on it, Chase. Our intel team is already working on portfolios of the men from yesterday. I'm going to have Matt see you back to your room so I can drop this off at the lab. I'll let you know as soon as

Sheldon checks in," he says before heading toward the far side of the resort with my drink.

Matt takes up vigilance outside Chase's room and as soon as we're alone in the privacy of his suite Chase takes me in his arms. "Baby, are you okay?" he asks, pulling me tight against him.

"I'm just bewildered. I have absolutely no idea what is going on. I can't believe someone would want to poison me, but Jay seems so sure of it. I wasn't going to argue with him or make him feel bad, but there must be some mistake, Chase."

"Katarina, I hope for everyone's sake it turns out to be nothing, but I've known Jay a long time. He's seldom wrong and I trust him completely," he says, pulling me closer into his arms before capturing my lips with his own. He pulls away slightly to check an incoming message. "Jay and Dr. Mederea are leaving the clinic now and on the way up."

"Alright, I'm going to get changed before they arrive," I say, wishing I could instead crawl into bed and go back to sleep. Hopefully we can get the situation cleared up relatively quickly and then Chase and I can have a conversation about what is and what is not acceptable about all this security.

Jay and Dr. Mederea are seated on the couch in the living room when I return and Jay's face is grim. "Chase, the test results were positive. I'll let Dr. Mederea explain the technical aspects and then we'll need to talk about logistics," he says.

Dr. Mederea gets straight to the point, foregoing preamble. "When I ran the test I found that it was heavily laced with GHB. It's the street name for a drug called gamma-Hydroxybutyric acid. It comes in the form of a clear and odorless liquid and can cause severe damage, or even death. The drug is frequently used to overtake sexual assault and rape victims because it's quick. It takes effect in about fifteen minutes, and it's hard to detect after the victim wakes up. It's usually completely untraceable after twenty-four hours with a urine test, so unless the victims report it right away, it's hard to prove they were drugged. You are one very lucky girl. I don't mean to scare you, but the levels of GHB contained in that drink were extremely high. I don't believe you would have survived had you ingested it," she says.

Chase's arms tighten around my shoulders and I feel the rock hard tension in his body. She asks me a few questions about my head and ribs before turning to Jay. "I'll keep the evidence along with the results in the lab until the police arrive. Please let me know if you need anything else, but I must return to the clinic," she says as Jay walks her to the door.

I feel nauseated and slump on the couch. "I want to know how the fuck they knew where she would be yesterday and how they got onto the grounds today, Jay," Chase says, ominously quiet as he sits next to me and pulls me into his arms. "I want a plan by the Ridalgo security team submitted to me by tomorrow morning outlining the steps they plan to take to ensure the safety of its patrons going forward. Likewise, move forward with Katarina's security plan. She and I will discuss it later," he says, taking in my uplifted brows.

"Chase, the police are going to be here momentarily. I've already contacted our teams at home and we're in the process of deploying additional men to the island. They've been instructed and should be in the air momentarily," he says.

"Good. I can't thank you enough for what you and the team did today," Chase says.

"Jay, I think I'm still in denial, but I really do appreciate everything you have done. I would be dead if it weren't for you," I say, tears slowly slipping down my face as the reality of the situation starts to sink in. Chase's arms tighten around me.

"You're welcome, Kate. That's what we're here to do. We'll find out who is behind this and why it's happening. In the meantime you're in good hands," Jay says.

"Do you think the mugging was random now or do you think someone is targeting me?" I ask, noting the cursory look of hesitancy flash in Jay's eyes as he glances at Chase.

"Baby, it's really too early to know for sure, but they are working on every lead we have right now. Jay and I need a few moments to talk," Chase says, pointing the way toward his office in the back of the suite.

I pour myself a glass of white wine and settle into one of the overstuffed reading chairs hoping to calm my nerves. It's all so surreal. I don't understand who would want to hurt me or why. I am pulled back from my thoughts by a knock on the door and the sound of Jay inviting the two uniformed police officers in. They each remove their hats in unison and introduce themselves as Detectives Hasan and Ahmad. Chase shakes hands with both of them while Jay explains what happened on the beach and informs them of the test results. There is a sharp rap on the door and Jay answers it letting Sheldon in. He appears disheveled and there is a rather large cut on the right side of his lip. The officers take notes of Sheldon's recount of pursuing the perpetrator. He stayed with the man disguised as a bartender as he left the resort, but the guy must have realized he was being trailed and called for assistance. "I was almost on top of him when two thugs jumped me in the alley right behind the Altera Sports Bar. I was able to hold my own, but by that time he was long gone," he says.

"Miss Meilers, I'm sorry for your distress today," Detective Ahmad says. "You can rest assured that we will be putting out an island-wide search for whoever did this. The Ridalgo has security cameras and we'll be able to use them to help us identify him. I know you've been through a lot already, but we're going to need to ask you questions about today and the attack yesterday and also, we'll need a detailed written statement from each of you for each incident." When they finally leave Chase pours himself a glass of wine and me another one. "I am sorry this is happening. I'm not going to let anything happen to you, Katarina."

"Do you think the police will find out why someone is trying to hurt me?" I ask.

"I'm not sure if they will, but Jay and his men will get to the bottom of this. What Jay didn't mention to the police was the real bartender noticed right away that he didn't have a resort wristband, but thought the guy had wandered onto the wrong beach area and let him buy the drink not to cause embarrassment to him or the others patrons. He recognizes him from one of the local bars where they shoot pool. Jay is getting teams in place to stake it out, as we speak."

"Are you hungry? It's been a long afternoon and you really should eat after two glasses of wine," he says.

"I'm not hungry, but I am incredibly tired," I say, trying to suppress a yawn. "I was planning to get through some email after I got back from the beach, but I'm not feeling as motivated now."

"It's too soon for you to be working, Katarina. Why don't you rest for a while? I'll wake you later for dinner."

"I think I'm going to take you up on that. I'll rinse off quick and then lay down for a little nap," I say, kissing him gently on the lips.

The water is refreshing and I put a little moisturizer on my skin after drying off. I notice my bag has been emptied and look around for my clothes. I open the top drawer and find my panties, bras, and a couple nightgowns have been folded neatly inside of it. I slip into a lacy peach-colored nightgown with matching panties, before sliding under the covers and drifting off to sleep.

I try to ignore the constant rocking of my shoulder again. "Baby, wake up." I rouse enough to realize that Chase is lying next to me. "Hi," he says, pushing the hair out of my face. "I just wanted to make sure you were okay before I go to sleep."

"What time is it?" I ask, surprised he's going to bed so early.

"It's almost midnight. I've woken you up a couple times, but wanted to check on you before I went to sleep," he explains.

"I'm okay," I assure, curling into his arms before falling back asleep.

I wake to the smell of coffee and follow it to the dining area where Chase is working on his Mac. He looks up as I walk into the room. "I was wondering how long you were going to sleep. Dr. Mederea said it's normal to sleep a lot the first couple days of a head injury, but even so I was about to come wake you up," he says.

"Surely you didn't call her, did you?" I say, sitting down across from him and selecting a delicious looking croissant from the assortment in front of us.

"Of course, I did," he says, eyebrows raised inquisitively.

"I guess she was right about laying low for a few days," I admit as he pours a cup of coffee for me.

"She said you may feel this way for a couple more days especially with all the stress from the last couple of days. If you're feeling up to it we'll take the yacht out and get a little fresh air. Jay's had quite a bit more security flown into the island. If you'd like to go, I'll make arrangements after breakfast," he says.

"I do feel much better and it sounds like fun," I say between bites of fresh pineapple and mango.

"Good. It's a perfect day to be out on the water and if you get tired you can rest under the cabana or indoors," he says.

"Breakfast was excellent. I was starving when I woke up. I think I'll jump in the shower and get ready while you're making arrangements," I say.

"Sounds like a plan, and pack a swimsuit," he says, grinning at me enthusiastically.

Chase assists me into the awaiting Jeep before pulling himself into the driver's side. Jay and Matt are in the car behind us as we drive through the island and out to the coastal highway, turning down a sloped embankment. Chase brings the Jeep to a halt and helps me to the ground. There is an enormous yacht moored just off shore and he guides me in its direction. The exterior is bright white and appears to be about three stories high. Along the side is a circular black emblem with the name Prestian emblazed upon it in gold lettering.

As we approach, I recognize Mickael. "Chase, good to see you again my friend," he calls out.

"Mickael, it's nice to see you again," Chase says.

"You remember Katarina?" he asks.

"How could I forget someone so lovely," he exclaims while extending his hand to shake mine.

"If you will excuse us Mikael, I think I'll give Katarina the fifty-cent tour," Chase says. I follow him up the stairs and onto a large deck. I'm sure my gasp is audible. Splayed out in front of us is a pool that spans almost rail-to-rail and all the way to the end of the yacht overlooking the ocean below. "Chase, it's absolutely incredible," I say.

"Come on, I'll show you the rest," he says, taking my hand as we head down another set of steps. The living area boasts of glass from one end of the room to the other, revealing the expanse of multi-hued ocean beyond them. The living space is furnished with a corner fireplace, leather sectional and impressive mahogany bar. The adjacent kitchen is adorned with dark granite countertops, glass backsplash, and stainless steel appliances. He shows me a total of three cabins, two smaller which both have nice sized double beds and adjoining bathrooms. The master suite is incredibly spacious with a king-size bed, reading chair and ottoman, a desk and walk-in closet. The views of the sea mirror those in the living room and as we walk into the master bathroom, I'm not surprised to see a marble whirlpool, in addition to a shower.

"This is the biggest boat I've ever seen in my life," I exclaim.

"Do you like it?" he asks.

"I love it. I saw the Prestian name on the side. It belongs to your company?"

"Katarina, the yacht is mine. I love to spend time in the Caribbean and I like to be on the sea as much as I can when I'm here."

"Why did you take me out on the public catamaran over the weekend if you own a fricken yacht?" I ask.

"A few reasons perhaps," he says thoughtfully. "Mikael makes the best coffee in the world," he says, as we enter the kitchen and the smell of hazelnut permeates my senses.

"Let's take our coffee and go up on deck. Did you bring your suit?" he asks.

"Yes, it's here in my bag. I'll get changed and meet you upstairs," I say, taking it into the bathroom with me.

I find the suit Jenny picked out on our girls' shopping trip. It's a little risqué but I'm secretly hoping he likes it. I pull on my cover up and find him on the deck, already lounging on one of the double cabanas.

"Why are you smiling?" I ask.

"I'm happy that you're out with me today," he says, patting the lounge chair beside him.

I feel the warmth spread through my body at the compliment and slowly pull the cover up over my head and place it on the lounge chair, watching his eyes scan the exposed areas of my body.

Did you remember to put sunblock on?" he asks huskily.

"I think you worry way too much," I say, slipping into the lounger hoping to distract from my almost nude attire.

"The glare from the sea can act like a magnifying glass out here and in combination with a bright sunny day could quickly burn and blister your skin." He tilts my head up and his eyes soften as they find mine.

"I've come to realize that listening is not your most adept skill, is it?" he asks.

I manage a slight shake of my head and realize how attracted I am to this overbearing but thoughtful man. "I'll put some sunscreen on if it makes you feel better," I concede, pulling it from my bag.

"Yes, it will make me feel better and it will prevent me from spanking that beautiful ass of yours for not listening. Actually, you should put it on quickly before I decide it would be exceptionally more pleasurable than to enjoy coffee with you on deck."

I turn away before he can see my blush and wonder if he would really do that to me.The thought is pretty hot and leaves me wondering if that may be one of the experiences he wants to show me...hmm, God he is so fun and sexy.

"Chase, why did you take me on a rented catamaran with Mikael the other day and not your yacht?" I ask again, spritzing on sunblock to the exposed areas of my skin that I can reach.

He appears thoughtful and for a moment, I'm not sure if he intends to answer me. "I realized you had not recognized me from the tabloids and newspapers, and I wasn't in a hurry for you to know who I was. The prospect of having a normal relationship was exciting to me, so I took you out on one of Mikael's catamarans. I'm sorry if it felt deceitful to you. I just wanted to experience being with someone who appreciates the simple beauty of the island and enjoyed spending time with me, and didn't give a shit about my money," he says, watching me warily.

"Well, I have to admit you somehow looked familiar, but I never really gave it too much thought. It's probably a good thing I didn't know who you were, otherwise I doubt if I would have ever given myself a chance to get to know you."

"Why do you say that, because I employ the company you work for?"

"Yes, because I technically work for you and if I had known who you were I would have put as much distance as possible between us," I say.

"And now?"

"I'm working through that, but I have to tell you, the fact that you employ the company I work for, own an entire resort and have this yacht is absolutely overwhelming to me," I say.

"How so?"

"I can't even imagine how much things like this would cost. Probably more than I will make in a lifetime. If it's any indication of your lifestyle it's more than a little intimidating if I'm honest."

"Katarina, it's only money, don't let it bother you," he says.

Chase jumps up when he hears Mikael call for him and grabs my hand. "Mikael has spotted dolphins," he says, guiding me to the rail so we can get a better look. We can see the tail of a dolphin, then two ... and then three of them. They are following our wake and one flips into the air, then... as if not to be outdone, another follows suit, flipping even higher out of the water. We watch until they tire of playing and slowly move out to sea.

"They're so beautiful... and I didn't realize they were that big," I exclaim.

"I love the way your eyes light up when you are excited, Katarina," he says, bending to kiss my lips gently.

"Chase, get Katarina down below," Jay calls, dashing across the deck with Matt and Sheldon close behind him. Before I have time to react Chase has me securely in the stairwell and we are headed downstairs. Two men that I have not met before are right behind us and as we get into the living room, they push some buttons and like magic, all the blinds in the room come down.

"Chase, we've got a large ship less than a mile out and it wasn't registered anywhere earlier. We've got a sniper team up on deck and another group in the helicopter heading this way. Jay wants you to stay below with Kate until we understand their intent," he says.

"Thanks, Keith. Greatly appreciate the update. Please keep me apprised. I'll have my phone with me," Chase says.

"No, I'm sorry, sir, but my orders are to stay with you and Katarina, as we may need to move you further below," he says.

"Chase narrows his eyes at him but does not argue. "Very well, Keith, we appreciate your help in the matter, but Katarina and I need to get dressed. Can you make sure my bedroom is secure and we'll get changed and go wherever you need us to go," he says.

I am appreciative of his gesture since we didn't take the time to get my cover up from the chaise lounge where we left it on deck.

"Sorry, Chase. We can't allow you to move towards the back of the yacht. Just give me a few moments and I will get you some clothes," he says as he heads for the master bedroom. He no sooner gets into the bedroom then comes out holding up a pair of shorts, a t-shirt, and a bathrobe.

"Will these do? We've just got word to be on standby and may need to move you below, fast," he says.

"All right, give us a second," Chase says.

"Here, Baby put this on," he says handing me the robe and sliding his shorts over his swim trunks.

"Any word on the boat's destination?" he asks Keith.

"No, that's why Jay is taking extra precautions. There's nothing registered at all. Not that it's unusual in these waters, but we're not taking any chances, given the last couple days."

I am scared. I've never been in a situation where my life could be in jeopardy, and now I have experienced it three consecutive days.

"Chase, there must be a reason that we are being targeted this week. Do you know why?" I ask.

"Baby, I'd be lying to you if I told you that we don't encounter resistance and have to take added security precautions every once in a while, but I don't have a fucking clue why there have been attempts on your life," he says.

"Do you think it has something to do with the project we're working on?" I ask.

"Very few people know about it and the only ones, at least initially, who will get stoked over it are the unions and pharmaceutical companies. The unions are going to want to make sure they get a chance to bid on the construction work. Unfortunately, Prestian Corp has some other contracts that are tied to individual construction companies, similar to what we're experiencing with Martel Designs. We've got our legal department reviewing and working on revising the contract to ensure it's not a barrier in the future, but for the short term, it's going to appear as though we are trying to shut the unions out. Likewise, when we start looking at the reimbursement model for drugs, the pharmaceutical companies are going to have plenty to say about it. We're not looking to decrease the amount of revenue they receive since we know much of the profit margin gets funneled back into research, but we are looking for an alternative to the patient needing to make up the difference. If the med isn't part of the covered package, we will continue to have patient non-compliancy resulting in compromised care and readmissions to the hospital."

"Then who do you think is after us, Chase?"

"We have a couple projects overseas that we are starting to meet a little resistance with, but I don't believe you've been with me long enough that they would see you as an opportunity to get to me, but I may be wrong. Just in case, Jay and the team have all of those possibilities laid out and are working every possible lead," he says.

Keith answers his phone as we are talking and nods every once in a while. "Sounds good, Jay," he says.

"Chase, we've got the all clear. The boat has moved south and appears to be heading into the South Atlantic Ocean. We've got eyes on it from the air and are confident that it's not a threat," he says.

"Great news, Keith. Thanks for your help this afternoon. We're going to head upstairs. It's beautiful out and I don't want to spend any more time than is necessary indoors," he says.

"Completely understand, Chase. Give me a few moments before you do that," he says sending out a message on his cell phone. It takes a short while to get all the confirmations that security needs to feel safe about us returning to the deck, but once we have it, Chase leads me upstairs and back to our lounge chairs. I don't see Jay or the security teams around so I slide out of my robe.

"Let me spray a little sunblock on your back, Katarina," he says, spritzing it onto my skin as I turn around for him. He rubs it into my shoulders and down my back, and then slowly rubs it in along my exposed cheeks and back of my thighs. There, I think that will do," he says.

Chase discards the shorts he was given and lays beside me on the cabana under the shade of the protecting cover. I realize that he's probably right. A person could get burned in the intense heat of the sun and I'm appreciative of the cabana's protection. The rest of the afternoon is relaxing and just what the doctor ordered: no television, computers or distractions and Chase seems relaxed regaling me with some of his escapades on the island. I try to stifle a yawn later in the day, but it does not go unnoticed. Chase takes me by the hand and leads me across the deck and down the stairs toward the master bedroom.

"Where are we going?" I ask.

"I'm going to tuck you in so you can rest before dinner," he says, closing the bedroom door with his foot and pushing a button on the wall that slides the blinds into place over the expansive windows. He kisses my lips with a checked urgency and unties the straps of my swimsuit from around my neck, slowly pulling it down, exposing my breasts and letting it fall onto the floor. His hand caresses the top of my bottoms, slipping his fingers into the sides and slowly working them past my hips, exploring the length of my body as he allows them to find the floor. He lays me back on the bed and gently pushes my thighs apart revealing me further to his smoky gaze. His finger finds the sensitive spot between my legs, stroking me until I am heatedly aroused and moist. He takes his time and then slowly begins caressing me with his tongue, following the same pattern until I am writhing with desire.

He pauses momentarily, "Still, Baby, or I might need to tie you up," he says huskily against my skin. He slowly inserts two fingers inside of me, pulling out and then pushing them deep inside as his tongue continues its sensual journey. I am unable to control my hips as they rise to meet his touch or to hold back any longer, trembling and crashing uncontrollably around him. I attempt to close my legs, but he has them spread apart and continues to lick softly over the swollen and still trembling area, creating new waves of sensation. He maintains his grasp on my thighs, causing me to writhe against his tongue and the sensual strokes until he brings me over the edge, trembling against the warmth of his mouth. I am breathless as he pulls me up against his chest, holding me close while I catch my breath. As I reach for him, he shakes his head. "No Baby, I want you to rest now."

I curl into the down pillows, too tired to argue, exhausted from the aftermath of his lovemaking and fall into a sated sleep. I wake a couple hours later and decide to indulge in a warm and invigorating shower. I try to keep the giddiness from getting the best of me as I look around. A loofah, my brand of body wash, shampoo, conditioner and a fresh razor are resting on the stone ledge shelves of the shower and next to it sits a vase of lilacs. *My absolute favorite flower, but how did he get them in Aruba? He's great, but can I actually work for someone I'm in a relationship with?* I finish showering and reach for the long Cashmere robe hanging on the hook. I snuggle into it and throw my hair into one of the towels, wondering if he thought of a toothbrush. *Of course, he did.* I quickly brush my teeth, spritz on sunblock and slip back into my swimsuit. Jenny helped me pick it out thank goodness. It is a simple and classic black two piece with a little circle of gold nugget holding the front together. The bottoms are a Brazilian cut and skimpier than I would have chosen. I brush through my damp hair and pull on my cover up to go in search of him on deck. I do not see Chase or anyone for that matter so I quickly discard it and snuggle into the luxurious material on the chaise lounge, relishing in the feel of the sun's warmth on my body and the tranquility of the sparkling turquoise-colored sea.

I sense his presence behind me before I feel his hand pushing my hair to the side. He gently kisses my ear, pulling on my sensitive lobe with his teeth. "Baby, that swimsuit looks great on your ass," he compliments, flipping me over in the lounge. "Did you sleep well?" he asks.

"I slept amazingly well," I reply, feeling my skin warm with the memory of him tucking me in.

His lips capture mine gently, avoiding the side that is still bruised and puffy. "Let's go relax in the pool," he says, taking my hand as he guides me through the wood and glass arched cabana to the other side of the deck. He leads me into the cool water and into shaped seats by the edge of the pool, which allows us the perfect view of the turquoise and brilliant blue of the sea swirling around us.

"I don't think you could have brought me to a more relaxing place," I say, admiring the turquoise color of the sea and the feel of the cool water around us.

"You really think of everything, don't you?" I ask.

He looks at me with amusement. "Everything?"

"Well, aside from all this," I gesture with my hands..."I took the liberty of jumping into the shower and all my brands were on the shelf, not to mention a new toothbrush and robe. Oh, and not to forget the great tuck-in service. You just seem to think of everything."

His eyes are alight and his jaw quirks. "You think something as simple as making sure your brands are available is thinking of everything? Katarina, I have a difficult time thinking about shampoo and soap being things that please you."

"I love that you think of the little things. It makes me feel special," I reply.

"You're so refreshing, Katarina. You find my lifestyle and possessions overwhelming and love that I buy you shampoo. I am definitely a little out of my league here," he says grinning.

"I absolutely love that you notice what types of shampoo and conditioner that I use and care how I feel in the bedroom. It's something I've never had, Chase."

"Baby, it still amazes me," he says, kissing my lips gently. The water is refreshing, and we spend time talking about some of his business ventures in Aruba and different countries around the world. He glances at his cell phone and scowls before tapping out a response.

"What's the matter, Chase?"

He shakes his head. Just a little situation with one of our business deals. It's not moving as quickly as we would like and I may need to travel to get it resolved," he says.

"Don't you like to travel?" I ask.

"Actually, I do, but would prefer it be for pleasure. Brian typically travels for the business more than I do. Once negotiations are finalized he's more hands-on and in charge of developing structures and resources to support operations in the facilities," he says.

"Unlike the Prestian Medical facility venture, in which you seem to be very hands-on," I say.

His mouth turns up in a quirk attempting to hide his amusement. "This particular one requires my personal attention on many levels. In fact, why don't you relax, dry off under the cabana and I'll get the salads and wine. They've stocked the refrigerator with grilled chicken, vegetarian, and seafood salads for dinner. Do you have a preference?" he asks.

"They all sound delicious, but the grilled chicken sounds good tonight," I say as he heads to the kitchen. Left to my own thoughts Mark's callousness comes back to me, and I wonder if soon I will be the laughing stock of the industry. I ponder briefly if this is the way my mother felt when she was dating her boss years ago. Chase has come to mean too much to me, far too quickly, and I know I can't possibly give him up simply because I work for him, but can't help dwell on what that choice cost my mother so many years ago.

We watch the sunset, as we enjoy the grilled chicken salads that are accompanied with an orange vinaigrette dressing and a glass of white wine. The view is just as magnificent as promised with bursts of fiery orange streaks of color, merged with the blue and purplish hues that shimmer on the horizon. We watch as the great orange ball that is the sun, seemingly so near, descends and continues to reflect off the ocean from our seats on the Caribbean.

ELEVEN

I know I should tell him about my past and about what transpired with Mark. He's a good man and has a right to know why I ran off and why it's so hard to trust. *It's now or never.* "There's something we should talk about, Chase."

"What's that Katarina?" he asks, taking a sip of his wine.

"I told you that I haven't dated much, but there's more to it than what I've shared. You asked me why I have issues with dating someone that I work with, so I should probably tell you," I say pausing, wondering if it's too soon.

"I'd like to hear that very much," he says.

"My father wasn't a part of my life growing up and my mom fell in love with someone she worked with when I was a young teenager. While I can't remember all the details, the ones of her crying herself to sleep after it ended have stayed with me over the years. We had to relocate shortly after that and I vowed never to let that happen to me... but, I find myself not wanting to give up what we have," I say, watching his expression for some clue as to what he's thinking.

He lifts my chin and captures my eyes with his own. "Katarina, I won't let you walk away from this. We are both consenting adults and your professional career is not in jeopardy as a result of our relationship, either now or in the future."

"It's not that easy. My career is already in jeopardy. There's more that I haven't told you, but I'm scared that if you know, you'll react rashly and make it worse," I say hesitantly, gauging his response.

"What is it you are not telling me, Katarina?" I try to avert my gaze, but to no avail. "Tell me, Baby," he urges.

"Thursday you left the conference and I stayed to finish some work. I walked down to the restrooms after I got done and Mark was in the lounge. I stopped to say hello in hopes of getting back on the right foot. He was on the phone and I overheard a conversation he was having," I explain.

The firm set of his jaw and darkening of his eyes is intense. *Maybe I shouldn't tell him what he said...* "What did he say to you, Katarina?" *Too late...*

"What did that man say to make you so distraught, Katarina?" he asks again as I hesitate.

"It was vulgar. He had been drinking and said something like, ***'should've seen the bitch today, she clearly has Prestian by the balls. Fucking him hard, too.'***"

"Dammit!" he explodes. The anger on his face is palpable and the glint in his eyes is unmistakable. "Why didn't you tell me?" he asks.

"Because I don't want you to make it worse," I say.

"How the fuck can it get any worse? I'll be damned if I'll have him working on any project of mine. I don't want that man anywhere near you."

"Chase, if you fire him it'll appear he was let go for making some stupid comment about the person you're sleeping with. If word gets out it will be much worse for me," I say, trying to reason with him.

"How will it be worse for you? You won't have to listen to his foul mouth!"

"Chase, you have to let me deal with this. You can't just charge in and fire everyone that says something derogatory about me."

"The fuck I can't, Katarina. He's finished."

"Chase, this is exactly why I didn't tell you. Martel is a huge conglomerate and if Mark gets fired, he will make it known that I was the cause. It will affect the projects I get asked to do in the future. I need time to think about how to handle it and I'd like you to help me resolve it, but please don't fire him," I say.

"This is the second time I've wanted to let him go and you've intervened. It's really against my better judgment, Katarina."

"Chase, this is the stuff that can really affect my career."

His eyebrows rise in question. "Is this what happened to your mom?" he asks.

"I don't know, Chase. All I remember is her crying all the time. I could hear her through the walls of our bedrooms. Then we started moving, town after town, new school after new school and no friends."

"What about a compromise? We'll develop a plan for Mark tomorrow, but then I am going to go over a very detailed list of security items and I want you to agree with them," he says.

"Okay, we can look at the list tomorrow and see which ones we can agree on."

His eyes hold mine captive. "Katarina, I want you to agree to the entire list. Surely you understand my arguments around security with everything that has transpired the last couple days?"

"I do, Chase, but this is all new to me. They are complete strangers to me and yet they need to know all the intimate details of my life? You just need to give me some time."

"Unfortunately, we do not have the luxury of time. We need to have a plan in place for your security."

"Has Jay been with you a long time?" I ask changing the subject.

He narrows his eyes at me not fooled for a moment. "Yes, he's been with me for quite a few years and is a good man. As soon as you left the lounge he knew something was wrong. He just didn't expect you to come barreling out of your room like you did. He and his team followed you onto the beach. If he hadn't, it's hard to say what could have happened to you in that alley or if you had consumed that drink."

"I know, and I am very grateful to him."

We finish our salad and wine and I feel relieved that I told him. He was obviously angry, but at least he agreed to work through it together which was probably a huge concession for him.

"Thank you for not firing him. I know it goes against your better judgment," I state.

"I'm not going to allow you to be in danger, regardless of your fears, Katarina. I'll have Jay start a profile on him. It's highly unlikely that he had anything to do with the two attempts on your life, but I need to be sure."

I walk around the table and slip into his lap, kissing him gently. "Thank you. I know you are just trying to keep me safe and I will try to be more cooperative," I say.

"You are quite distracting sitting on my lap with nothing on but this bikini," he says, rubbing the sensitive skin of my neck.

"I'd much rather be sitting on your lap with nothing on," I confess.

"Careful, Baby, you're not wearing much and I am only human. Why don't you go change while I talk with Mikael? We'll be pulling onto shore rather soon and he and I need to discuss adding more fleets to his commercial catamaran business," he says, giving me one last kiss.

I slide off his lap, careful to press into his hardness as I do.

His eyes are alight with amusement. "I see this is going to be a long night," he says as I head toward his bedroom.

I realize I left my cell on the nightstand earlier. I pick it up and see several missed texts from Jenny.

Message: How are you feeling today?

Reply: Much better. I will call you later.

I should really have some fun tonight. I send Chase a quick text.

Message: Trying to decide if I should wear panties or not...

Reply: You are playing with fire tonight.

Message: I vote for no panties...

Reply: Spankings feel much better without them!

Message: Doctor ordered rest!

Reply: Quit tempting me or I might change my mind leaving you to explain your red ass in the event you have a relapse!!

Message: Maybe a little embarrassing, huh? I'm curious about this punishment thing...

Reply: I like the idea of punishing you when you deserve it. Like NOW!

Message: Why now?

Reply: Because you are deliberately arousing me when you know I want you to rest!

Message: I can't believe you would accuse me of such a thing. That behavior would certainly call for punishment.

R**eply:** It does! Are you almost ready?

Message: Yes, up in a minute without my panties...

Reply: A slow torturous punishment to compensate for the agonizing hard-on I've had all day will do nicely.

I smile at the last response, finish dressing, place my panties into my bag, open the bedroom door, and stop short to find Chase at the entrance. "Mikael is still mooring the boat, so we have a little time before we depart," he says, closing the door behind him. He runs his fingers down the side of my neck and traces the ties to my sundress before loosening them and letting it drop to the floor.

"You forgot to mention that you were also braless," he chides, exploring my naked body with his eyes. He gently pushes me down on the bed and opens the nightstand to pull out what appear to be suede ties.

"I'm going to tie you to the bed now, so you can't move that luscious ass of yours all over the place," he says. "If you don't like anything I'm doing or want me to stop, I want you to tell me right away."

I nod, barely able to contain my surprise and excitement. He watches me intently as he cuffs first one hand and then the other to the bedposts, spreading my legs slowly and cuffing my ankles one at a time to the bottom of the bedposts.

"Does it excite you to have your body restrained and exposed in front of me?" he asks.

I am excited and turned on...but nervous. I can only nod.

"I'm going to punish you for all the anguish you've caused me today."

I nod, wondering what it is that he's going to do. Holy shit... I suddenly realize I really can't move. He plants small kisses on my body starting at my neck, ears and nipples, continuing lower to trail kisses on my belly before his tongue finds the amazingly sensitive spot inside my navel. His tongue lingers there for some time, building my desire before trailing lower with his tongue. He nuzzles the soft auburn hair with his nose and by now my body is aching for his touch, right there on the spot he seems to know perfectly. His tongue is warm and wet on my skin and finally he lets it wash over me, finding his mark, creating a deep warmth and ache inside of me. He continues, with slow and deliberate strokes that run over my clit, igniting me, and then with strokes that are just off the mark. I try to arch to coax his tongue in the direction of that special little spot, but his skillful tongue knows exactly how to keep my body poised on the brink. I attempt to move my hips and meet his tongue, but am bound by the constraints and he holds my hips firmly. My body is on fire by now and I hear myself softly moan. He lifts his face, gently kissing the soft hair between my legs, and then my belly button, making me squirm with desire.

"Don't stop, Chase."

"Baby... patience and anticipation. We'll finish this later. Right now I want you as turned on as I have been all day," he says, trailing kisses over my body as he slowly unties the restraints. I'm left with an aching desire that I fear is not going away anytime soon. He pulls me up gently and easily slides my dress over my head before he pulls me close so I can feel how aroused he is.

"Do you feel what you do to me, Katarina?" he asks, his smoky eyes capturing mine and holding them with the intensity of his gaze.

I nod, captivated by him and the way he makes me feel.

"If we don't go up shortly, Mikael will be down in search of us," he says, as he takes my hand and guides me above deck.

We head back to the resort in the Jeep and when we arrive he takes me by the hand. "Let's go to the tiki bar and have a glass of wine," he says, eyes watching me intently.

"Okay," I say, my heart only half in it. *What I really want is for him to take me back to his room and finish what he started.*

He looks mischievous. "All in good time, Baby," he says. We find a table overlooking the water. "What are you thinking, Katarina?" he asks.

"We've known each other for a week and we met in this very bar. Is that why you brought me here, tonight?"

"It's one of the reasons I brought you here. I enjoy this bar and meeting you here just makes it that much more special. I didn't want to take you upstairs just yet," he says, gauging my reaction.

"So you brought me here to prolong my agony?"

"I thought it was pretty well suited since you wouldn't stop tormenting me today," he says.

"I don't like this punishment very well," I say, pretending to pout as the waitress brings us our wine.

"Baby, you're such a delight. It's a punishment that will provide you greater pleasure in the end," he says.

"I'm not sure about that. I need to go to the restroom," I say.

"Can I come and watch?" he asks softly.

"No, I think you've done quite enough already," I retort, smiling as I head toward the ladies restroom. Jay is standing by the far wall appearing to look at a tourist pamphlet. As I make my way back to the lounge area, I almost stop dead in my tracks as I see Mark at a table with other members of the event team. I recall Chase gave them the choice of flying back to the states or staying on the island until the event resumed. Mark notices me right away and leaves the table to come and talk to me. *Be cool*, I admonish myself. *Do not show that he intimidates you or he will sense it.*

"Hey, Mark," I call out as he reaches me.

"Kate, I didn't expect to see you around until Monday. We were told you were in an altercation on the beach. Hope it wasn't anything too serious," he says, appearing sincere and friendlier than normal.

"I took a pretty bad hit to the head and I'm banged up a little, but feeling much better."

"I don't know how much you overheard the other night, but I had been drinking for almost an hour and was just blowing off some steam. I'm sorry if you heard something inappropriate," he says, shifting his weight from one foot to the other.

"Mark, I'm not quite sure what you're referencing. I was in such a rush to go for a run that I'm afraid I wasn't paying much attention." Chase is standing at the door glowering into the room at the two of us.

Mark appears to visibly relax. "A few of the physicians flew back to the states and will travel back in, but the rest of us took Chase up on his offer to stay at the Ridalgo until the event resumes. We were just going to order another round of drinks if you would like to join us," he says.

"Thanks for the offer, but I believe Chase just ordered a drink for the two of us, but maybe a different night," I say before heading towards Chase, who meets me halfway into the room, puts his arm around me and guides me back to our table.

"What did he say to you?" he asks as we reach the bar.

"He said he wasn't sure what I overheard the other day and apologized for any inappropriateness," I reply.

"Katarina, do you really believe he is sincere?" he asks.

"No, I don't. Right now he doesn't know what I heard or what I've said to you."

"You shouldn't have been talking to him alone like that."

"Jay was right outside the hall and obviously texted you the moment he saw Mark approach me or you would not have come rushing in like that. Am I right?"

"Katarina, what am I going to do with you?" he says. The quirky smile that is becoming so familiar appears.

"Chase, you're going to have to pretend you don't know anything about Mark. He isn't sure if I've told you and I don't want to give my hand away."

"I'll think about it, Baby," he says.

The band begins to play an island rendition of a well-liked song and Chase takes my hand, leading me onto the dance floor, holding me close to his body and skillfully weaves me among the other guests. My head rests comfortably on his chest and I can hear the sound of his heartbeat as we dance to several numbers.

"Let's go upstairs for the night, Katarina," he whispers as another song comes to an end. He nods to Jay as we head to his room and we've barely entered the room when he pulls me into his arms, capturing my lips gently with his own.

"Does it turn you on to walk around and dance in public with no panties on?" he asks. I feel the hot blush on my cheeks.

"I'm sure I should be punished for such brazenness," I tease.

"You're going to have to stop tempting me or you're going to find yourself across my knee or in my bed all the time," he says.

"What if I want you to put me across your knee?" I ask, hearing an audible intake of breath.

"Have any of your former lovers spanked you, Katarina?"

"No, nothing like that," I say, feeling the blush rise to my cheeks.

"I'm curious about your interest, Baby. If you want to experiment, I'm more than happy to oblige," he says, guiding me to the couch and onto his lap. "But when I say punish I mean it in the sexual context of driving you absolutely crazy, nothing more. You'll need to tell me if there is something that you don't like, Katarina."

"I can barely think straight I'm so turned on, Chase. I'll tell you if I don't like it," I assure him.

He brushes the hair out of my eyes, kissing me gently before laying me face down on his lap and slowly pulling my dress up to my waist. I am completely exposed in this position. He caresses my ass with gentle hands, before crossing one of his legs over the back of my thighs, easily restraining me. His fingers follow the curve of my back from the waist down to my highly exposed ass cheeks, tracing around each, sending shivers of delight through my body, building the anticipation.

"Your ass is so beautiful, tight and firm..." He reaches between my legs so he can explore me with his fingers. "You're so wet and ready," he says, pushing a finger deep inside of me, and then two, making me squirm before he pulls out. "Are you sure you want to do this, Baby?" he asks, again.

I nod, my throat dry and hoarse with eagerness.

"Okay, I am going to spank you a total of eight times, but if you don't like it, tell me and I will stop.

His hand lands firmly on the right side of my cheek, startling me and at the same time sending a tingling sensation deep into my body. He rubs the spot lightly before delivering another smack to the left side, and again he rubs the spot before the third is felt in the center of my ass, as well as the fourth and fifth and then the rest. He parts my thighs and enters me with two fingers...pushing in deep and slowly pulling out.

"Baby, you are absolutely soaked."

He increases the rhythm of his fingers inside of me and begins rubbing my clit. I am almost immediately lost to the trembling that overtakes my body. He caresses me through it, extending my release until I am completely spent and breathless "Baby, I love being intimate with you," he says, kissing me gently.

"Have you ever used toys, Katarina?" he asks.

I shake my head. "I haven't except for the ties today," I say.

"Come with me," he says, guiding me into the bedroom and pushing me into the softness of the down comforter before he opens the nightstand. He pulls out a dildo with an attachment on the end. I've seen it advertised in magazines and even entertained the idea of purchasing something similar at one time, but was too shy to go through with it.

He pulls a bottle of lubricant out of the drawer and opens my legs, positioning himself between them so I am completely exposed and on display to him. He bends down, eyes still holding my own captive, and blows on my clit, before inhaling deeply. He has not touched me, but I feel myself moistening in anticipation, as he opens the top of the lubricant bottle, dribbling a few drops onto his fingers before warming it with his breath. He glides his index finger over my clit, ever so slightly, and then allows it to enter me slowly. He pushes it in deeper, twirling his finger inside of me, ensuring the lubricant is well dispersed. He repeats the pattern, pushing into me deeply with one finger, and then begins to caress my clit with his thumb. "Chase," I moan, lifting my hips to take his finger in deeper.

"There, now you're ready, Baby," he says, rubbing the large dildo against the moistness of my body, before sliding it into place. I gasp at its depth and rigidity. He does not move it but gives me a few moments to acclimate before gliding it slowly out of me and then back in. The end of the attachment rubs against my clit each time he pushes it into me and my body is shameless, rising up to meet him thrust for thrust.

"Don't stop, Baby. I'm going to turn the vibration on and you're going to need to tell me if it's too intense," he says.

He turns it on and it is intense. The pulsing sensations are fast, rubbing deep against my insides while grinding and almost squeezing my clit with every down stroke. My breathing has become ragged and I cry out, but he does not stop. "Cum for me, Baby. I want to see you shake again," he says, pushing me over the edge as another orgasm overtakes my body. He gently repositions me to the end of the bed before rolling a condom onto his engorged penis. His body is magnificently chiseled and I reach up to stroke him.

He groans, lowering himself to me, taking possession of my lips as he pushes into me. "Baby, you are so tight... I can barely think straight," he says, his eyes dark with passion. He pushes in deeper, exploring with each penetrating thrust. I wrap my legs around his back and pull his body closer as we find our rhythm. He is intentionally slow, bringing me right to the edge and then changing course, keeping me poised and wanting, shamelessly arching to meet him stroke for stroke. He grasps my hips firmly, lifting them and I gasp as he penetrates me even deeper, over and over until I am crying out and he releases deep inside of me. He holds me close against his chest, as our bodies recover, pushing the hair out of my face and gently kissing my lips. "Let's relax a little in the whirlpool," he says, guiding me into the bathroom, discreetly discarding the condom before turning on the whirlpool and sprinkling bath crystals into the warm and inviting water.

I look into the full-length mirror and gasp with feigned shock. "Chase Prestian, you have spanked my ass red."

"Get into the bath, Katarina. Your playfulness makes me hot for you, Baby. I'll pour us a glass of wine," he says.

I smile and slide into the water and can't help but admire his washboard abs, muscular thighs, chest and arms as he returns with our wine and slides in.

"Baby, I want you to tell me how you felt today when I put you in restraints and spanked you."

"You really want to know?" I ask, embarrassed.

"I need to know Katarina, but I have a difficult time thinking about anything except fucking you when you're blushing at me like this."

"Well, you ask such embarrassing questions. I've never talked to anyone about stuff like this."

"My intent is not to embarrass you, but to make sure your needs are met, Katarina."

"I can try. I'm just not used to talking about these types of things," I explain. *Here goes...* "It made me feel completely exposed and on display this afternoon. When you restrained me earlier, I didn't know what to expect. I've never been held in place by anyone, but I trusted you. The way you made me feel was like nothing I've ever experienced. It was the same feeling tonight when you pushed my dress up around my waist and my ass was uncovered. It almost felt like I was on exhibit and when you were spanking me, I felt a little embarrassed at first and having said that I have never felt so liberated, wanted and sensual in all of my life," I say, looking into his intent and steely green eyes. "I absolutely love how you make me feel, Chase."

He reaches for me and kisses me long and hard.

"Baby, you don't know how good that makes me feel. I was worried we might have taken things a little too fast. I was hoping that I did not scare you."

"Scare me?" I ask. "Nothing could be further from what I feel. When you say things like, 'I'm going to spank your ass red,' it makes me hot, not that I would want you to hurt me. And it does embarrass me talking about it. I've never done that with anyone before."

"The only way I can make sure your needs are met is if I know what you like and don't like," he says.

"Do you really want to know what I want now?" I ask, urged on by the effects of the wine.

"I'm listening, Katarina."

"I would like to have another glass of wine, lie in your lap, and have you rub my ass," I say, trying to keep my blush under control, but to no avail.

"I personally think that's an excellent idea and if you keep blushing, I'm going to have a hard time not fucking you again."

"You're not going to give me a protest about another glass of wine?" I ask.

"No, as you so aptly mentioned there's been plenty of time between drinks today." I wrap up in my robe and head for the couch as he pours the wine. He places the glasses on the coffee table and pulls me into his arms, kissing me and finding my nipples below the soft material of the robe.

He laughs. "That's what I thought I might find." Are you turned on just thinking about me having your ass exposed while I rub it?" he asks.

I nod as he slowly pushes the soft material over my ass and up to my waist. I feel his hands on my hips and then a trickle of warm liquid that he begins rubbing into my skin. "Katarina, I do believe I've been duped into thinking your ass was sore," he says.

I smile to myself, stretching leisurely and enjoying the feel of his hands on my body.

"I love your ass, Baby. I want to feel it around my hard cock."

"I don't know if it will fit," I respond warily, thinking of his girth.

"It won't at first. We'll work with some small devices and lubricants until you get used to it. They will stretch you so that when we do you'll be ready and it won't be painful," he explains.

"If you say so," I say.

"Have you ever felt anything inside of your ass before, Baby?" he asks.

"No," I respond.

"I want you to relax and trust me," he says. I lay my head on a couch pillow and enjoy the exploration of his hands over my ass and lower back. He adjusts slightly and shifts so his fingers can explore between my legs and rub my clit.

I moan softly. "Chase, that feels good."

"Stay focused on the feel of my finger," he instructs. I feel warmth drizzled over my ass as another finger starts to rub its opening. I tense a little at first.

"Trust me Katarina, it's only my finger," he says, rubbing the opening with a circular motion while he positions his other hand underneath me and uses his finger to caress my clit.

"How does it feel, Baby?" he asks.

"Very nice," I respond, slightly embarrassed and glad he isn't able to see my face.

"You're going to feel a slight bit of pressure, and I want you to breathe through it," he coaches, gently inserting a small finger into my ass. He doesn't move but lets me acclimate. "Does that hurt, Katarina?" he inquires.

I shake my head. "No, it feels different... full," I respond. He pushes in deeper, again pausing to let me adjust. He continues, slowly fucking me in the ass with his finger while maintaining the slow and sensuous rhythm to my clit.

"Oh, please don't stop," I say.

He continues the leisurely and persistent pace with his fingers, rubbing and pressing firmly against my aching clit, allowing my urgency to build again before gently beginning to increase his rhythm, pushing deeper into my ass until I am moaning and trembling uncontrollably. He repositions himself and pulls me into his lap and I watch while he rolls the condom down his shaft before lifting me over him, bringing me down atop his swollen cock.

"The thought of you inside of my ass one of these days is such a turn-on," I whisper. His eyes are molten, reflected with the passion that I feel.

His hands tighten around my hips, guiding me as the urgency builds and our rhythm increases until we are left breathless, completely overcome by our physical exertion of the day. We are freshly showered and as we crawl into bed he pulls me close against the steady beat of his heart, and that's the last thing I recall as I drift off to sleep.

TWELVE

I wake to find Chase already at the table working on his Mac with a cup of coffee.

"Morning," he says, stretching back in invitation. I crawl into his arms. He hugs me tight and kisses me deeply. "How you are feeling this morning?" he asks.

"Much better and completely satisfied," I respond, running my hand across his broad shoulders and up the back of his muscular neck, gently pulling his face closer to my own and kissing him back, caressing his bottom lip with mine.

"We have a lot to discuss and I can't think straight when you're on my lap kissing me like that," he says.

I pretend to pout and rub the back of his neck coaxing his face closer to mine again, kissing him once more.

"Good try, Katarina, but we are going to talk about security details," he admonishes, seeing right through my delay tactics.

"I'll order brunch and then we can discuss security and Martel," he says, watching me, probably waiting for an argument.

"I know how anxious you are to do this and I'll try to be as open-minded as I can," I say.

"The security team is eager to have a plan in place before we leave for the States. I've started a very basic list but I'm sure it's going to feel like an invasion of your privacy," he warns, turning the Mac sideways so we can both read the screen together.

The list is not an invasion of my privacy, it eradicates any existence of privacy I've ever had. I am sure I must be in a state of shock as I reread the Word document and try to absorb the content. I can feel the intensity of his gaze, waiting for some reaction. I attempt to keep my mounting frustration in check. My heart is racing and I am trying to maintain some semblance of control.

"Chase, I wouldn't have considered any of these items before the last few days. I can agree to some of these security measures, but not to them all."

"They are necessary for your protection and simply aren't negotiable, Katarina."

The dam breaks. "You're serious ... my family and friends need to go through a screening process? You want me to live in an apartment with a safe room? Are you kidding me? What the hell would I need so much security for? What the hell do you do for a living that would require me to have this much security?" I ask, losing the battle to maintain my composure.

"Katarina, calm down. The work I do can be contentious and the people closest to me can easily become targets. Your family and friends will not even realize they're being screened. Jay and his team are superb at what they do. They are working round the clock to find out who has targeted you and why, but until we get this resolved, I need to make sure you are safe."

"This scares me to death," I say, rereading the list, trying to comprehend and make sense of it all. He wants me to live in an apartment with a safe room. I thought that was only in the movies. I will have a driver assigned to me, can't run the same routes every day, and need to have someone with me at all times. Not to mention bugging my phone, keeping me on GPS, and the rest of the list.

"Katarina, the work I do and decisions I make often affect global environments. As a result, certain groups would like nothing better than an opportunity to exert pressure to influence those decisions.

The best strategy to combat that is to eliminate the ability for those opportunities to exist," he explains.

"Chase, I know Prestian Corp is a very successful conglomerate, but I think you are intentionally vague. I don't understand what it is that's so dangerous and contentious."

"The integration of global markets has been almost entirely funded by financial institutions, non-governmental organizations and multinational corporations such as Prestian. The issues that arise from the global business are many and complex, ranging from labor issues to environmental issues and in any of these factions conflict can occur quickly. It often turns violent in countries that are adapting to changes in their lifestyle or culture. Katarina, in layman's terms some countries don't like a change in the workforce rules and they will stop at nothing to keep control over the workforce. Prestian Corp is committed to doing its part in the global market while maintaining a high level of quality both in its products and environmental practices. The safety and welfare of the workforce are imperative to me, and this can be quite controversial when it means a change to the current host country's standard practices. You can liken it to cultural changes in our own city as we look at building the first multidivisional health facility that challenges the status quo. It's going to shake things up a little, Katarina, and there's always a danger in that. Security is not an option in the world that I live in, Baby. I know it's invasive, but it's necessary."

"I appreciate that you're worried about me, but these rules eradicate any existence of privacy I have at all. Besides, I can't afford the security you want."

"Katarina, I will be paying for your security. You wouldn't need it if it weren't for me and the work I do."

"The hell you will," I say, getting up from the table and trying to put some distance between the two of us. I don't give a damn why you think I need a safe room and the rest of your security rules. I am not about to let you pay for my apartment," I say, furious at the level of control being proposed.

"Katarina, be reasonable. The security you need is expensive and you can't afford it. The money is minimal to me."

"That's not the point, Chase. I can pay for my own apartment and I don't care how much money you make."

"Calm down. This is getting us nowhere fast. You must realize the necessity for security."

"After this week I can understand and appreciate the need for security, at least until we figure out why I'm being targeted, but I can't let you pay for my apartment. It's just too much, too soon. We've only known each other a little more than a week," I say.

"So you are agreeable to full-time security, as long as I am not paying for your apartment," he says.

Did I say that? "I'm looking at a few places on the outskirts of the city that are very nice with a forty-minute commute. How about if you go with me so you can take a look at the security in the apartments that I can afford? If you do that, I will compromise on the security."

His eyes darken before me and his jaw is firmly set. "Katarina, I want you to have a safe home, security when you are not at home and if I'm honest having you on the road for an hour and a half each day seems ludicrous."

"Chase, you have to give me some time for all of this to sink in. Really, it's all a little overwhelming. In my world, I go wherever I want, whenever I want. The only person I need to check in with is me. You're asking me to give up all of my privacy, and my financial independence just like that."

His eyes are dark, slightly guarded making it difficult to know what he's thinking. "I know you are a very self-sufficient and strong woman and this is all new to you. I am trying to be as patient about the security as I know how to be, but it frustrates me greatly that we won't have a secure place for you upon our arrival in the States. I'd like you to look at the apartment options in my neighborhood that come with security provisions. If the meeting wraps up by four, we can be back in Chicago by ten thirty. You can stay the night with me, and then we can look at apartments together in the morning," he says.

"I thought the team was heading back on Tuesday morning?" I ask.

"They are, they'll be picked up by another of the corporate jets in the morning," he says.

"You have more than one jet?" I ask.

He reaches out and tilts my chin up so that my eyes are looking into his. "The team is having fun on the island. They'll have another night to enjoy themselves courtesy of Prestian Corp and I will have you all to myself on the way back. They are scheduled to leave a little later in the day so they can enjoy their last night on the island. As an added benefit that will keep Mark safely out of my way."

I nod, resigning that everything is just so different when someone has money.

"Now let's talk about your plan for Mark," he says.

"Mark is worried right now. He doesn't know what I heard and isn't sure if I told you. He probably assumes that I haven't since he didn't get sent packing. I'm hoping this earns me a few points, and his position on the process can be turned."

"Katarina, he was pretty straightforward with you. He's clearly not the slightest bit supportive of the process we intend to use. I wanted to cut him loose at that point and against my better judgment agreed to wait. He has not changed his position, but has instead, turned nasty. When you heard him on the phone, he was probably talking to someone at Martel, which means it's a bigger problem than just Mark. We're going to need another design firm."

"Chase, I don't want you to let Mark go over this, yet. If they don't produce a plan based on the processes then that's different, but we don't know that, yet," I argue.

"Katarina, don't you think he's already discussed this with others, given the way he referenced you on the phone?"

"I just don't think cutting ties with Mark or Martel is a good idea. You don't have any reason to believe all the people on Martel's payroll feel the same. Look at the way Terry has been busting his ass all week. He's engaged," I counter.

"I don't trust the son of a bitch, Katarina. Mark probably doesn't think you've told me and that means he knows you may at some point. That makes him even more dangerous. I would prefer to cut him loose now, but I'll agree to wait until we see the designs they produce."

"Thank you. I know it's a huge concession and you're just trying to protect me," I say, hoping we can now focus on something other than my security. The weather is warm with a slight breeze and we spend the afternoon catching up on work, even opting to take lunch outside on the balcony. Chase is on multiple calls throughout the day and excuses himself shortly before three thirty to take another call. I finish up for the day and I know he is in a meeting with Brian, who decided to stay at the resort over the weekend.

Message: Hi... heading to my room for a while.

Reply: I'll pick you up there at 5 p.m. Pack what you need until we leave. We'll drop it off in the suite before dinner.

Message: It sounds like you're inviting me to spend the night with you?

Reply: If it makes you feel better to think of it as an invitation...

Message: What if I said no?

Reply: I would carry you back.

Message: Well, in that case, I accept the invitation. I was planning to go for a run, but I find that my hips are still a little achy.

Reply: You will have plenty of exercise and stamina building for one day, Baby. It's too soon to start running again.

Message: Hmm... I'm getting all wet again.

Reply: I'll need to confirm this.

Message: See you at 5.

My mom calls to see how the trip is going and we talk for a little while. I am still wrestling with how to tell her about Chase. I want her to like him and don't want her to be biased by her past and the fact that I work for him. I opt to keep it to myself for a little while longer and give her a call to talk about it once we're home. When I get to my room I pack my clothes for the return stateside. I have just enough time to freshen up and apply lip gloss before I hear the knock on the door. Chase is in khakis and a sports shirt, which does nothing to conceal his tremendously cut muscular legs and arms.

We drop my belongings off at his suite, before heading toward the outdoor restaurant where we are escorted to a secluded table in the corner overlooking the sea. When the waitress arrives, Chase orders a bottle of wine.

"Does Jenny know your plans for tomorrow night or does she need to?" he asks.

I hadn't really thought about that, and he's right, I am sure she will ask. "I'll tell her I'm staying with a friend for now. I haven't said too much about us since she's also my boss."

He looks up, surprised. "That Jenny," he says, with raised eyebrows. "I guess I didn't put two and two together. So, it's not okay to date someone you work with, but it is okay that your best friend is your boss? I don't know if I can follow the logic."

I can't help the blush that creeps slowly along my cheeks. "So, tell me, how did it happen you are best friends with your boss? I'm intrigued by this, given the resistance you've shown me."

"She hired me right out of high school. I needed employment while I was attending college and she let me work flexible hours to accommodate my school schedule and gave me assignments that fit with my interests and career plan. I use to go straight from school to Torzial and Jenny was always in the office late into the night. I guess our friendship just developed over time.

He takes my hand from across the table. "So you avoided dating altogether and focused on your work," he says quietly.

"I definitely wasn't looking to repeat the past experiences. I guess it was a way for me to avoid dating. Well, that and pay the rent and trivial things such as food," I say.

"I love the way your eyes light up when you're being playful, but it saddens me that you thought you were lacking in any way," he says as his finger circles the top of my hand.

I shrug. "Mom's experience, my own, you know, it sort of leaves its mark," I say.

"Your friendship with Jenny is the reason you stayed at Torzial instead of signing on with some of the larger architectural firms?"

"Not entirely, those companies were interested in creating facility designs that could be reproduced, at least in part. Torzial provided me with a way to help the firms integrate the philosophy of getting the experience right for the customer and then designing the facility around that. I enjoy what I do and Jenny gives me free reign to take the assignments that make a difference. It's worth much more than money to me. She was actually the one who encouraged me to take this project," I say.

"I see. Remind me to thank her," he says.

"You may not mean that when we get back to the states and start changing the processes that everyone is accustomed to."

"Yes, I will. It's exactly what we need," he states.

The waiter arrives and Chase orders dinner for both of us. "It's a traditional meal in Aruba called Pastechi. Many times it is served as a breakfast food, but I particularly like it filled with marinated beef and goat cheese for dinner," he explains before ordering.

"Why do you have such an interest in funding a healthcare facility of this magnitude?" I ask.

"You heard the patient stories and the tragic failures happening in healthcare. Changing the model and building a new infrastructure to support it is expensive and it needs to be funded and driven by the private sector. If government cuts continue as a way to force reform, hospitals will be unable to sustain their existence. I recall sitting in a waiting room one day years ago with my mother. One of the women going through chemo with her could not afford a wig, another had to choose between meds and food. Fortunately, my father was in a position to provide anyone in my mom's support group with whatever was needed, but most people aren't that fortunate. Once a model is developed that can demonstrate increased quality and service with reduced overall costs it won't take long before others get on board," Chase says.

The waiter arrives with the Pastechi, which smells deliciously of cumin and nutmeg as he places the meal in front of us.

"The combination of marinated meat, raisins, and goat cheese are delicious," I say to Chase surprised at the flavor of the pastry.

"I'm glad you like it. It's one of my favorites," he says.

"I'm not sure if you saw the results of the original patient interviews, yet. We held a lot of patient forums that included many of our elderly populations. I was shocked at the number of patients who are choosing between buying meds or more food."

"I did see them, Katarina. Brian sent them to me and they were alarming. If our reimbursement and care models were aligned the cost of the drugs would be included in the overall expense just like other supplies. People like my mother's friends would not have to choose between meds and food and from an employer's standpoint the cost of coverage would not be cost prohibitive. It's not going to be easy to change the status quo. The pharmaceutical companies rely heavily on the revenue to pay for research and continued testing. We're anticipating significant pushback in this area, which is why we're keeping the project so quiet at this point. We need to provide a way to care for patients that they can afford, but that aligns with other long-term goals and needs."

The waiter has cleared the table and arrives with dessert. "It's called banana na binja. The plantains are grilled and then glazed with a port wine and brown sugar mixture," Chase says. I taste a bite and can see why it's considered the island specialty. When we finish with our meal, he guides me down a set of stairs that leads to the private beach area where we leave our sandals. We walk hand in hand for a while enjoying the feel of the water and sand underneath our feet, the scent of sea salt, and the warm breeze on our skin. It is our last night together on the island and I can't help feeling a little sad as we head back to the resort.

I organize my belongings for the next day before showering and get into bed for the night. Chase pulls me into his arms and his fingers caress the side of my neck.

"Katarina, I'm curious to know what you liked in the past few days. You've told me some things, but I want to know more. You said you loved it when I spanked you. What else did you like or not like?" he asks.

I'm thankful the room is relatively dark. "I see we're going to jump right into the uncomfortable conversation," I say, trying to control my blush.

He laughs out loud, obviously enjoying the conversation immensely. "What about when we were in the shower and I had my way between your legs?" he asks.

"I loved that," I respond.

He kisses the top of my head. "And when I was fucking you in the ass with my finger?"

"Maybe a little nervous about how you are going to fit, but I trust you and it felt great," I say.

"When we used the vibrator?" he asks.

"Honey, you can do that to me anytime. Especially when I see the look in your eyes watching it," I say.

"And when I was deliberately licking just around your clit, not allowing you to climax?"

I'm not sure how to respond.

"Katarina, what is it?" he asks, turning my face towards his.

"You really want to know?" I ask, trying to overcome my embarrassment.

"Yes, I want you to be honest with me, even if you think I won't like what it is that you have to say. I need to trust that our communication is open and honest, Baby," he says.

"I didn't like it."

"Katarina, what about what I did makes you say that?" he urges, sitting up on his elbow so he can see my face.

"I've never experienced orgasms until I met you. It's like this beautiful and magical gift. I used to lay awake at night wondering what was wrong with me. When you kept teasing me, it felt like you were taking the gift back."

He pushes the hair out of my face and caresses my cheek. I'm glad you told me how it made you feel, Baby. I don't want to do anything you don't enjoy, but it greatly enhances the sexual experience and I want to make up for everything you've missed," he says, kissing me deeply and pulling me astride his powerful thighs.

In the morning, I arrive at the conference area a little before everyone else feeling refreshed after a long run. It felt odd knowing so many of Chase's security men were out on the beach, but at the same time, comforting given the last few days. The members of the team begin to drift in and I apologize for the delay of the event and spend time sharing what happened to me on the beach as people inquire. Chase is the last to arrive having been in an early conference call and I close the doors to get the team started.

The group is engaged and animated throughout the morning, developing the front end process with little or no conflict. As they get farther along the workflow, there is deeper discussion around the right thing to do for patients, but do an excellent job keeping the patient's perspective and have almost completed the workflow before we break for lunch.

As I'm walking down the corridor, I notice Jay not too far off. I smile to myself, wondering if I was supposed to let someone know I was moving. Swoosh...

Message: Where are you, Katarina?

Reply: Almost to the ladies room, why?

Message: I have an intense desire to kiss you. I've had you all to myself for days and I like it that way.

Reply: I wish the day were already done and we were by ourselves, Chase.

Message: Careful, Baby or I will cancel the rest of the day.

Reply: You wouldn't.

Message: Don't tempt me, Katarina. I most certainly would.

As I get back to the event, I decide to have a little fun and send Chase a message.

Message: I changed my mind. We should cancel this afternoon!

He reaches for his phone as it starts to vibrate and I like the smile that plays across his lips as he reads my message. His eyes light up with amusement as he begins to type a response.

Reply: Katarina, are you intentionally provoking me?

Message: Yes!

Reply: Behave yourself before I do cancel the afternoon!

The team is highly energized and we make significant progress finalizing the new patient-centered workflows. When we return from the afternoon break we develop an implementation plan so everyone understands what needs to be done and how it will occur.

Chase acknowledges his appreciation of everyone's contributions to the project and congratulates the team on a job well done. "The future state workflows will help us create a facility that far exceeds patient service needs in our city while decreasing health care costs associated with providing care," he says to the team at the end of the day. Chase and the administrators of the Chicago Medical facility talk while a few members of the team assist me in collecting all the exercise material from the surrounding walls before we wish everyone safe travels home and leave the conference center. Jay is already waiting at the resort entrance and takes us to the airstrip, expertly dodging the late day tourists and vendors. As we approach the plane, I notice the same gold and black Prestian logo on the side of the Gulfstream that I saw on the side of the yacht.

"Chase, your luggage is on board. They are running a few last minute checks and we should get the all clear momentarily," Jay says.

Chase takes my hand leading me up the stairs and into the plane introducing me to a young stewardess, the pilot, and copilot. He talks with them for a few moments before guiding me to the main cabin. "This is the newest living space design in the Gulfstream G650," he says as we walk into an impressive living room with two couches and large overstuffed leather seats adjacent to the exterior windows. The fireplace in the center of the room is three sided, but is not turned on at the moment.

"We sent one of the planes with a boardroom layout to bring the team home. That plane has a conference table and can seat about ten around it, and has all the latest Internet capabilities. It saves our executives an enormous amount of time. Many of them are starting to book long conferences right over the top of travel blocks now. It allows them to spend more time with their families once they do get home." He guides me through the cabin, past the seats and bar area before opening a door, which leads into another suite. The sleeping quarters are impressive, with a nice sized mahogany bed, matching dresser and a floor length mahogany trimmed mirror. "All the amenities of home," he says grinning, while opening the closet door where my dresses are hanging up along with his business suits and ties.

"I asked them to take our bags to the plane," he says, noticing my look of surprise.

"Thanks," I say, wondering why in the world someone would go to the trouble of unpacking everything just to repack it several hours later.

"We better get seated. We'll be lifting off soon," he says, guiding me back to a table with two leather seats across from each other. I look out the window as the pilot turns the plane and we are soon taxiing down the runway and airborne, gaining altitude and flying high above the multicolored sea. At this distance it's easy to see the patterns of white sand, which create the lighter turquoise reflection in the ocean.

It is not long before the stewardess brings each of us a glass of wine and a tray of crackers, cheese, and smoked fish. I find myself nervous, twirling the stem of my crystal glass, contemplating reaching the States, the public scrutiny, and my mother. I take a long sip of wine, but the thought of food does not appeal. I take another long sip of wine and look up, drawn by the magnetism of Chase's eyes locked on mine.

"Katarina you're so very quiet. Tell me what's wrong, Baby," he urges.

"It's just your lifestyle is so different than mine. I don't even fly first class. I purchase my airline tickets online and change layovers just to get the best price. You have your own airplane, excuse me... multiple jets and your own pilot. It's more than a little intimidating."

"Katarina, I am the same man you were attracted to before you knew who I was. I don't know how to react to your feelings about the money. I've never dealt with someone that saw the money as a negative," he says, concern registered on his face.

"I think it's just hitting me that when we get stateside things will change. You have absolutely no privacy. Are they going to plaster our pictures all over the tabloids? I'll have security around the clock. What are they going to call me, the latest girlfriend, and another conquest? I don't even know how to explain our relationship or what to expect when we land," I say, aware that I am now rambling.

He puts his drink down and lifts my chin across the table, so I have no choice but to look at him. "Katarina, I should have known you were going to be worried about this. What do I want to call you? You excite me on a level that surpasses anything I've ever experienced and I'm not about to let money, security or anything else come between us. I don't have all the answers, but I know that I want to call you mine," he says, coming around the table and guiding me to the nearby sofa.

"I love that answer," I whisper as he pulls me into his arms. As he holds me close, my anxiety about moving our personal relationship from a private island to front-page news starts to subside a little.

"When we get to the airport we'll travel from the plane to my home on the outskirts of the city. If we go to the condo, we'll attract more attention. I'm hoping that by arriving this late, we'll avoid the press until tomorrow."

"Chase, are you sure you want me to stay the night with you? I can take a cab back to Jenny's and meet you at Prestian Corp tomorrow, if you like," I offer.

"Katarina, first I am not worried about what the press thinks or writes about me. My only concern is for you. There were enough people on the island with stateside connections and word about us could have gotten out. Jay has men set up at the airport and they will let us know what we can expect in the way of paparazzi before we land. Secondly, I want you to stay with me tonight, at least until we can get a lead on the incidents in Aruba and finalize a security plan that we can both live with. We'll check out a few apartments in the morning and take it from there."

"Chase, we need to be realistic, too. I told you I can't afford the apartments in your neighborhood."

"The money is of no concern, Katarina. You require security because of your involvement with me and I will pay for the apartment."

"Chase, I can't let someone I have known for less than two weeks pay for my apartment," I insist.

"Katarina, we've been through this already. You can't afford the level of security I want you to have and you only need it because of your relationship with me."

"What if I still say no?"

"I will renegotiate the contract for Torzial Consulting to state all project consultants will be required to live in an apartment provided by Prestian Corp Monday through Friday."

"I'm not sure how to feel about that, Chase. Do you always get your own way?"

"If I'm honest, most of the time I do. I can learn to compromise about some things, but surely you understand the need for security after the last few days, Katarina?"

"I appreciate their protection, but right down to planning out my running routes? It just seems a little much."

"You could always run on a treadmill, Baby," he counters.

"That's not going to happen, Chase. I love running outside!"

"Katarina, you can map out your own running routes, they just need to know them so they can have security in place and Jay wants you to switch it up so anyone watching patterns doesn't get a fix on you. That doesn't sound unreasonable to me."

I sigh. "Chase it's not unreasonable given the situation. You just seriously need to give me some time to acclimate to all of this," I say, finally starting to relax a little.

"We should talk about how we're going to approach work since I'm sure it weighs heavily on your mind," Chase says.

"I have been giving that a lot of thought," I admit.

His eyes are intent, waiting. "Things are happening fast, but I want to be with you and don't want to sneak around. I don't think you would intentionally hurt me, but sometimes things change. I need your assurance that if you wanted to end our relationship you would do it in a way that would not impact my career," I say.

"Katarina, you have my word. When I said I want you to be mine, I meant exactly that. I want to take care of all of your needs, not just the physical ones. If anything happened to our relationship, your career would be of my utmost concern. I would never do anything to damage your reputation, Katarina. In fact, we're most certain to run into the paparazzi either tonight or tomorrow. If you like, I'll let you handle them however you see fit," he says, gauging my reaction.

"Chase, I have never dealt with paparazzi."

"Katarina, you speak in front of large groups all the time. They are nothing to be concerned about, although they will ask all sorts of questions, especially about our relationship. Once the Paparazzi know who you are they will dredge your family history for anything newsworthy," he explains.

"I've had a pretty boring life until I met you, so there's not much to dig up. I'd really rather you deal with them," I say.

"I'm happy to handle it if it reduces your anxiety level. However, we've got another couple hours before we land and I have something guaranteed to relieve your anxiety right now," he says playfully as he takes my hand and guides me into the bedroom.

THIRTEEN

"I was secretly hoping you would bring me into the bedroom on the way home," I say as he closes the door. His eyes do not leave my body as I slip out of my dress, letting it drop to the floor in front of him. I find the look in his deep green eyes mesmerizing and the intake of his breath at my nakedness pleasing. As I get closer his hands glide over my body, touching and cupping my breasts, caressing my nipples.

"Did you intentionally go without panties to seduce me tonight, Katarina?" he asks.

I am enjoying taking charge and am so turned on that I can only nod.

"Were you thinking about this today?"

"That's all I've been thinking about," I say, moaning softly as his fingertip trails across one erect nipple sending a shiver of anticipation along my spine.

"Whatever would you like to do with me now that you have me under your spell? Tell me what you want, Baby," he says.

"I want you to feel how wet I've been walking around with no panties," I say somewhat hoarsely. His eyes darken and he captures my lips passionately while his fingers explore lower, through the fine soft hair. "Baby, you are already so wet and ready for me," he says, running over the sensitive spot with excruciatingly slow strokes. It is hard to concentrate as I begin to unbutton his dress shirt and slip it over his shoulders. I slowly stroke one nipple while taking the other playfully between my teeth. The scent of fresh soap and his crisp cologne fill my senses as I let my tongue make its way down the light path of hair to his navel, teasing, as I unbutton the clasp of his dress pants and push them off his narrow hips to the floor below. I rub the bulge in his underpants lightly with my fingers, marveling at the size of his desire. I look up, watching him, as I stroke his cock, rewarded with deep green pools of passion. Encouraged, I slide my fingers into their waistband, slowly pulling them down, kneeling as I go. I trace my fingertips along the length of him, relishing in the way he twitches under my touch. He is hard and erect and I am anxious to taste him. I gently lick the end of his cock, savoring the pre-cum that is glistening on the tip. He is salty and I feel my insides clench with longing, thinking about his desire. I take him in my mouth, covering my teeth with my lips, allowing them to glide the length of his shaft.

"Baby," he moans, stroking the sides of my face as I slide over his length with my lips, caressing him with my tongue.

I am enthralled with the experience and cup his ass cheeks with my hands pulling him in deeper as I do. His hips begin to move on their own accord pushing in deeper, but I do not want him to cum yet. I want to pleasure him in many ways tonight.

"Honey, you are so hard and ready. Can I put it on you?" I ask, taking the foiled wrapper from his hands, captivated by his size and obvious need. His eyes turn darker with unspoken desire as he nods and I gently roll the condom over the tip and down the shaft the way I've seen him do it. He pulls me up and into his arms, capturing my lips hungrily with his, holding my naked body closely.

"I want you to experience how you make me feel, so wanted and desired, but I've never done this before," I whisper, taking the moment to push him towards the bed so he is sitting at its edge before I crawl into his lap and straddle him. His arms come around me, holding me tight as he captures my lips with his own, allowing me to rise slightly, lowering myself slowly and deeply onto him. He audibly gasps as I take him in as deep as I can, slowly raising my body around him, using his shoulders to maintain my balance and rhythm. I continue this slow and sensual pattern while his mouth finds my erect and extended nipples, fueling the desire between my legs.

I am so wet and he is so hard that I slide easily down the length of him, savoring the way he feels as I take him in fully, resting against his thighs before coming back up, squeezing his length as I do. I moan softly and begin to increase my rhythm.

"Baby, slow... like this, I want to feel all of you," he says, grasping my hips to pull me down deep, until he is completely rooted, holding me there, and then helping to guide me up and back down over his hardness, slowly. I am overcome with desire as he lets me take over. He captures the delicate skin of my neck with his lips, kissing along the side until he reaches the hypersensitive area between my neck and shoulders making me squirm with longing.

"Are you ready?" I ask breathlessly.

He nods and I increase our speed, hands grasping his shoulders as I come down deep and hard, over and over until we're left trembling with a climax that leaves us both breathless and spent. I rest against his chest and can hear the pounding of his heart in my ears as we recover and our breathing eventually starts to return to normal.

"Baby, that was more than amazing," he says, rolling me over and curling me into his arms.

"Did you like being in charge?" he asks, his eyes searching mine as he rubs a finger down the side of my cheek.

"I'm not sure about the being in charge part, but I love the look in your eyes," I say feeling the warmth of a blush rise to my cheeks.

"Baby, that's my favorite part of taking charge. Seeing the look on your face and in your eyes when you are right on the brink," he says, nuzzling my ear with his lips. "Now, close your eyes and sleep, because I have plans for you when we get home," he says.

I wake a little later confused at my surroundings and to the sound of Chase opening the door. "You must have been tired, you've been asleep for almost an hour and a half," he says, looking down at me.

"Hmm... I think someone took all of my energy. That and I didn't sleep very well last night. I was thinking about the event and our last day on the island."

He caresses my cheek and kisses me softly. "Who took whose energy?" he asks, swatting my ass playfully through the sheet.

"As much as I would like to keep you in my bed deliciously naked, you better get up and dressed. We're going to be landing soon and it's hard to say who we'll encounter," he warns.

I get out of bed and feel his eyes on my body as I walk into the bathroom. I'm grateful my clothes are hung up and not wrinkled. When I finish dressing, I turn in the mirror. The dark blue dress has black color block accents and is business casual, yet professional enough in the event I need to brace myself against the paparazzi. I slip into a pair of black slingbacks and find Chase working on his laptop.

"I thought you had an aversion to working long hours or does that only apply to my working habits?" I ask.

"My aversion is definitely to you working long hours, Baby. I see you've regained some of your energy as well as your feistiness," he says. I reach down and kiss his lips, thoroughly enjoying the look of appreciation I see in his eyes.

As soon as the plane touches down Jay begins talking to Chase about logistics. Chase wraps his arm around my shoulder, pulling me into the conversation.

"Jay, once the reporters catch sight of Katarina, they are not going to leave us alone so we're going to switch things up a little. Instead of avoiding them, I'd like to speak with them."

"You're going to do what?" Jay asks.

Chase raises his eyebrows. "I am going to spend a few moments talking to them so we don't spend the next few weeks avoiding them. It doesn't appear they have caught wind of our arrival tonight, but make sure the team knows my intent," he says.

"You're the boss," Jay says, shaking his head as he guides us out of the plane and into the back of a long black limousine. Security is everywhere. We have a team in front of us and another group of men that get into the car behind us. I feel more than a little uncomfortable knowing the need for precaution is real. He takes my hand pulling me close, and I squeeze it appreciatively.

The traffic is not heavy since it's late, and once on the highway, we're able to make the drive northeast in about fifty-five minutes. We pull onto a side road and Jay navigates the limo over a long stretch of road through great lengths of pine trees. The wrought iron gates open as we approach and the limousine slows while the driver speaks with the man at the door. We continue down the lengthy drive and a sprawling three-story chateau lit up against the night's darkness comes into view. Even from the car, the architecture is breathtakingly impressive with massive pillars and archways that encompass the entire home.

"It is absolutely beautiful, Chase."

"I'm glad you like it. The architecture is not contemporary and not something everyone finds appealing." The driver pulls around the large semi-circular driveway to the front entrance of the home where we are greeted by a middle-aged, slightly rotund woman with porcelain skin, deep blue eyes and short dark hair. She embraces Chase with a warm hug as we get out of the car and extends her hand to me with a large welcoming smile. "You must be Katarina. I'm so glad to meet you, dear." I shake her hand, immediately taking a liking to her. "Thank you for such a warm welcome."

"Katarina, this is Gaby. She lives here and takes great care of me and the house."

"I'm so happy to meet you, Gaby. Please call me Kate," I say.

"I thought you would arrive a little earlier than eleven o'clock at night," she says to Chase.

"I thought so too, but we spent a little time talking to the facility team after the event and it took longer than normal to get in the air," he says.

"Well if you are hungry I left soup in the refrigerator," she says.

"That sounds great. I think first, I'd like to give Katarina the fifty-cent tour," he says, leading me through the grand entrance over hardwood flooring into what he describes as a great room. The fireplace mantel is fashioned from natural stone in keeping with the chateau feel while the adjacent wall is almost all windows.

"The house was designed to maximize views of Lake Michigan. You'll be able to see what I mean tomorrow. There is another great room along with a library and gym that have almost the same views as these upstairs. I like to work out on the treadmill and watch the sun rise over the lake. You're welcome to use it if you like, but right now I'd like to show you the master bedroom," he says, leading me up an arc of ivory marble stairs. When we reach the top, there is another spacious living area with expanses of glass from one side of the room to the other and another sprawling fireplace that takes over the entire corner of the room designed with natural beige stone, rising from the floor to ceiling. A large Mac screen sits atop a mahogany desk in the opposite corner; two large sofas and an overstuffed reading chair give the room a comfortable feel. There is a floor-to-ceiling bookcase in the corner and it is filled with hardback books of all genres.

"I could spend days in this room," I say, spying the perfect wing-back chair by the fireplace and imagining how cozy I would be curled up with a good book and a roaring fire while it snowed outside. "Do you read a lot?" I ask.

"It's one of my favorite pastimes," he says, taking my hand again as we walk through the living area and past several rooms until we reach what appears to be the master bedroom. It is nicely furnished with a four-poster bed crafted out of mahogany wood and covered with a battleship gray comforter. There is a heather and gray colored over-stuffed reading chair with a matching ottoman in the corner by the window, and a floor length mahogany mirror adjacent to the bed. The bedroom floors are the same wood that is throughout the house, but the bathroom floors are stone, and dark granite with flecks of gold adorn the dual-sink counter top and the edge of the whirlpool. The stone shower is designed in a circular shape eliminating the need for a door or curtain. I can't help smiling as I spy my brand of shampoo and conditioner and a loofah on the shower ledge.

"You really do think of everything," I say.

"I have a lot of fun with that little loofah," he says, pulling me into his arms and looking into my eyes.

"You like it, Baby?"

"I love it, Chase."

He captures my lips, expertly parting them with his tongue as he explores deeper, slowly pushing my dress over my hips, hands sliding over my thighs, ass and waist as he lifts it over my head, leaving me standing before him in only bra and panties. His eyes turn smoky as he frees my breasts, gently kissing each nipple as he slides my panties over my hips, letting them fall to the floor.

"Baby, I've been thinking about getting you into my bedroom all day," he says, settling me on the bed before removing his clothing to lie down beside me. He parts my legs with his powerful thighs and gently rubs between my legs, slowly igniting my desire. My hands are free to explore and they travel from his neck and shoulders over erect nipples to his rock hard abdomen. They follow the trail of dark hair that leads to his manhood. He groans as I slowly stroke him, traveling from the tip of him down lower to the base of his cock. I let my body slide down the length of his; my lips travel the path of my hands across his nipples and abdomen as I continue to stroke him. "Baby," he moans softly. I look up at him, letting my tongue explore the soft patch of hair extending to the lower side of his abdomen, watching his eyes turn molten. My lips search out the tip of his cock, licking gently before taking him deeper between moistened lips. He groans, and with one quick movement repositions me over the top of him, his tongue finding the sensitive spot between my legs while I continue my discovery of his swollen cock. He grasps my hips firmly, holding me in place while his tongue continues to ravage me. Our rhythm increases as desires flare and I take him in deeper, sucking faster... urged on by the feel of his strong and engorged cock throbbing with need.

As I feel myself begin to tremble around him, he increases intensity, extending my release, taking my clit between his lips, and sucking hard. I gasp as an extended round of orgasm hits me, and only then does he allow his own warm, salty release, exploding deep and hard between my lips, as I continue to suck and caress him through his pleasure. He softly trails his tongue along the still tingling area between my legs, kissing her softly before moving positions. He turns me around, pulling me close to his body so my face is lying on his chest. I can feel the steady beat of his heart beneath me matching my own breathing as he presses me close.

"Baby, I don't like thinking about how you learned to do that, but it was incredible," he says.

"Mmm... for me, too," I say, nuzzling into his chest. "I love your home, Chase. I can't wait to see the views you talked about earlier. So, what did you tell Gaby about me?" I ask.

"That I met someone I spent the week with and that I was bringing you home. Now, you've taken all my energy today. Let's get cleaned up and go downstairs. I'm sure Gaby has left something out for us and I need to replenish," he says, scooping me into his arms and into the bathroom.

"I love the way you pick me up and carry me where you want me," I say laughing, but slightly embarrassed by my nakedness.

He smiles broadly. "Well, I'm certainly glad it meets with your approval. It's all part of the Prestian control package," he says as we get into the warmth of the shower to rinse off. He is quicker than I am and I've just rinsed the conditioner from my hair when he hands me a towel to dry off with. "I thought you might like this, too," he says, pulling a long robe just like the one in Aruba from a hook behind the door.

"I absolutely love it, Chase," I say, snuggling into the luxurious material and using the towel to wrap my hair. Do I need to get dressed or can I wear it downstairs?" I ask.

"Wear the robe. We may run into Gaby, but she won't care," he says, pulling on lounge pants and nothing else.

As we walk into the kitchen, I look around amazed at the sheer size. There are two Viking stainless steel ranges and an oversized Sub-Zero stainless steel refrigerator. "It's like a restaurant kitchen," I exclaim.

"We usually have the Boys and Girls Clubs for meals during the holidays. Gaby cooks everything right here," he says, opening the refrigerator to pull out a large bowl of soup. The note on the top says *Potato Dill soup. Heat for 2 minutes per bowl. Fresh bread is in the breadbox.* Chase places the dish on the counter and begins ladling it into two ceramic bowls.

"I'll cut the bread while you heat the soup," I offer having found the breadbox on the counter by the range. I finish slicing the loaf, place it on a plate and bring it to the table as he puts both of the heated bowls in front of us. "It's delicious," I say, savoring a piece of the fresh dill bread.

He smiles. “She’s a magnificent cook. I worry that she does too much sometimes, though. She’s got her hands full managing the household and all the staff we employ,” he says.

His phone vibrates on the table and he turns it over, scowling briefly at the message. “Excuse me, Baby,” he says, hitting the number to one of his contacts.

“Sid, Chase here, what’s going on?” he says into the phone.

After a slight pause, he appears frustrated with the conversation. “I don’t care how many people it takes, Sid. Draw him out of hiding, and find out who he’s working for. There has to be a reason, some connection we’re missing,” he says before disconnecting.

“Was that about the guy in Aruba?” I ask.

“It was. Jay has intel teams working to find any connection between some of the work we are doing overseas and the attempts made on your life, but nothing’s coming up,” he says.

“What do you mean by that, Chase? You think someone is trying to kill me because of a job you are doing overseas? I don’t understand.”

“We’re not sure yet ourselves. It doesn’t make a bit of sense that someone would want to fatally harm you. Some traffickers prey on young women and use the same drug that was found in your drink, but the doses were too high just to knock you out for a while, so we’re looking into other reasons. The teams are working round the clock, but they haven’t been able to turn up anything, yet,” he says.

I crawl into his lap and kiss him gently. “Finish your bread so we can go back to bed,” I whisper, wanting to forget the incident and be in his arms.

I WAKE CURLED up with his arms wrapped around me from behind. “Good morning,” he whispers into my ear, pulling my body closer, cupping my bare breasts in his hands, slowly and deliberately rolling my nipples between his fingers. “I like waking up with you in my bed,” he murmurs playfully.

“When Dr. Mederea came to take care of me after the accident I asked her to prescribe the same birth control pill I was on a few years ago. I’ll be covered from pregnancy, but she asked me a few questions that I wasn't able to answer," I say aware of the warmth rising on my cheeks.

"What did she ask you?" he asks.

"Well, um, you know about sexual partners and ensuring we wouldn't transmit anything to each other," I say.

"And you are embarrassed discussing this with me?" he asks, sitting up on his elbow to look at me.

"Maybe, a little bit. It's not like I've had many experiences in this particular department," I say.

"It's a perfectly reasonable question. You can be assured precautions with previous partners have been taken, along with routine lab work," he says.

"I see, and are you taking precautions with me, aside from the condoms?" I ask.

"I didn't think it was warranted given your limited experience and the fact you haven't slept with someone in three years," he says, his eyes rising questioningly.

"I guess I didn't think about the risk of you and your other partners and probably should have," I state, annoyed at the petulant sound of my own voice.

"Katarina, don't tell me you're jealous," he says and this time, the quirk of his lips reveals his amusement. I try to avert my gaze. *Is this what jealousy feels like?*

"Look at me," he says, turning my chin to face him so that I have no choice but to look into his eyes. "There is absolutely no reason for you to be jealous. I am completely monogamous and these relationships happened before I met you," he says.

"I don't know what's gotten into me. Your previous partners really shouldn't matter to me. A couple more days and I will be covered from the birth control aspect," I say, wishing the thought of him with other women didn't leave me feeling so covetous.

"I can't wait to be inside of you and feel you around me without a condom," he says, kissing me on the lips gently. "Now, let's go downstairs and see what Gaby has prepared for breakfast. We have an appointment with the realtor mid-morning," he says.

"You're really quite fond of her," I say as I reluctantly slide out of bed and we get ready for the day.

"Yes, I am. She's been with me for about seven years," he says.

"So, what does Gaby usually make for breakfast?" I ask hoping to lighten the conversation.

He grins sheepishly. "Bread pudding, egg and hash brown casseroles, strawberry cream cheese, french toast or blueberry pancakes," he says with a large smile.

"I think someone is completely and thoroughly spoiled," I say, laughing as we enter the dining room just as Gaby is placing a plate of blueberry pancakes and fresh fruit on the table.

"Breakfast looks amazing. We had some of your potato soup and fresh bread last night and it was excellent," I say.

"A woman with such good taste in men and food," she exclaims. Her slightly broken european accent is hard to place, but her smile is warm and beaming as we sit down to eat.

"Gaby, Katarina and I have an appointment in the city and won't be back for lunch. We should be home for supper, though, but I'll let you know by this afternoon if not," he says before she heads into the kitchen and his phone vibrates.

"Chase here," he says, sipping his coffee while listening to the person on the other end of the call. I take a few bites of pancake and fruit. "Soo good, taste this while it's warm," I mouth to him, putting a generous forkful of warm blueberry pancake to his lips. He slides the entire forkful into his mouth and nods his agreement.

The voice on the other end seems to go up an octave or two. "Let's hold tight and see if they accept the contract by the deadline. We'll know more about intent once we get to that point. Until then, stay firm on the offers we've made, and thanks for the update, Sid," he says before disconnecting.

"I am going to have to run more than an hour to wear her cooking off," I say.

Chase looks around and Gaby is coming back into the dining room to clear the table. "Baby, I'll give you all the extra exercise you need later," he says, leaning towards me and whispering so as not to be overheard."

"Gaby, thanks for breakfast. I'll give you a call this afternoon and let you know what the plans are for tonight," he says, guiding me through the great room, into the large open foyer and outside.

A silver Jaguar XJL has been brought around to us and Chase helps me into the back seat before joining me. Jay navigates the mid-morning traffic with relative ease and the forty-five-minute drive into the city passes quickly. "There are a couple vacant properties that I'd like you to look at," Chase says, taking my hand.

"I'm still torn about the expense, Chase, but it won't hurt to look at them," I say.

The driver drops us off at the front entrance of a tall sky-rise and the doorman greets Chase by name. "My condo is upstairs," he says in response to my surprise. The one just below mine was recently vacated and I am hoping you will like the location. It's a quick walk to Prestian Corp, and the views are great," he says, watching me warily as we get out of the elevator and I see it's the only condo on the floor. The realtor arrives right behind us and I hold my tongue about the expense as Chase introduces us.

"Penny has other properties we can look at, but I am partial to the ones in this building for obvious reasons," he says as she unlocks the door for us. The living room and dining space have spectacular views of the city and Lake Michigan. A brick fireplace in the corner gives the room a warm and inviting feel. The kitchen has a Viking stainless steel range, dishwasher, and Sub-Zero double refrigerator, although nothing as grand as Gaby's kitchen.

"How many bedrooms does it have, Penny?" Chase asks.

"This unit comes with four where I believe yours has five, but it does have a gym area and office space in addition to the bedrooms. I've taken the liberty of speaking to the owners and if you decide to purchase, the same contract related to modifications could be assumed with this property and alterations can be made before moving in. The list is seventeen million, but as you know, there's room for negotiation given the sellers' situation."

I inwardly gasp at the price and he takes my hand, following Penny as she leads us through the living room into a large office area. The master bedroom is as big as my last apartment and includes a corner whirlpool. The accompanying oversized bathroom includes a walk-in shower and smaller whirlpool bathtub. The farthest room down the hall overlooks the water and is equipped with an elliptical, treadmill, and a fifty-two inch flat screen hangs on the wall.

"All areas of the home have in-room speakers with the newest digital technology," Penny explains.

"How do you like it, Katarina?" he asks.

"It's beautiful, Chase, it's just a lot more than what I was looking for," I say.

"Penny, Katarina and I will need to discuss the condo and we'll let you know what we decide. Thanks for taking the time to show us around," he says.

"Kate, let me know if you would like any more information. It's one of the most coveted in the area," she says as Chase guides me toward the elevator. Penny stays behind to secure the door and I wait until we are out of earshot and safely into the elevator before I speak.

"I can't let you buy another condo just to have me live in it. I had no idea they were that expensive. It's absolute craziness."

"Katarina, it would be yours. I would not want you to be obligated to me for anything," he says.

"You are definitely not going to purchase a condo for me. It's an incredible amount of money."

"We haven't even looked at the other options," he says.

"Why do you want to see the others, you obviously like this one."

"The condo we just looked at would be my second choice, Katarina. I'll show you my first, as I find it has quite a few more advantages," he says, entering a passcode to the thirtieth floor. I immediately know where we are going and he has barely gotten me through the door of his own condo before he pulls me close to him, capturing my eyes with the intensity of his own.

FOURTEEN

"I don't want this to be an argument. I just want you safe and close to me."

"How the hell do you expect it not to be an argument? I have told you repeatedly I am uncomfortable with the thought of you paying for an apartment. I agree to go out with you to look at apartments against my better judgment and you have a realtor show me an apartment you've already apparently discussed purchasing for me? How do you expect me to feel, Chase? You completely disregarded my concerns."

"Katarina, it frustrates me that you don't have a place to live that I consider safe with everything that has transpired. Jay is doing his best to keep security a step ahead of you, but you need to be in a secure environment, at the very least until we know who is behind the attempts on your life. We've already gone through this," he says, raking his hands through his hair.

"I told you I was willing to look at different apartments, even went so far as to concede that you may pay for it until this was over. I never said that it was okay for you to buy me a fricken apartment just because you can afford it though. It makes me feel cheap."

"That was not my intent, Katarina, and I'm sorry if that's how it made you feel. I just want to take care of you and keep you safe," he says, pulling me into his arms and holding me close.

"I'm sure you didn't intend to, Chase," I say, feeling my irritation start to subside.

"I need you to trust that I have your best intentions at heart. Why don't we relax and talk about how we want to proceed with the condo," he says, taking my hand and leading me to the bathroom. He begins to run the whirlpool while I stand in perplexity.

"I thought we could relax in the tub and solve the problems of the world," he says, clearly amused.

"Chase, it's the middle of the day. I really should be working," I half-heartedly protest, my earlier anger starting to subside.

"Katarina, you work entirely too much. We need to talk and get this resolved," he says, sprinkling violet crystals into the water that turns the tub into a sea of frothy foam.

I am not surprised to see my shampoo, conditioner, body wash and a loofah on the ledge and shake my head in resignation. "Did you know you were bringing me here today?" I ask.

"Yes, I was hoping we would end up here," he says.

I narrow my eyes at him still smarting from his high-handedness.

"I want to see what you have on under this dress," he says, bending slowly, making sure I am not opposed, before lifting the dress over my head. "You have no idea how stunning you are, do you?" he says, pulling my black lace panties down and allowing them to fall to the floor before releasing the clasp on my bra. "I have to admit I've been thinking about you sexually all morning, but right now, I am much more concerned with your emotional needs," he says, kissing my lips gently. "Slide into the water with me, Katarina," he says, encouraging me before I sink into the water, luxuriating in the lavender scent and bubbles as he gets into the square shaped bath across from me.

"I'm not going to draw this out, Baby. You could just move in with me," he says, eyes watchful... gauging my reaction.

"Chase, we've only known each other for such a short time."

"It's been two weeks and you've been living with me for over a week. I'm trying not to rush you, but I am admittedly not a patient man. I want you under my roof so I can take care of you. If you are not ready to move in with me, then I want you just below me which is why the condo we saw earlier would be my second choice."

"Have you ever lived with anyone before?" I ask.

"I lived with my parents until I went away to college, but otherwise, no. I've never really wanted to spend more than diversionary nights with someone until now."

"Chase, we know so little about each other. My mother has done exceptionally well for herself, but we're not wealthy by any means. She's the only family that I have and..."

"What's bothering you, Katarina?"

"A few things," I say not sure if I'm prepared for this depth of conversation.

"Katarina, you can tell me anything."

"I work for you and I haven't told my mother, yet, and I'm worried that she won't like you very much once she learns that you employ me."

"Because of her past relationships?" he asks.

I nod. "Yes, well, that and I've always stayed well away from men I work with and she knows that."

"Katarina, it would appear that you've stayed away from all men in general, not just those that you work with," he says.

"Okay, especially men that I work with, then."

"Is that all that's bothering you?"

"No."

"Katarina, this is the participative part of the conversation," he says, looking slightly bemused.

"It's just that you are very wealthy. I've worked for Torzial since I was eighteen years old and while it's an excellent job, I will never be in the same class as the women you've probably dated."

"That's for damn certain. One day I will share with you my definition of classes of women, but let's suffice it to say that you're in a class of your own, and I wouldn't want it any other way. There's a reason I'm not with the women I have dated in the past. Unfortunately, there's nothing I can do about the money, Katarina. It's sort of a package deal and I have never dealt with a partner who had an aversion to it," he says, pausing for a second.

"Now that we've covered that, tell me what you like," he says, smiling widely.

"Well, you're everything I ever wanted in a partner— caring, gentle and kind. I even like it when you're a little overbearing and possessive... it makes me feel like you really care," I admit, feeling the flush rise in my cheeks.

"Baby, I do care or I wouldn't be asking you to move in with me," he says, capturing my eyes with his own. "And what about the sex?" he asks, grinning.

"Oh, God, I seriously never dreamed it could be this good," I say, bemused at the smile on his face.

"So, with all that, you still need to think about moving in with me?" he asks.

"Chase, I don't want you to purchase another condo for seventeen million dollars when we would probably spend most of our time together anyway. I know you care about me and I would feel much better about living with you than having you buy me a condo."

"It will not take the paparazzi long to make the connection once they see you coming in and out of the condo. They will put articles about us in all of their magazines and people will talk. Are you sure you're ready for all that?" he asks.

"Yes, I know you are concerned about the security, but for me, it's about not feeling kept, if you can understand that," I say.

He kisses me gently. "I don't ever want you to feel kept, I want you to feel protected and cherished. I didn't think you would want to move in with me given your aversion to having a relationship with someone you work with. That's the only reason I showed you the condo downstairs. I would much rather have you under my own roof," he says, caressing my cheek.

"I'm still trying to work through some of this. I need to talk to my mom and get our relationship out in the open. I'm just nervous about how she'll take it," I say.

"You'll find a way to discuss it and once we meet each other, I'm sure it will be okay," he says, tracing his finger from my cheek, along my neckline, and across my erect nipples. My body moistens in response and I moan softly as he takes a nipple into his mouth, sucking until I can feel the moistness of my arousal.

"I want you right now, Katarina, fast and hard," he says, his eyes darkening.

My body responds shamelessly, losing sight of everything but him as he guides me above the water and onto his rigid cock. His arms are supportive, holding me in place, as he pulls me upon him. I am overcome by the feeling of fullness as he penetrates me. He caresses my clit with one finger while keeping one hand on my hip helping me maintain our rhythm. I am so close and can't help but grind myself onto his finger and only then does he increase the pace grasping both hips firmly, beginning a steady rhythm at first and then increasing the pace as he skillfully builds the intensity, driving us both over the edge with a passion that takes my breath away. We lay together, sated, my anger long forgotten, joined as one below the warm, silky feeling bubbling water until our breathing returns to normal.

He kisses me, caressing my neck with his hands. "I'm glad that you decided to move in with me," he says, keeping me held close to his chest and I relish in the way his heart beats strong and steady against my cheek.

"Baby, we better put some clothes on, or I am going to end up having you again right here in the whirlpool. Besides, you've taken all my energy and I need to replenish. Do you mind having a light lunch and working from here for the afternoon?"

"Sounds like a good plan to me. I'll see what's in the refrigerator and put something together," I say.

"So, you think you can stand the country house on weekends?" he asks, helping me out of the water and into a robe. "I try to get home at least once during the week, too," he says.

"I don't mind at all. I absolutely love it there, Chase. I just hope Gaby will like me."

"She already likes you," he says, kissing my forehead.

"I hope so, she's important to you."

"She is and you will both get along fabulously."

I find roasted chicken breast, lettuce, and vegetables for a salad in the refrigerator and in no time at all we are enjoying lunch on the balcony.

"I have some documentation to complete this afternoon. I don't typically have the owner in the room all week, so I generally develop a presentation."

"Having the owner in the room sounds like it saves a lot of rework," he says, grinning.

I laugh at his apparent attempt to show me his Lean learnings. "I'm impressed, you were actually listening."

"Of course, I was. I believe in the process or I wouldn't have hired your company. The only reason I didn't intend to stay was because Brian was planning to be there all week. He manages the operational aspects of the business well. I am definitely glad you invited me, though," he says. "I'll get some calls out of the way while you're working and we can celebrate moving in together with an evening out. I'll have someone bring your briefcase and laptop up from the car," he says.

I'm just finishing all of the event documentation when I hear the familiar swoosh...

Message: Almost done?

Reply: Almost... about 20 minutes or so.

Message: Trying to decide on your punishment in the event I don't see you in less than 20 minutes.

Reply: Anyone ever tell you that you are totally overbearing?

Message: I think you also said it makes you hot.

Reply: I am never going to get done if you keep messaging me!

Message: Ironic, then I would need to punish you.....

I laugh and decide not to respond to the last text. I finish compiling the last of the documents and find him in his office. "So did I make it?" I ask.

"Barely, in a couple more minutes I would have been forced to haul you into the bedroom and have my evil way with you," he says, eyes alight with amusement.

"Hmm, maybe I should have waited a couple more minutes," I tease.

"While I would love to scoop you up and take you to my bedroom,

I made reservations at the Noor House for this evening. They have excellent food and the views are the best in the city. I need to sign into one more call, though. I've had a dress and heels delivered for the evening. If you don't like them, we can always do an exchange." As I walk into the bedroom, I see the package immediately. It contains a short strappy little black dress with sequins and heels to match.

The shower is invigorating and I apply a generous amount of coconut oil as a moisturizer, liking the sheen it gives my legs before I put on the dress and slip into the heels, amazed that they fit perfectly. I sigh at my hair, unruly as ever, falling past my shoulders in a mass of curls and waves. I decide to go with a straight look for the evening and spend time with the blow dryer and hot iron. A little dusting of face powder, some mascara, colored lip gloss, and I feel ready.

Chase glances up as I walk in. "Baby, you look hot... and those legs. I almost don't want to take you out in public," he says, eyes dark and smoldering.

"I hardly doubt anyone will be looking at me."

"Baby, there's not a man alive that won't be looking at you. You're stunning," he says, lifting my face to kiss me. "Jay's going to pull the car around and we'll drive to dinner ourselves."

"Will they be with us?" I ask.

"Why do you ask? Are you nervous?"

"Not really. I think the stuff that happened on the island was probably random misfortune, it's just we haven't gone anywhere without them since we've been stateside," I say.

"You think two attempts on your life were random misfortune? Forgive me if I don't take your optimistic view and instead ensure that we get to the bottom of it before leaving your life to chance. The security teams will always be with us, even if they are not in the same car. Jay will have a team in front of us and one behind us this evening. They're excellent at what they do," he says.

Matt pulls up in the Jaguar and gets out of the driver's side. Chase opens the passenger door for me and I slide into the amazingly soft leather seat. The front dashboard looks like a cockpit lit up with navigational controls.

"So, you do think someone is targeting me," I counter as he slides behind the wheel and closes the door.

He sighs. "Katarina, it can't be coincidence. Although we don't know why, we can't rule out the possibility that someone is intentionally trying to harm you. It's a precaution and a necessary one."

"I have to admit, I do feel better knowing they are with us," I say.

"I'm very glad to hear that. The iPad in front of you is synced into the stereo system, so if you want to listen to something on iTunes or Internet instead of the radio you can select what you wish to listen to." A phone rings and he answers it as we pull away.

"Go ahead, Jay. I've got you on speaker."

"Do you have an update on your plans?"

"Katarina and I still need to discuss the logistics for tomorrow. Most of my work can be done remotely, but I'll let you know a little later about plans once we've had a chance to discuss it."

"Jay usually drives you around, doesn't he?" I ask once he's disconnected.

"He does most of the time. I usually get a lot of work done while traveling, but I felt like driving tonight. The team is with us and the car is completely secure. All of the Jaguar XJL Ultimates come standard with a 510 horsepower, 5.0 liter supercharged V8 engine and we had a custom security package designed for this one," he says.

"Of course you did. I know absolutely nothing about cars, but am duly impressed by the sound of a supercharged engine and custom security package," I say, trying to suppress my smile as he turns to narrow his eyes at me.

"I think I have just the punishment for sarcastic wit in mind," he says, pulling into traffic.

"Whatever would that be?" I ask as he navigates us through the heavy city traffic.

"Something too intense for words, I'll need to show you," he says, changing lanes and pulling up in the front of a magnificently tall skyrise.

The valet assists me while Chase gives the keys to another young man. Jay and Sheldon get out of the car behind us as Chase guides me toward a small group of reporters gathered at the entrance.

"Gentlemen, let me introduce you to Katarina Meilers. She is the Lean consultant who has been working on the Prestian Medical Facility project, which is intended to change the face of healthcare in the city of Chicago as we know it. Tonight, however, we are celebrating our personal relationship. As you may already know, we have been seeing each other and she has agreed to move in with me. I couldn't be happier." The reporters ask for a picture and he pulls me close, allowing photographers to snap a few rounds, before answering a few questions, saying goodnight and guiding me into the restaurant.

"One of the young reporters I was speaking with is beginning to develop quite a reputation for his credibility," he explains, pushing the hundredth floor. We exit the elevator into a grand entrance with marble flooring and chandelier lighting.

"Good evening, Mr. Prestian. We are expecting you and Miss Meilers and have your table ready, sir," she says, leading us past open tables adorned with white linens and crystal wine glasses to a table in the back of the restaurant by the window. It is situated behind a magnificent black marble wall and affords the occupants an increased level of privacy.

"I don't think I've ever seen such an incredible view of the city," I say, taking in the expansive view of lit up sky-rises laid out in front of us.

"The view is nothing compared to you, Katarina. You are absolutely breathtaking and you've made me a happy man today," he says before the waitress takes our order.

I am embarrassed, but his words make me feel giddy inside.

"Thank you," I say at a complete loss for words. I have never experienced a man that openly says what's on his mind like this before and feel the warmth of a blush rising to my cheeks.

"Your face is absolutely lovely when you blush," he says.

"Are you intentionally trying to embarrass me?" I ask still flushing.

"Baby, my intent is not to embarrass you."

"I'm not used to talking so intimately with people," I say, lowering my voice.

"Clearly something else we'll need to practice and experiment with," he says, clearly bemused.

"I think I'll save my experimenting for the bedroom," I whisper.

I reach under the table and text his phone.

Message: Like not being able to move...

He reaches down to look at his cell phone and types something.

Reply: So shy when we're talking and so uninhibited when texting. I will restrain you, Baby. You are not in the least bit safe.

Why is that so hot?

His eyes are dancing with delight as the waitress stops to take our order before progressing to the next table.

"I'm glad you decided to move in, Katarina. It will save me from carrying you back to my condo each night."

"I'm happy about the decision, too, and I don't think you would have had to carry me," I say, still slightly embarrassed. "I do need to go to Jenny's to collect my clothes and personal items unless your plan is to keep me undressed," I say after the waitress pours each of us a glass of white wine and leaves a platter of shrimp and oysters on ice in front of us.

"I personally think keeping you deliciously naked in my bed sounds like an excellent plan, but clothes may be needed once in a while. Have you and Jenny always shared an apartment?"

I am not sure how to tell him that I was living with Matt, one of my dearest friends from college, and that he asked me to move out because I wouldn't marry him. I do not want to spoil our special evening. "I moved in with Jenny until I could find a different apartment after my roommate and I parted ways. Long story... but on a serious note, I do need to stop by Torzial, too. I'd like to scope out meeting rooms and get them penciled into the calendars. As soon as we get the baseline design complete I'll want to bring the users together for the detailed design drawings. They have excellent meeting rooms, but I don't want to wait too long or they won't be available."

"We have an entire floor of Prestian Towers the teams can work out of if you like. If I recall correctly, the floor has approximately sixteen administrative offices and six different conference rooms all equipped with Wi-Fi, digital video and big screen monitors. The space is empty right now, so if it meets your needs, I'll have the broker take the availability off the market."

There is really nothing to think about. The project will last for at least two years and having a space adjacent to the worksites with the capacity to hold all of our key stakeholders will be invaluable. "That would be perfect, actually. It takes a while to get back to Torzial, especially in rush hour traffic and most of the contractors are on this side of town."

"Yes, approximately forty-one minutes each way on a good day," he says.

"What, did you have someone time it?"

"No, but I Googled it," he admits, grinning. "I anticipated more of an argument about this and thought I may need to convince you that eighty-two minutes of travel is non-value added," he says.

"I'm not going to squabble about the space. I like the idea of less driving time and having a space the team can collaborate in, especially since the project work will span over the next couple of years.

"Pity, I anticipated an argument and had such a delightful punishment in store," he says.

"Inquiring minds want to know what that might entail."

"A sound paddling with an implement of your choosing," he says.

"Really? Well, as you know, I'm quite innocent and inexperienced. I might need you to go over my options," I say.

His eyebrows raise and his mouth quirks. "Indeed? I think we can arrange a viewing of said implements and if you desire, a trial of each," he says.

I feel the heat rising to my cheeks talking about such intimacy in a public place. "I think I might need to reconsider my original agreement. I'm sure I can find something to squabble about," I say.

"You are delightful on so many levels, Katarina. I'm glad we'll be able to put our new toys to good use so quickly," he says, taking in my widening eyes. "I'm anxious to have you moved in. Jay will drive you to Torzial and help you bring back anything you need from the office. He can also run you by Jenny's if you need to pack your personal belongings."

"That would be nice. I don't have anything in the way of furnishings. When my roommate and I parted ways I left anything we had purchased together. I just have the usual. Clothes, makeup, and lots of shoes," I say.

"I think we can make room, somehow," he says, grinning. Dinner arrives and smells delicious. The rack of lamb is served on a large oval platter surrounded by gremolata, cumin spaetzle and shaved roasted brussels sprouts. The lamb is tender and the lemon and garlic in the gremolata intensify the taste. The brussels sprouts are slightly caramelized bringing out their own sweetness, and providing a lovely balance to the meal. Chase this is so good," I say, finishing another bite.

"I'll have him pick you up early so you can be back to Prestian Corp for the project meeting," he says.

"What project meeting?" I ask.

"Martel scheduled a meeting for tomorrow afternoon. I assumed you were included," he says, looking at his cell phone.

"I don't recall seeing one, but I'll check," I say, pulling up the calendar on my phone.

"It's scheduled for one thirty tomorrow in one of the Prestian conference rooms. It doesn't appear that you were on the invite Katarina, but you should be there. I'll forward the planner to you and Jay can have you back from Torzial and Jenny's in plenty of time," he says before my calendar loads.

"I can be there," I say, wondering what Mark Martel is up to.

"Enough about work, though, tell me a little about your family, Katarina. You said you grew up without a father and you and your mom are close. Where does she live and what does she do?"

"Well, I never knew my dad and Mom didn't talk about him. She never remarried and only dated a number of times, at least that I can recall. So it's a pretty small family, just the two of us. She worked long hours to support me growing up and now she's a very successful publicist and runs her own business in Naples, Florida. We don't get to see each other as much as we'd like with work schedules, but I'm planning a surprise trip to go see her for her birthday in a few months." I say.

"Seems like a long time to go without seeing each other," he says.

I sigh. "You're probably right. I've literally thrown myself into work the last several years. I should really make her more of a priority," I say, contemplating on how time passes so quickly.

"What about your family, Chase?" I ask.

"I told you about my mom already. She died of cancer when I was nineteen. My dad lives in New York and spends a lot of money funding research and technological advances in the hopes that one day they will find a cure. He's been dating a woman named Emily and spends a great deal of time with her when he's not working at the office. We talk on the phone quite a bit, especially lately. I gave him an iPhone for Christmas, so he's been trying out the FaceTime features," he says, laughing.

"Are you texting Jay?" I ask as they clear our table and he messages someone.

"Yes, I usually let him know when we're moving." The manager stops to talk to us for a few minutes and apparently knows Chase well. They spend a few moments chatting and Chase compliments him on the food and service before we leave. The Jaguar is waiting for us as we exit the building and Jay is already in the driver's seat as Chase and I get into the back. "Are you ready to go home, Baby?" he asks.

"Yes, please," I say, curling into his arms as Jay pulls away from the sky-rise and into heavy traffic. As we begin heading out of the city Chase pushes a button on a remote control and the privacy glass slides into place.

"Do you need to let Jay know if I plan to run tomorrow?"

"You don't like the treadmill?"

"I love being outside and we only have a couple months left before it gets too cold."

"We have to talk about a plan if you're going to be running around at five o'clock in the morning," he says, the twitch of his jaw evident.

"I don't mind using security, Chase. I'll even map out a couple routes and alternate them. I will actually feel much better knowing they are with me after everything that's happened," I admit.

"So you don't mind if Jay's team keep you and your family under surveillance?" he asks.

"I never discussed it with my mom, so I'm not sure if she will mind, or not, to be honest.

Have you heard anything from the police in Aruba, yet?"

"They were able to identify the man that gave you the drink. They have his place of employment and apartment staked out, but he has not been to either. Jay has an entire team dedicated to finding him, but nothing has turned up yet," he explains.

"Your team is doing that and not the police?"

"The police are inundated with many crimes. This is my team's highest priority. They've gone through his history and believe he's under contract. They are cross-referencing bank files, data feeds, and Internet communications with people on our watch list. We need to find out who hired him and why."

"You have a watch list? What is that, like a list of people that might want to harm you?" I ask.

"Baby, it's complicated, but we'll get to the bottom of it. Until then, Jay has instructions that you are not to move without them."

"I won't give them a hassle then," I say, grinning and hoping to lighten the mood.

"Good. We'll synchronize your phone with the security software we have once we get to Prestian Corp, but I want you to carry one of mine in the morning, agreed?" he asks.

"Agreed."

"What if we truly compromise? You take security, develop some outside routes and I will punish you for being so obstinate," he says.

"It sounds like that may have potential," I say, excited about the game.

"So do I still get to pick out the implement?" I ask.

He smiles. "I think that can be arranged," he says, pulling me against him until we arrive home.

FIFTEEN

We've barely entered our room when his lips capture mine, parting them under the pressure and urgency of his tongue. I moan softly against his lips.

"I love how passionate you are," he whispers, pulling the dress over my head, leisurely running his fingers against the lacy thong, cupping my ass cheeks and pulling me closer to him before lowering it over my hips and letting it fall to the floor. He unhooks the strapless bra, exposing my breasts and already extended nipples. His eyes darken with appreciation and I can feel my body warming at his gaze.

"Katarina, you are so brave texting and so shy otherwise," he says, lightly running his fingers against the erectness of my nipples.

"I like that you want to explore different pleasures with restraints and toys," he says, kissing me gently on the lips. "I've purchased some toys we can experiment with, but I'm going to need you to guide me, Baby. I don't want to go too fast with you or do anything you find uncomfortable emotionally. I'm going to need you to tell me what you like, and what you don't like," he says, opening the drawer of the nightstand and pulling out the suede cuffs. I blush at the memory of the last time they held me.

"I see you recall these," he says, placing them on the bed and pulling a kidney shaped eye mask out of the drawer. "Katarina, sensual deprivation is something I think you may enjoy, but I need to know how you feel about being unable to see what I am doing to you. When a person has diminished sight, other senses intensify including your sense of feel, but it and other things we try will require trust. If I put this mask over your eyes, you will have a heightened awareness as I touch you, but I need to make sure you are comfortable with it first." His questioning eyes have mine captured, and he waits patiently for a response.

The fact that I am nude, standing before him and talking openly about things I have never experienced are both embarrassing and exciting. "I like what you do with the set of suede cuffs very much, and I do trust you with the mask," I say, attempting to keep the blush from rising to my cheeks and failing miserably. "I'd like to see what else is in the drawer," I say, gaining boldness, walking towards it nude, in anticipation of what I may find. I bend over the nightstand drawer with a particular satisfaction feeling his eyes on my body.

"The drawer is full of different toys: tiny, medium and large sized dildos and ones that are even larger with external vibration systems. I rummage through the assortment and recognize nipple clamps, which I have seen in magazines, some other clamps that I do not recognize and a device with a ball at its end. I pull it out, curiosity getting the better of me. "What is this for, Chase?" I ask.

"It's a ball gag. Its purpose is to eliminate the ability for you to speak," he says watchful, gauging my reaction.

I eye it disdainfully. It is not attractive and I have a hard time visualizing what I would look like with it in my mouth. In fact, I am not sure if it will fit in my mouth. "How does it fit?" I ask.

"While it appears a little large it's not, Katarina. When you open your mouth, it actually fits nicely and you close your mouth around it. It's not intended to be uncomfortable, only to keep you from speaking which allows us to experiment with different forms of communication," he says.

"I like the idea of experimenting with you and I do trust you,

Chase," I say, trying to keep the excitement and anticipation from my voice.

His voice is deeper and I find myself mesmerized by it. "Tell me what you find appealing and why," he persists.

"I love the cuffs, and I like the mask and the gag. The idea that I wouldn't be able to move, see what you're doing or tell you to stop appeals to me," I say.

"Katarina, I want to go slow with you. We're going to progress from one to the other and I want you to guide me," he says, lowering me onto the bed.

"I am going to put this mask over your eyes first. I don't want you to see what I'm doing, just feel it," he says, slipping it into place.

He slips a soft cuff around one of my wrists and then the other, extending each above my head in opposite directions. He does the same to my ankles, leaving me completely naked, exposed and vulnerable. His fingers trail along my inner thighs, avoiding the spot between my legs, already moist and aroused. His tongue lingers, traveling from my navel, along my waist and erect nipples, sucking and teasing. I hear the clink of glass before he kisses me, pushing an ice cube from his mouth to mine.

"I want you to feel how sensual warm and cold can be, Baby," he says, swirling his tongue in my mouth, taking the ice back from me. The ice clinks in the bottom of the glass again and his fingers rub my aroused nipples, rolling them firmly, extending them. He kisses one nipple, licking it with his cold tongue while his fingers continue gently squeezing my other nipple until it becomes warm. He begins rolling the chilly nipple, warming it between his fingers. He lays something on my stomach. It feels coarse and bristly. I hear the ice clink, and tense, waiting as he places the ice cube in my navel. He removes what seems like rope from my stomach and rubs it gently across one of my sensitive breasts. My nipples must be connected with my most private nerve endings because I can immediately feel myself getting moister. I've never felt anything like this. It's softly abrasive. He continues rubbing it against my nipples, creating an exhilarating friction. The ice in my navel is causing a sweet burn. He removes it before it becomes painful, slowly rubbing it across my heated nipples, while his tongue explores my navel, warming it. I feel a mildly sweet burning sensation as he rubs my breasts with the ice and then switches to the abrasive rope to warm them. I try to move, but he has secured me well. His tongue explores the length of my waist, traveling towards my navel, removing the ice cube long enough to warm the sensitive area with his tongue, before placing it back. His tongue feels slightly cool against my heated skin, running it through the delicate hair between my legs and exploring my clit. I want to raise my hips and meet him, but am unable to move. Just as the ice in my navel begins to burn, he removes it, rubbing it against my excited clit, before switching to his tongue. I try to raise my hips again, but to no avail. He shifts back to cold and leaves it on longer, this time, creating the same sweet burning feeling before removing it and taking my clit back into his mouth.

"Chase, stop," I moan.

"Baby, I just started. I'm going to use another restraint now and you'll be unable to talk. He places a ball in my hand. "We will communicate with this. When you squeeze the ball, it makes a sound. Try it now," he says.

I squeeze the ball. It emits a small squeaking sound. "Good, now I'm going to insert the gag. We'll go slowly and if you want me to stop all you have to do is squeeze the ball and I will stop and immediately remove it. Ready?" he asks.

My body is poised with anticipation and a slight apprehension. I nod though, assuring him I am ready before he kisses my lips.

"I want you to open your mouth for me. It will feel slightly awkward at first so you'll need to relax," he says, inserting it into my mouth and instructing me through it before fastening the device. He is right, it seems large in my mouth.

"Do you trust me, Katarina? Squeeze the ball once for yes and twice for no."

I squeeze once and it produces the same squeak.

"Is this making you hot? Squeeze once for yes and twice for no."

I squeeze once.

"If you want me to stop for any reason, I want you to press the ball," he instructs.

He captures my nipple in his mouth, exploring the sensitive flesh with his tongue before moving to my other breast. I feel all the anticipation in my body pool as he moves his tongue down the length of my body, exploring my navel, licking the hypersensitive skin in a circular motion. He holds me firmly in place, continuing his ministrations, allowing his tongue to circle around my mound, gently teasing me, finally focusing on my clit. His tongue runs over it lightly, and then moves away, and then back again, teasing me, licking gently, and then moving just off the mark again, creating a desire I can no longer stand.

Chase, stop... I can't take it anymore...

He continues the pattern, bringing me to the brink and then adjusting to allow my body to cool; I squirm in an attempt to grind against his tongue, but to no avail.

Chase, stop... I can't take it anymore....

His tongue finds my clit, lingering, building my pleasure until I tremble around him, and continue to shake as he extends my release. He removes the gag, and releases my legs from the restraints, lifting my hips to enter me deeply and urgently. "Wrap your legs around my back. I want to feel you cum with me," he says, pushing deeper inside of me, still stroking my oversensitive clit. I can barely breathe as my desire intensifies and he sends me spiraling again before finding his own release deep inside of me.

"You were amazing," he says, pushing my hair out of my face and pulling me into his arms. My heart is racing and I curl against his chest, placing my face against the beating of his heart while my breathing returns to normal.

"That was amazing," I say, leaning up to kiss him gently on the lips. "I love how you make me feel, Chase. It's beyond anything I ever imagined," I say, resting my head back onto his chest and looking into his eyes.

His dark green eyes meet mine, holding them in the hazy light. "I like hearing about what makes you hot. What you like and what you don't," he says.

"I liked being tied up, but you already know that, don't you?" I say, feeling the rising blush warm my cheeks. *Why is talking intimately with him so embarrassing?*

"I guessed, based on how wet you were that you enjoyed it," he admits. "What else did you like, Katarina?"

"I loved what you did to me when you used the ice and that rope. I've never felt anything like that before." I am pretty sure my face must be crimson.

"Did you feel it between your legs when I rubbed the rope over your nipples?"

How did he know that? "I did, it was incredible."

"What else did you like?"

"I love being tied up, but I always want to move and it forces me to take the pleasure if that makes any sense."

"That's exactly the intent, Katarina. It's our body's natural instinct to move when things become too pleasurable or painful," he says.

"What else did you like?" he asks.

"I loved that you gave me a way to communicate with you and made sure I was comfortable when I couldn't talk."

"Anything you didn't like, Katarina?"

He senses my hesitation. "What is it Baby, tell me," he urges.

"The gag is not very attractive looking at all. I can't imagine what I looked like with it in my mouth," I say.

"Baby, I wasn't exactly looking at your mouth," he says smiling. "I did, however, miss hearing you beg me to stop when you were getting close," he says, capturing my lips.

"Did anything else bother you?"

"I still didn't like that you made me wait when I was ready."

"So you were ready to climax and I prolonged the experience when you wanted it to end?"

"Well, said like that, no. It's hard to explain."

"Did it bother you as much this time?"

"Not as much. It felt fantastic. I never realized you could have an orgasm of that magnitude, but it's almost like a control thing."

"Katarina, it is very much a control thing. If you cum right away, your pleasure will not build and your climax will not be as pleasurable and I very much like to control that," he says, pulling me closer and kissing me deeply. "Baby, I want to show you how pleasurable different experiences can be and make up for all that you've missed."

"It's all so new to me, but I love that you want to know these things. It makes me feel so connected to you. What did you like, Chase?" I ask.

"That you put your complete trust in me. You couldn't move, talk, or see what I was doing to you, but trusted me to pleasure you. It's an incredible turn-on," he says, pulling me close and kissing the top of my head.

"I'm glad that you liked it, too," I say, feeling sated and a little drowsy.

"I don't know about you, but I am famished. Want to help me raid the kitchen?" he asks, lifting up on one elbow and grinning widely.

"Absolutely," I say, pulling my robe on as he slides into his lounge pants for the trip downstairs. Chase pulls a peach and rhubarb pie from the refrigerator. "Want to try a little of each?" he asks.

"Half a slice of each sounds good," I say, shaking my head at his antics.

He places the pie on our plates and proceeds to swirl a mound of whipped cream onto his pie. "Whipped cream?" he says, grinning like a schoolboy.

"Sure," I say, laughing at the large slices he has in front of him. "What will Gaby think when she sees half of her pie is gone?"

"She's going to think we appreciated her efforts."

"Did you ever get an agenda for tomorrow's meeting?" I ask.

"I haven't seen one. You're planning to attend, though, right?" he asks.

"I am, but I don't know why Mark called a meeting without the users and can't help but feel like he purposely excluded me from the invite," I admit.

"I'm sure that he did, but do try not to worry about it. You have to trust that I am going to take care of things and have your best interests at heart. I need to be in the air by six thirty to make it to an early meeting. If you like we can take the helicopter together and I'll show you around after that, or you can sleep in a bit."

"No, I'd like to get an early start. I can finalize some other work while you're in the meeting. I have a lot to catch up on and things to do in preparation for the user group meetings."

"I'll let Jay know then," he says, guiding me into the formal dining room. I'm not sure what he pushed, but a panel slides open exposing an elevator. He gestures me in and enters a code. When the doors open, we are in the dining room of his own personal suite upstairs.

"Jay will show you the ins and outs of the elevators and security panels soon," he says, gauging my look of surprise as we head into the bedroom. I brush my teeth and am almost asleep when I feel his lips on mine. "Good night, Baby," he whispers.

The alarm wakes me and I pull on my running clothes and lace up my shoes. Chase is at the kitchen table talking on his cell and in his gym clothes. It's obvious he just got off the treadmill. "No, it didn't sound like he was thrilled about the human resource agreement. We'll have to see how this one plays out, Sid. Okay, keep me posted," he says before disconnecting.

"How long have you been up?" I ask.

"Quite a while. I usually go over stock accounts and global reports on the big screen while I get a workout in. It saves time and gives me something to do while I'm on the elliptical or treadmill."

"How often do you run?"

"Three or four times a week. The other days I like to use the elliptical for changes in muscle groups and free weights three times a week."

"That's why it's so easy for you to cart me around," I say laughing.

"Maybe I should add you to my workout routine."

"I'll be back in an hour. Wouldn't want to miss my helicopter ride," I tease.

"Do you mind if we make the trip back here tonight?" he asks.

"Not at all. I would generally be driving an hour each way anyway."

"Here, take this phone for your run. The team is already outside. When we get to Prestian Jay will sync yours with our intelligence software," he says.

"I feel like I'm in a James Bond movie with all of this security, but not arguing," I say, kissing him.

"Glad to hear that. When you get back let's have breakfast together. I'll let Gaby know we'll be home tonight," he says before kissing me goodbye.

I find a path lined with pine trees and follow the property toward the lake. The moon is relatively bright, but I'm glad Jay insisted on the reflective vest. It's much darker in the country than in the city with all the streetlights. I am soon lost in the run and my mind drifts to my mom. I know I should call her and tell her about Chase before she sees our faces plastered on one of the magazine covers in her office or at the local grocery store. I resolve to call her before day's end as I come to the end of my run, slowing to a walk and removing my vest. I see lights in the woods ahead of me. I turn around and see lights in the forest behind me, and then recognize Jay, Sheldon and Matt. What the hell...

I'm still thinking about the reality of the effort to keep me safe as I get out of the shower. I decide on a black skirt, multicolored blouse, and flats and go in search of Chase when I'm ready. I pass what appear to be other bedrooms and a large library, and poke my head into the gym room. On closer inspection I see it's equipped with an elliptical, free weights, treadmill and circuit machines. There's a large flat screen on one wall, computer monitors affixed to the equipment, and an adjacent shower room. Swoosh...

Message: Where are you?

Reply: In the gym...

I can't help admiring the treadmill and Chase walks in looking every bit the hot CEO in his dark suit and tie. "It really is a nice way to get a run in when it's cold," he says.

"It is a pretty fancy unit and the view is absolutely incredible now that it's light," I say, admiring the Michigan shore.

"You're welcome to use whatever you want, anytime. A heated pool and sauna are located on the lower level. I like the view from this window so had the gym moved upstairs," he says.

"I'm never going to find my way around this house," I say, following him downstairs towards the kitchen.

"You'll get used to it. In fact, Jay will go through the floor plan along with that of the condo to review the security aspects with you."

"Chase, you can't be serious. Don't tell me he's going to make me memorize the floor plan," I say.

"Shhh ... Baby," he says, putting his finger across my lips. "It's not Jay's fault, it's mine."

"Why can't I just get used to the house without all that?" I ask.

"Katarina, I thought you understood the need for security," he says.

I recall the attempts on my life and surprise at the amount of security applied to my morning run. I look up and his dark green eyes are hooded and resolved. "It's important to me that you know how to navigate through the house and use the safe room equipment, Katarina."

"Well, then I guess I'll spend the day tromping through the house learning how to lock myself in rooms," I say, smiling as the tension in his face appears to subside.

We enter the kitchen to find a clucking Gaby. "Whatever happened to my pies last night? It appears we've had late night visitors," she exclaims, feigning displeasure.

"We were starving last night. How could we resist?" I ask.

Gaby smiles at me and looks down at her half eaten pies. "My goodness, you are a bunch of pie heisters! Now I have two of you to deal with," she exclaims, clucking as she swishes about the kitchen. "I made a quiche for breakfast, good thing I put that in the back of the refrigerator last night," she says, narrowing her eyes at us.

"Gaby, I am seriously going to have to start running twice as long to wear off all your delicious meals. I have never tasted a better rhubarb pie in all my life, honestly," I say.

"It's my mother's recipe. I'm glad that you like it," she says, bringing us each a plate of quiche made with spinach, goat cheese and paired with fresh fruit. We devour the breakfast and as we're leaving Chase gives Gaby a warm hug. She beams up at him and it's clear to see how much he means to her.

I reach over instinctively and give Gaby a hug, too. "Thank you for such a warm welcome and lovely meal. Did Chase tell you we are coming back tonight?" I ask.

"He did mention that," she says warmly.

"Okay, we'll see you tonight then," I say.

Chase hands me earplugs before we get to the helipad. "The helicopter will be noisy, put these in and keep them in until we land," Chase says. I adjust the earplugs after we're seated and I'm surprised when he hands me a set of headphones. They are cushioned and I place them over my head as he does after buckling in. I take in all the instrumentation on the panels and over the pilot's head. The whirring of the blades barely penetrate the earplugs as we lift off, hovering at first, and then gaining momentum, height and altitude, clearing the tops of the trees. We are flying parallel to Lake Michigan and from this far up in the air, the water appears to be a deep dark blue as we approach the city. As we near Prestian, I can see the outline of their crest on the side of the sky-rise before the pilot lands on its roof. Chase assists me out of the helicopter and guides me out of the wind and toward the rooftop entrance to the Prestian building. As we enter the elevator he pushes numbers on the security panel. The light turns green and we begin our descent one floor lower. The doors open into the reception area and we walk through what appear to be administrative offices.

"Katarina, you can use this office for now, but we'll look at different space arrangements in the future. Right now I need to go meet with a group that has flown in from overseas, but it shouldn't be more than an hour. Matt and Sheldon will be outside in the corridor if you need anything," he says before departing for his conference.

I open my Mac and sign onto the network, quickly becoming engrossed with the project updates and replying to those that require it.

I feel his eyes on me and glance up from my computer, surprised that an hour and a half has already gone by. "I didn't realize so much time had passed," I say, glancing at the clock on the wall.

"Yes, I can see why. You've responded to more than forty emails, and provided teams with good direction as they work through the next steps. Are you always so involved in every aspect of the project?" he asks.

"Title, project consultant," I say as if that should explain everything.

"Job scope," he says with a wide grin.

"Regardless, I'm caught up now and won't feel guilty taking some time off to go pick up my personal belongings today," I say.

"You have absolutely nothing to feel guilty about. You work more hours than most of our executives. Now are you ready for a little tour?" he asks.

"I'd love for you to show me around," I say, packing my MacBook into my black leather bag. Chase leads me to the executive suites, introducing me to a few members of his team before taking me through the vacant space that can be utilized by the team working on the Prestian facility.

"Chase, it's absolutely perfect. The smartboards will work great for the work we have left," I say thrilled with the layout of the space and the technology we'll have.

"I'm glad it will work nicely for your team. I told Jay you wanted to leave fairly early this morning, so he could get you back for the meeting. He will have the car pulled around shortly so we should probably head downstairs," he says, taking my hand as we walk toward the elevator. As we reach it, Sheldon appears out of nowhere and enters the elevator with us.

The limo is waiting for us right outside the building and Chase opens the rear door for me so that I can get into the backseat. "If you want to use the computer to get some work done or just go online, feel free. He flips down a leather cover and exposes a computer monitor inlaid in the back of the seat. You just press the power button, sign on with this password, and you should be all set," he says, giving me a piece of paper and a quick kiss before closing the door. The computer is intriguing and since it's at least a forty-minute drive I boot it up and am soon online accessing my worksite.

There is a new email from Martel Design and I see that it is from Mark responding to my request to begin putting group meetings together with the design team and the users of the space.

I quickly review it and then reread it slowly, digesting the information within it.

TO: KMeilers@TorzialConsulting.org

From: MPowers@Martel&Sons.org

CC: CHPrestian@PrestianCorp.org,
JWarling@TorzialConsulting.org

MISS MEILERS,

My colleagues and I have had an opportunity to meet and review designs. We believe we will be able to deliver a design that meets your needs by the end of the week.

Thanks,
Mark

MARK POWERS

Project Coordinator
Martel and Son Design

TO: MPowers@Martel&Sons.org
From: KMeilers@TorzialConsulting.org
CC: CHPrestian@PrestianCorp.org,
JWarling@TorzialConsulting.org

MARK,

I would be interested in looking at the design in coordination with the future state flow, SIPOC, and spaghetti diagrams created by the team. It's exciting that you may already have a design that incorporates all the newly identified services.

I look forward to reviewing.

Thanks,
Kate
Kate Meilers
Project Consultant
Torzial Consulting Firm

TO: KMeilers@TorzialConsulting.org

From: CHPrestian@PrestianCorp.org

I WONDERED how you would respond.

CHASE H. **Prestian**

Chief Executive Officer

Prestian Corporation

I PONDER CHASE'S response based on my plea for him to keep Mark on the project. I am the one that wanted to make sure he had every opportunity to design this facility using Lean methodologies. His email leads one to believe that his intent is just to pick a pre-drawn design. I decide not to focus on it until he responds and I see what he wants to meet with Chase about later in the day.

TO: CHPrestian@PrestianCorp.org

From: KMeilers@TorzialConsulting.org

He apparently doesn't realize I will be at the meeting. I'll hold on opinions until then.

Love this computer!

Kate

Kate Meilers

Project Consultant

Torzial Consulting Firm

FROM: CHPrestian@PrestianCorp.org
To: KMeilers@TorzialConsulting.org

GOOD! If you spend drive time working, you will have more time to devote to important things when you get home.
Chase H. Prestian
Chief Executive Officer
Prestian Corporation

TO: CHPrestian@PrestianCorp.org
From: KMeilers@TorzialConsulting.org

IMPORTANT THINGS...LIKE entertaining you with how I shower alone?

KATE

KATE MEILERS
Project Consultant
Torzial Consulting Firm

FROM: CHPrestian@PrestianCorp.org
To: KMeilers@TorzialConsulting.org

BABY, I love the way you think. Yes, exactly like that. Text me when you leave Torzial.

. . .

CHASE H. **Prestian**

Chief Executive Officer

Prestian Corporation

TO: CHPrestian@PrestianCorp.org

From: KMeilers@TorzialConsulting.org

ANYONE EVER TOLD you that you worry too much and are just a little overbearing??

Kate

Kate Meilers

Project Consultant

Torzial Consulting Firm

From: CHPrestian@PrestianCorp.org

To: KMeilers@TorzialConsulting.org

YES, and they were right. Do what I say!! I also happen to know it makes you hot!

CHASE H. **Prestian**

Chief Executive Officer

Prestian Corporation

TO: CHPrestian@PrestianCorp.org

From: KMeilers@TorzialConsulting.org

INCORRIGIBLE!

Kate

KATE MEILERS
Project Consultant
Torzial Consulting Firm

SIXTEEN

"Kate, I'm going to drop you off at the entrance while I park the car. We've got people stationed around Torzial, and someone outside each floor of the elevator, so you won't be alone," Jay says.

"I appreciate that, Jay but Torzial is pretty safe," I say.

"Kate, Chase and I have our numbers programmed into the phone he gave you. A call to 9-1-1 trips a call back to us. If you ever find yourself in real trouble hit the button programmed to 9-1-1. It's labeled here," he says, showing me the button. "Then you only have to worry about one button and we'll know," he explains.

"I'm sorry, Jay. I don't mean to sound ungrateful, it's just a little overwhelming at times. I will try to make things a little easier for you guys," I state, feeling a little guilty knowing he is only attempting to do his job.

"No need to apologize, Kate. We just want to make sure you're safe," he assures.

I recognize one of the security details, whom I have not been introduced to yet, as I get into the elevator and press the 16th floor for Torzial. I greet Melinda, who has been with the company for more than five years and is always smiling and pleasant. We talk about her family and the recent trip to Aruba for a few minutes before I make my way to Jenny's office.

She is behind her desk poring over papers in front of her. Her shoulder-length brunette hair falls in soft waves around her face and her green eyes show her surprise at my arrival as she looks up.

"Kate, I was so worried about you. Are you okay?" she asks, coming around the desk to hug me tightly.

"Yes, I left you a voicemail that I wouldn't be home last night. Didn't you get it?" I ask.

"Kate, I got it. You haven't seen the newspapers today, have you?"

"Jenny, I haven't seen anything this morning except email."

"Shit, I hate to be the one to break it to you, Kate, but you're all over the papers this morning," she says as she walks over to the cabinet and pours each of us a cup of coffee from the carafe. She turns on the big screen with the remote as she sits back down and pulls the story from the Midwestern up.

CHICAGO MIDWESTERN

Chase Prestian Returns to Chicago
Nate Collins

CHASE PRESTIAN HAS ARRIVED back in Chicago after a 10-day visit to the isle of Aruba where he participated in a week-long Lean event to determine the future of the Prestian Chicago Medical Facility. He was accompanied by hospital and clinic administrators, clinicians, nursing home, government, and pharmacy leaders, as well as designers, mechanical engineers, and Torzial representative Kate Meilers.

Kate is a process consultant hired by Prestian Corporation to drive the design of the new Prestian Chicago Medical Facility. It is rumored that she and Prestian spent the better part of the week together. Prestian is a strong advocate for design using Lean methodologies. He personally participated in each of the sessions and spent the other days with Kate as she recovered from an altercation on the beach, which was broken up by his security team.

After having arrived stateside, Chase shared with this reporter that he and Kate were celebrating after making the decision to move in together. He said and I quote, "I couldn't be happier," before escorting Kate into Noor's restaurant.

There is a picture of Chase holding me around the waist and I have to admit the photographer captured a very nice photo of us. I'll have to remember to ask Chase if we can get a copy of the picture from Nate.

I feel bad that I didn't give Jenny a heads up. "I should have known the photograph from last night would be in the papers. I'm not sure how you feel about me dating Chase related to my employment with Torzial and our contractual relationship with Prestian Corporation, but I was going to tell you today," I say.

"Kate, there's nothing in the employment agreement that says you can't date someone from a company that we have a contract with. I'm just concerned about you, and frankly surprised that you're going out with someone that has anything to do with your job. It's just, well, I mean your mom, and well, you know you've always steered well clear of that," she says.

"I didn't know who Chase was when we first started seeing each other. I don't know how to explain the chemistry we have, but it's like nothing I've ever felt before. The story is pretty accurate. We haven't spent much time apart and I've actually agreed to move in with him. I haven't even told my mom yet. I need to call her before she gets wind of this, although she's probably going to flip either way," I confess.

Jenny gasps. "Kate, this is just one of the stories that hit the papers today. It happened to be well written, but I'm afraid the others are not," she says, pulling up another article on the big screen.

SIZZLE PUBLICATIONS

Chase Prestian Ensnared

Brent Korska

. . .

CHASE PRESTIAN SPENT 10 days in Aruba with Kate Meilers, the representative for Torzial Consulting assigned to the Prestian Chicago Medical Facility project.

ACCORDING TO CONFIDENTIAL SOURCES, they spent every moment together, dancing and partying the week away. Police records show she was assaulted by three men on the beach and was moved into the Prestian suites shortly afterward. Another police report was filed the very next day citing details of an attempted poisoning of the consultant. Members of the team were delayed in getting home until she recovered and could finish the event. It's hard for this reporter to sift through all the rumors and various opinions about what happened. One team member who asked to remain anonymous shared thoughts from the group that these attacks may have been part of a ploy to get close to the elusive Chase Prestian. Others suggest she may have become a target because of her relationship with the billionaire who is under suspicion of drug trafficking.

Chase Prestian is well renowned for his exotic tastes in women around the globe. He and Kate were interviewed outside of Noor's last night and he shared with reporters that he and Kate are moving in together. The question for most readers is how long will it last?

I FEEL sick as I look at the images on the monitor. There must be at least twenty pictures of Chase with different women on his arm. Blondes, brunettes, and redheads from around the world, all drop dead gorgeous.

"Kate, there's more of the same in different tabloids. Do you want to see them?"

"No, I can't see anything else and I'm not really sure what to say, Jenny. I didn't know who he was when we first started seeing each other or we would never have started dating, but it happened, and I've never felt like this about anyone before. I have no clue what they are talking about related to the drug trafficking. I just hope that Torzial does not come under scrutiny because of it," I say, hurt and embarrassed by the articles.

"Fuck that, Kate! Torzial is a stable, reputable company and it stands on its own merits. This won't hurt the firm. If anything, it will give it more publicity. I just want to be sure you are okay. I mean, Kate, I don't have a clue about the drug trafficking stuff, but honestly hon, the guy's in the tabloids with a different girl every night," she says, hugging me tightly.

"I'll have to talk to him about the articles, but in the meantime, I'm going to pack up some of the Prestian Facility documents and facilitation materials to keep at Prestian Corporation. Chase offered to provide the teams with a floor in the compound and I looked at it this morning. It'll work out perfect when we start modeling some of the rooms. I was also hoping to stop by your apartment and pick up my personal belongings," I say, hoping that I don't seem as desolate as I feel.

"Whatever you need, Kate. You've got the key and you know you can stay for as long as you want to," she says.

"Thanks Kate, I just need to talk to Chase about the articles," I say before I set out to find some boxes. The mailroom is humming with machinery when I go downstairs and I can hear the women in the back cubicles chatting. I stop walking when I overhear my name.

"Did you see the articles about Kate and the guy who owns Prestian Corporation? She's all over the tabloids. A week in Aruba sounds like a tough assignment. Looks like she snagged Chase Prestian. What a little gold digger. The guys downstairs have a pool going to see how long it takes for Prestian to dump her," says a voice I recognize as one of thc Torzial accountants.

Her voice drops slightly, and I have to strain to make out what she is saying. "Pete from IT said his uncle works for the Chicago P.D. He may be a great upstanding entrepreneur in this country, but he is the number one suspect in a large drug trafficking incident that happened last year. I guess the guy's got a security system on par with the police and they couldn't make anything stick. He's sure got the perfect cover to move in and out of the country."

"Stop it. I feel sorry for Kate," says a woman I recognize as Sue.

She has worked in the mailroom for as long as I have been with the company. "She probably doesn't even know what he's up to in his spare time. Last year when I was home sick with pneumonia she brought me containers of fresh soup, so all I had to do was pop them in the microwave for a warm meal. She's a real sweetheart. You can't believe what you read in those trash magazines. What's concerning to me is that Pete said Mark told him that Prestian is going to use their templated designs. If that's the case why would they keep Torzial on for the project?" she asks.

I close the door and walk quietly out of the mailroom and take the back stairs to the second floor, glancing toward the elevator where the security detail is still staked out in the waiting area. *Drug trafficking?* What the hell. I knew it was strange he had so much security, but nothing like this ever crossed my mind. He can't possibly be into drugs. Maybe this is the reason someone is targeting me and why we need so much security.

I head to Jenny's office hoping she can put some perspective on the situation with Martel, but as I reach her office I stop short, hearing her on the phone. "Chase, you're not really leaving me much choice in the matter. Are you going to announce details of the new contract at the meeting today?"

"I see," she says after a brief pause. "Then you can be the one to break the news to Kate. She's not going to take it lightly, though. She prides herself on her ability to handle multiple complex projects such as the Prestian Corp Facility."

I back out of the hallway and head toward my office feeling confused and frustrated with the way the morning is turning out. I sink into my chair and fire up the computer to see if I have any messages from Chase or Mark and find absolutely nothing to give me a clue as to what Jenny and Chase were talking about. Jenny apparently wants Chase to be the one to fill me in on whatever is going on. I type Chase Prestian in Google images and am overwhelmed by the surge of jealousy I feel at seeing him with a barrage of other women. As I'm scrolling through the hundreds of images one of the security details pokes his head in to see if help is needed with the boxes.

"I'm no longer in need of them," I say, thumbing through the multitude of pictures splashed all over my screen.

"Yes, ma'am," he says, leaving the office.

A few moments later the swoosh of my phone interrupts my thoughts.

Message: I'm told you aren't packing?

Reply: You were told correctly. We need to talk.

Message: You have my attention.

Reply: In person. I'm on my way.

Message: I see.

I CLOSE out of the pictures and head toward the elevator. The proximity and even the need for security are more annoying to me at this moment. He has apparently alerted Jay, who already has the car pulled around.

"Jay, can you take me back to Prestian? And, when did the other car join us?" I ask, getting into the backseat of the limo.

"The second car has been with us the entire day. We weren't taking any chances with what's happened to you in the past few days," he says, pulling into the heavy city traffic.

"I didn't recall seeing it on the way to Torzial."

"It's a different car, different team than we used on the way in," he explains.

Of course... more teams. "Do you have any leads on who may be targeting me, Jay?"

"I think it would be better if you ask Chase. I'm really not at liberty to discuss it," he explains apologetically.

"What the hell, Jay. Why can't you tell me? If I recall correctly, it's my life that is in jeopardy. I don't see anyone going after Chase," I say.

"Kate, I understand you are upset, but please talk to Chase. I'm really not at liberty," he says.

I realize he is only following orders and out of frustration decide to text Chase.

Message: Would you give Jay permission to tell me who the hell is targeting me and why?

Reply: I would prefer we discuss it when you arrive at Prestian.

Message: Security is in the car, behind the car, in the elevator, waiting rooms. EVERYWHERE!

Reply: Katarina, they are making sure you're protected.

Message: Which I wouldn't need if you didn't lead the life you do.

Reply: We've had this conversation.

Message: And I think you may have left out a few details...

Reply: You obviously have something on your mind.

I decide not to respond and instead get some work done. I need to think. I push shuffle on my iPhone and put my headphones on during the ride across town.

Jay pulls up in front of Prestian and the car doors are opened for us. There is an awkward silence as we ride the elevator to the top floor. Once in the administrative suites, Jay tells me that Chase is expecting me and that I should go straight in. I open the door to his office and he looks up from his work.

"Katarina," he says, walking around his desk to stand in front of me. "So, you have something on your mind?" He is standing so close that I can feel the warmth of his breath against my cheek.

I walk to the opposite side of the room, and look out the window trying to put some distance between us.

"I'm not sure where to start."

"Katarina?"

"So much has happened that I don't even know where to begin. I was at Torzial and overheard people talking about us." He's moved behind me again and now I am between the window and his body, so I turn to face him. "They said some pretty callous things about me, in fact, called me a little gold digger." His eyebrows rise in concern and he looks as though he is going to say something.

"No, please, last week that would have upset me greatly. I know it's not true and so do you and that's all that matters to me. But a lot more happened today, Chase."

"Go on," he urges.

"I saw the newspapers and some of the tabloid articles. I couldn't bring myself to read all of them, though."

He moves to pull me closer and I put a hand on his chest. The sight of him with all of those women in his arms is too fresh.

"I'm sorry, Katarina. I was hoping to show them to you later this evening. The pictures were taken over a lot of years and put together to project a particular image and point of view," he says.

"The articles also made reference to you being a drug trafficker. Then I went to the mailroom and people were talking about us and the fact that you are a suspect in a drug trafficking operation. I don't know what to think, Chase. I need you to tell me what's true and what's not."

"I see," he says, the deep green eyes penetrating and holding mine captive. "Is that all?"

"No, actually, it's not all. One of the Torzial workers also said Mark made reference to Martel Design getting a large contract with you on the Prestian Medical facility and they're worried that Torzial will no longer be needed for the project. I went upstairs to talk to Jenny after I heard that, hoping she knew something that would put some perspective on it, but then I overheard her on the telephone with you. All I know is what I heard Chase. She apparently wanted you to explain this to me so I didn't ask her for details. I don't want to step over any boss and friend lines," I explain.

"What do you think happened with the Torzial contract, Katarina?"

"I don't have a clue, Chase. I thought you were pleased with the work Torzial has done, specifically the work of the team in Aruba. You even told me you were happy with the outcome. I wasn't intentionally eavesdropping, but I overheard Jenny's conversation with you. I don't know what to think right now."

"The contract negotiations Jenny and I were discussing have absolutely nothing to do with Martel. When we were in Aruba and the caregivers expressed their desire to have a medical facility in the heart of where their sickest and most socio-disadvantaged patients were, I put out a few feelers. There is land available in that area, and our offer was just accepted, which means we will be designing and creating two facilities in the city of Chicago."

"That would eliminate so many of the transportation barriers that we currently have, but what does that have to do with the Torzial contract?"

"I contacted Jenny to revise the existing contract and have a full-time consultant dedicated exclusively to the Prestian Medical facilities. Your other accounts will be given to different members at Torzial if she agrees to the contract."

"Why would you talk to Jenny about something like that, instead of me?" I demand.

"Katarina, the Prestian facility is more than a full-time job and now there will be two running simultaneously. You can't possibly think you can continue to manage the other projects you have for Torzial."

"Chase, this is not your decision to make. I am a grown woman and this is my career. How dare you?"

"With all due respect Katarina, it is my decision to make. I want a full-time person dedicated to the Prestian facilities. This project is going to need to be up and running fast as soon as we get state approvals. The fact that I want you in that role is due solely to your skill set and abilities and not our personal relationship which is why I did not discuss it with you."

"You are absolutely infuriating. You think you can just snap your fingers and I will do your bidding? Well, newsflash, I am not about to give up my other projects and you should have asked me before you talked to Jenny."

A voice from the intercom interrupts my thoughts. "Mr. Prestian, Martel Design has arrived and they are in conference room six."

"What are they doing here? I thought we weren't meeting with them until later in the day," I say.

"Katarina, you saw the note Mark sent about the design. He's apparently still intending to pitch us a prefab design and I didn't think you would want to be included in the conversation. I moved the meeting up to spare you the discomfort. However, since you're here now, why don't you join us?"

"Please let the team know I will be there momentarily," he says into the intercom.

"Chase, this doesn't change anything about the contract. I am not giving up my other projects."

"The Prestian Medical Center facilities are going to be the biggest projects in the state. I want you in charge of their efforts, but dedicated only to them. Why don't we agree to disagree and talk about this after our meeting," he says, walking toward the conference, leaving me no choice but to follow in his wake.

He guides me to one of the open seats around the table and sits in the chair next to mine. Mark Martel and a few others from the design team, including Terry, who was at the event, the hospital president, and Brian, the chief operating officer are already in attendance.

Mark pulls up a presentation on the overhead and starts the meeting. "Martel Design is excited to be part of such a great community venture. We know this is one of the most important projects in the state and understand the urgency of getting shovels into the ground quickly," he says, moving through key points on the PowerPoint before revealing the next slide, which displays four options for the facility layout. He walks through what appear to be completed designs for the new facility demonstrating the layouts and attributes of each of the four models. The designs have not utilized the information from the event. The departments which should be located near each other are not, and the lab still has an enormous wait area. It's clear now why I was not invited to the meeting. He finishes his presentation and asks the team for their questions and thoughts.

Chase begins to speak. "Mark, thank you for setting up the meeting and sharing your work. Unfortunately, the designs do not include any of the critical to quality attributes defined in the weeklong event. The lab and x-ray departments should be centrally located, but with a much smaller floor space since the patients will be drawn in the exam room. The urgent care setting should be adjacent to the emergency department since it will be critical to share the same staff at times. The social services department appears to be a stand-alone service on the floor plan, instead of being integrated into the practices. While I do believe there is a market for these template designs, they will not be used for the Prestian facility. This project will be utilizing information gleaned from the event and weighing heavily on the voice of the customer data to make healthcare better in our community.

"I have been in contract negotiations with Torzial and Martel

Design since our return and have secured dedicated resources for both design and Lean expertise. Mark, I want to thank you for your efforts here, and I am sure that Martel Senior will be in touch with you related to the contract. Have a good day, everyone," he says, getting up and pulling my chair out for me. He places his hand on the small of my back as we leave the conference room and return to his office.

"What the hell just happened, Chase?" I ask as he closes the door behind us.

"Katarina, you know exactly what just happened. I am not going to continue working with a designer who clearly does not understand the process we are using. Martel Senior will let Mark know he is no longer on the project later today and Terry will be taking over designs."

"You didn't think to talk to me about this before you did it?" I ask. "Now word will spread that you fired him and put me in charge of the project because we're sleeping together."

"I fired him because he did not deliver the intended product, which if I recall correctly is exactly what we agreed upon. He doesn't believe in Lean methodology even though he's been provided with a week to become engaged *and* I'm not going to condone behaviors such as the ones he has displayed on our team. Secondly, you have always been in charge of the process we used for the facility when Mark was in our employ and now."

"And how do you think I'm going to explain this when word gets out that he was fired because of me?" I ask.

"You fight back, Katarina. You tell the truth. He was removed from the project because he didn't produce the agreed upon designs and has no desire to do so. The only person that thinks he's getting fired because he said something about you is you. Your insecurities around what people think about you and your working relationships is something you're going to have to deal with at some point, Katarina, but him being fired has nothing to do with that. I gave you my word that I wouldn't let him go unless he did not deliver. He did not and was fired as a result."

"You are the most infuriating person I have ever met. You had no right to talk to Jenny about my projects and you should have at least talked to me before you decided to fire him," I state.

The phone on his desk rings and he answers the call as if dismissing me. He has got to be the most insufferable, arrogant asshole that I know. Two can play at this game. I leave the office and not seeing security around, head for the elevator in need of some fresh air. The arrogance of that man! It's breezy outside and I search in my purse for a hair tie, quickly pulling it into a pony and wishing I had my running shoes on. I hear the swoosh of an incoming message and check my phone as I exit the building.

Message: Where are you?

My phone rings and it's Chase's ringtone so I turn it on vibrate and keep moving at a good pace until I get to the next block and out of securities reach. I hear a buzzing sound and realize it's the other phone that Jay gave me this morning. *You have got to be kidding.* I fumble in my purse and lay the phone on a park bench as I pass by. *Let Jay and his team track that!*

There are lots of people milling around the lake taking advantage of the fall weather and brilliantly colored leaves before winter sets in. I'm thankful that I wore flats today and decide to walk the lake path. I'm sure Mark knows by now that he won't be working on the project and I can't imagine what rumors he'll spread given the way he talked about me in Aruba. Pretty soon the whole architectural world will think that Prestian Corp is advocating Lean methodologies because I'm sleeping with him.

The guy has some serious control issues. *Yes, and you usually like it...* and, why am I so set on protecting Mark? Maybe Chase is right, I haven't even told my mom about him for fear of what she may think. I'll have to call Jenny and talk to her about the Prestian Corporation accounts. It's not as if I have that many others and some are wrapping up. He could've asked me though, or at least, told me what he was thinking instead of going to her first. And what if he really is doing something illegal? I try to keep my thoughts at bay, but it would explain so many things. As I reflect back to the conversation, I realize he completely circumvented the discussion about his illegal activity.

I glance at the time and realize I've been walking for over an hour and head to the local bookstore that I frequent. It's almost five when I realize I am famished since we were supposed to have a late lunch after the meeting. I decide to eat at one of the restaurants within walking distance before dark settles in and determine how to handle the situation.

The restaurant is not overly crowded and after a short while, the waitress takes my order. The creamy dill tomato soup arrives with a small basket of fresh bread. I ponder going to Jenny's for the night, but that will be the first place Chase looks. I need some time away from him to get my thoughts together and decide to get a hotel room for the night. It's early and I hail one of the available taxis lined up along the street. The cab driver is older and seems friendly. "Where to miss?" he asks.

"Can you please take me to one of the nice hotels?" I ask.

"Sure, ma'am, anything you like," he replies. In about fifteen minutes he pulls up before the entrance of one of the best hotels in Chicago. *I'll stay here for the night and it'll give me time to think about what I want to do. Thank God, I have my laptop and my iPad in my tote with me. I can get some work done and try to get my head screwed back on.* I give the cab driver fare and a generous tip thanking him for the drive. The hotel entrance is grand and I try not to think about the cost. Luckily they have availability and I ask for one of the suites. As long as I'm staying at this hotel I might as well go all out. Although I am without luggage, the bellboy escorts me to my room. I give him a tip, put my tote down on the floor, and sink into the inviting overstuffed armchair. I feel like an emotional wreck and just need time to calm down and think about my next steps. I decide to call Jenny and let her know what's going on and fish my phone from the bottom of my purse and power it up.

Message: Where are you?

Message: Katarina, where are you?

Message: I'm going to turn on the tracking device.

Message: Damn it, Katarina. The receptionist saw you leave by yourself. Turn around and head back. You're not safe in the city by yourself.

Message: Where are you? Chase called to find out if you had contacted me. Text me... I need to make sure you are okay. Love, Jenny.

My phone vibrates and I glance at it, expecting it to be Chase again, but answer when I see it's Jenny.

"Kate, where are you and what the hell is going on? Chase was blowing up my phone earlier to see if you had contacted me. Now, Matt just called rambling on and on that he can't live anymore without you in his life. He didn't have your new phone number so called me and didn't sound like himself at all, Kate. He wants you to come to his apartment and talk. I seriously think it's a cry for help… he sounds utterly dismal."

My heart sinks in my chest. "I'm heading to his apartment right now, Jenny," I say, already halfway to the elevators. The damn things are as slow as waiting for a watched pot to boil and seem to stop at every floor. As they reach the ground level, I hurry out and dash across the lobby and into the street to hail a cab. I give the man Matt's address and am impressed with his ability to quickly navigate the busy city traffic.

The cell vibrates again and this time, it's Chase. I turn it off not wanting to explain the situation to him right now. How am I going to explain my relationship with Matt to him? *Please hurry* I pray silently, wishing the streets were not so congested with traffic.

As we reach Matt's the driver pulls to the curb and I hand him some cash. Matt's apartment is on the lower level of the small compound and the lights are on. I knock on the door and realize it is not all the way closed.

"Matt, it's me, Kate," I call out, pushing the door open a little farther.

My heart sinks as I see him slumped forward on the couch, a piece of paper hanging out of his mouth. I fear I may be too late. As I reach him, I feel a forceful blow to the back of the head and fall into an enveloping world of pitch dark. I am unaware of how much time has passed but am acutely aware of the throbbing in my head and the pain of the restraints pinching the sensitive skin of my wrists as I come to. I try to concentrate on my surroundings as things begin to regain focus. Matt is next to me on the sofa, gagged, his eyes wide open and grave. The alarming smell of gasoline has permeated my senses and instantly sobers me. My heart is racing a million miles a minute as I watch Mark pouring it all over the furnishings in the room. I try to yell out, but the gag sufficiently hampers any attempts of being heard. My heart is pounding in fear as the smell engulfs the room and my senses. I look up in despair and see triumph on Mark Martel's face. "You won't be happy until you have taken everything from me, will you?" he snarls. "It wasn't good enough that you got Matt, but you had to get in the way of my business, too! You've cost me millions! Where are your precious Chase and his security team now? He's not going to save your ass this time, bitch. And you..." He turns to Matt. "You sniveling coward. Scared of what everyone would think if they found out we were a couple, you turn to this slut? Well now they'll believe you were so depressed over losing her that you took both of your lives and then Prestian Corp will have no other option but to buy the designs if they want to meet their deadlines. Right now, I want the pleasure of taking this bitch out while you watch. Once this place ignites there won't be any way to determine what happened. "

The pain in my head is excruciating and it's becoming impossible to focus. I vaguely hear the shattering of glass coming through the living room window, followed by short shots of gunfire and searing pain before I am once again enveloped in a world of darkness.

SEVENTEEN

There is shouting all around me, but all I can focus on is the excruciating pain. "He's down. Secure that lighter and get Kate the hell out of here, before the entire place lights up!" There is more pain when someone pulls at my restraints and I cry out as I am lifted into the air. The last things I hear are the sirens in the distance before I lose consciousness again.

As the stark white room comes into focus, I see the dark green eyes that I have been dreaming about. "Chase."

His hand strokes my cheek. "Finally... Baby, I have been so worried about you." His eyes are filled with concern and anxiety.

I look around the white room. Monitors are beeping above me and an IV pole is next to me. "Chase... is Matt, okay?"

"He's all right, Katarina. He was discharged earlier in the day."

"Mark?"

"After he heals he will be behind bars wearing orange for a very long time, Katarina."

I look around taking in the hospital room. "What happened, Chase and how did you find me?"

"You were shot in the shoulder and the bullet needed to be

removed. You also sustained another nasty hit to the head. You've been recovering, Baby."

"I'm so thirsty."

"Take slow sips," he says, easing me forward and putting the cup of water to my mouth. "I'm going to let the nurse know that you are awake."

I can't help but smile as he returns with a bristling nurse. The poor woman has probably been pulled away from another task by Mr. Bossy himself. "Miss Meilers, glad to see you're awake," she says kindly and begins asking me a series of questions to gauge my pain level.

A few moments later a tall man with graying hair and glasses who appears to be in his mid-forties shakes Chase's hand and introduces himself to me as Dr. Rouse.

"Miss Meilers, you were very lucky. The wound you sustained to your shoulder did not injure any major arteries. You were most fortunate it did not hit the scapula or any other bones, which could have shattered. The smaller muscles and blood vessels were quickly repaired and you'll be up and around in no time at all. You sustained a traumatic blow to the back of your head and, unfortunately, another concussion. We've been watching you carefully given this is the second one in as many weeks. The initial tests look good, but we are going to want you to limit physical activity for a little while and have you remain in the hospital until tomorrow, just to make sure none of the vessels leak. I'll leave orders for pain control and stop by to see you in the morning. The discharge planner will get you scheduled for a follow-up with me in three days and we'll evaluate therapy needs at that time. Do you have any questions for me?" he asks.

"None that I can think of right now. Thank you for taking care of me," I say as the nurse returns with a pill and pours a fresh glass of water for me from the pitcher on the table.

"You are more than welcome. Gunshots to that area can either cause minimal damage or leave someone paralyzed for life depending on the location of the bullet. You were very fortunate, Miss Meilers."

"Mr. Prestian, if you want to stay with her tonight I would suggest having them move in one of the rolling beds. They are much more comfortable than the chair you were in last night," he says before leaving.

"You were here all night?" I ask as the doctor and nurse leave.

"Where else would I be, Katarina?"

"How did you even know I was here?"

He raises his eyebrows and narrows his eyes at me. "Katarina, do you seriously think I would allow you to wander around the city without security after what happened in Aruba? When you didn't answer my calls or texts, I figured you needed some time alone. I tried initiating the tracking system so the security team could follow from a distance, but then you already know that don't you? They were following from the minute you left the building. They pulled in another team to follow the signals and much to their surprise they were tracking a young skateboarder who picked up the phone on a city bench," he says.

"I tried reaching Jenny a few times earlier in the day to find out if you had contacted her, but she must have been in meetings when I phoned. Jenny finally called me to let me know what was happening, when she couldn't reach you on your cell. She was worried that you had decided to go alone and scared Matt may try to hurt you as well as himself.

"He didn't try to hurt me, Chase. Mark must have called Jenny," I begin to explain.

"Baby, I know that. Jay received a call from the team in Aruba about the same time. They found the man who attempted to drug you and he provided a description of the person who hired him. It fit Mark, perfectly, right down to the mole on the top of his ear. Jay's team followed you from the hotel and ran the plates of the vehicles outside Matt's apartment building and one belonged to Mark. They created a diversion and moved in fast. If they had not, you and Matt would not be here today, Baby," he says, gently brushing my hair off my face.

"I asked Jay to gather intel on Mark when we first started to encounter problems with him, but it just appeared he was trying to venture into a business of his own. My team never made the connection between him and his former lover and you. My guess is you not only stole the heart of his lover but were also thwarting his plans of gaining my support in launching his facilities template design business. Millions of dollars' worth of motivation to get you out of his way when he thought he could sell Prestian Corp his designs, and after the meeting today, he knew there was no chance of that. He must have still been at Prestian Corporation when you left and thought that you had evaded security.

"It all feels like a nightmare and it doesn't make any sense at all, Chase. Mark said Matt was a coward and I wasn't satisfied with just getting Matt, but I had to get in the way of his business, too. He was ranting and raving about wanting to kill me in front of Matt. What does Mark have to do with Matt? He made it sound like they were a couple?"

"Katarina, apparently Mark and Matt were in a pretty long- term relationship."

"I can't believe I didn't know they were together or that it was Mark, even in Aruba. I thought it was because of what you do for a living," I admit.

"Yes, my illicit criminal activities," he says, rubbing his chin, watching me intently. "First things first, Baby, I need to know what Matt means to you."

"Do you really want to hear this now?" I ask, taking another sip of my water.

His face is grave and his eyes are dark. "Baby, I need to know, and I want to hear it from you, Katarina."

"Chase, he's just a very close friend, well at least he was. We met when we started at the university and had a lot in common. We took many of the same classes and he was working his way through school, too. We became great friends and were rarely home so it made sense to reduce our rent and share an apartment. We lived together for quite a few years."

His eyes are hooded and controlled and it's hard for me to determine what he's thinking.

"Chase, I never slept with him if that's what you're wondering. He was just my dearest friend. We went out to dinner one night and out of the blue, he proposed to me in front of a whole restaurant full of people. I had no idea he had those kinds of feelings for me and it caught me completely by surprise. I have never felt anything for Matt except the deepest of friendship. I tried to explain that to him, but he asked me to move out and I lost one of my dearest friends."

"That's why you were staying with Jenny?" he asks.

"Yes, I wanted to respect his wishes. I just took my personal belongings and moved in with her until I could find a place to rent. He has not been in contact with me since that night. We used to share the same phone plan, but I got my own contract shortly after I moved out and he didn't have my new number. I had just checked into the hotel when Jenny called to let me know that he had called her and sounded suicidal. I assumed he called Jenny because I just recently changed service and he didn't have my new phone number."

"Baby, apparently Matt and Mark were in quite a long-term relationship. Matt told me that the relationship was quiet and that he just couldn't bring himself to let his parents and employer know. He decided that he would break it off with Mark and decided to ask his best friend to marry him. He said he was admittedly a little messed up emotionally over the entire situation, but that he never thought Mark would take it this hard."

"I never knew he was in a relationship with anyone, much less Mark." My head is fuzzy and my eyes are weighted with the effects of medication. Chase pulls me into his arms and holds me tightly.

"I didn't think you were in a relationship with him after what you told me about your past experiences, but I wasn't sure if maybe he wasn't the person that it just didn't work out with," he says.

"No, nothing like that, Chase," I say.

"I flew your mother in when you were admitted, and she had just left for the cafeteria before you woke up. She's been by your side all night and will be relieved that you're awake. I'll go find her while you rest a little and let her know that you've rejoined us," he says, pushing the hair out of my eyes and kissing my lips gently.

I wake to conversation and smile at the sight of my mom bustling around the hospital room, chatting with the nurse. "Mom..." She starts as she realizes I am awake. "Oh, Katie, Sweetheart, I was so worried about you when you wouldn't wake up. They said everyone has different reactions to anesthesia, and with your concussion you needed the rest, but it just felt like you were asleep forever," she says, pulling me into her arms.

"Can I get some water, Mom?" I say, still so thirsty.

"Here you go, Sweetie," she says, putting the ice-chilled water to my chapped lips.

"So you met Chase," I say, still not fully understanding how he managed to get ahold of my mom and fly her in.

"He called me from the ambulance to let me know that they were taking you to the hospital and that you would be going into surgery upon arrival. He had arranged to have a driver at my house to pick me up and take me to the airport and then he flew me in one of his corporate jets to be here with you. He had everything organized before he even called me and I barely had time to grab a few necessities. My goodness, he's an intense young man," she says smiling.

I can only imagine what he put her and the rest of the team through. "You have absolutely no idea, Mom," I say, smiling at the thought.

"He also told me he cares very deeply for you. I am pretty sure moms are supposed to be the last to know when their daughters get into a serious relationship," she says, scolding me with one of her looks.

"I'm sorry I didn't tell you, Mom. I was actually going to give you a call and then so much happened. Jenny called me about Matt and I just left. I'm not sure how to explain my relationship with Chase. He comes with a lot of baggage that to be very honest with you I'm not even sure if I understand right now," I explain, trying to keep my emotions in check and tears at bay.

"Where is he, by the way?" I ask.

"I sent him home for a shower and a change of clothes, but I'm sure he won't be gone long. He's going to pick up a few of your personal items while he's there. The man has been worried sick about you and hasn't left your side since it happened. He carried you out of the house because it was soaked in gasoline and rode in the ambulance with you to the hospital. I shudder to think what could have happened if they hadn't gotten to you in time. Your friend Matt told the police that Mark was aiming at your heart and if he hadn't been shot he probably would have succeeded," she says.

"I didn't know that, Mom. Chase just told me that he was healing and then would be behind bars for a long time."

"Chase's security team shot him before he could hurt you worse. The one they call Jay," she says.

I sigh at all the grief I have put that man through over the past couple of weeks and vow not to give him such a hard time in the future.

"Chase hasn't stopped badgering the doctors and nurses with questions since I arrived. I seriously think your nurse is about ready to throw him out on his ears. She wasn't going to let Jenny stay because of the immediate family rule, but Chase intervened and she finally conceded. He refused to leave you and slept in the chair all night. Sweetie, he really seems to care for you," she says.

"I know, Mom, but things are really messed up right now. I just need time to sort everything out," I say.

"Sweetie, what is it? It's clear he absolutely adores you. You don't feel the same?" she asks.

"Mom, it's not that, it's complicated. I do care about him. In fact, I'm pretty sure I am in love with the man, but..."

"Katie, I saw the tabloids already. What's bothering you?"

Leave it to my mom to get straight to the point. Well, I guess there's no time like the present to have this conversation. "I've been struggling with how to tell you about Chase for a while now. I don't know how to say this without making you feel bad, but when I was younger, I remember you dating a man named Steve and listening to you cry on the other side of the wall after you guys broke up. Shortly after that time you had to leave your job, and I had to leave my school and all my friends. I remember all that stuff, so it's been really hard for me to trust men or even have good relationships with them. I have always steered clear of getting involved with someone I work with because of it, but I didn't know who Chase was when we first met. I had no clue he was in charge of Prestian Corp when we first started dating, and it really threw me for a loop when I found out. But the fact is, I love him, and I didn't tell you because I didn't know how you would feel about me dating someone I work for after everything that you have been through."

"Katie, I am so very sorry. I never realized that you heard me crying at night or that you thought Steve and I were dating. While you're right, he was my employer, we were just the best of friends and he helped me through a very rough time in our lives."

"Mom, I thought you were dating all this time," I say.

"No, he was the glue that held me together when I needed it the most. It's a long story Katie and I will tell you about it someday," she says.

"So, you probably already know if you have read the articles in the tabloids, Chase is rumored to be part of a global drug trafficking organization. It doesn't sound like he was indicted, but he's avoided conversation with me about it and I really don't know if it's true or what to think. I thought the reason someone was targeting me in Aruba had something to do with the criminal activities referenced in the papers," I say.

She takes my hand and holds it for a few moments, the turmoil in her eyes a reflection of her internal conflict. "Sweetie, I was very young when I met your dad and quite principled as a young lady. Your father was tall, dark and handsome and he absolutely swept me off my feet. We fell in love with each other almost immediately and he treated me like a princess. There isn't anything that he would not have done for me, and I know he would have absolutely adored you. We were not married long when I overheard a conversation that was not meant for my ears. I learned your father was the eldest son of the East Coast crime syndicate. I always thought he was a successful businessman on Wall Street, and he never told me any different," she says, pausing and looking out the window.

"Mom, I need to hear this," I say, urging her on.

"A week later I learned that he gave the order that killed two men and I didn't even think, I ran. I changed my looks, identity, and locations multiple times before I felt safe that I would not be found. My parents had passed away the previous year, so I didn't have anyone to turn to. I started a new life in a different city, but I never in a million years suspected I was pregnant."

My heart aches for the young woman who is my mother. "Mom, I am so sorry. You must have been petrified," I say.

"Katie, I know this is all probably coming as a complete shock, but I had to tell you. I can see the same contemplation and doubt in your eyes about Chase that I had with your father. As much as I tried to stop loving him, I couldn't. I have never felt a flicker that compares to the love I had for him, and I don't want you to throw your relationship with Chase away until you consider what loving him without having him in your life would be like."

There is a brief pause, and she fidgets with her hair. "You see, I learned years later that the two men your dad put a hit out for were targeting our family and he was trying to protect us. I knew I couldn't go back though because even if your dad took me back, members of the different crime families would want me dead for things they presume I know."

There is a pregnant silence, and I know I should say something, but the effects of the medication are making me drowsy, and the words just don't come in time.

"I'm so very sorry, Katie. I was young, no family to confide in and scared to death. I just ran," she says, wiping the tears from her face. "I don't expect you to forgive me for keeping your father from you, but I needed to tell you so at least you have all the facts as you consider a life with or without Chase," she says, leaning in close to me.

I hug my mom tightly. My head is swimming trying to absorb everything. My mom has spent the best years of her adult life pining away for a man that she left because he was a criminal. That love apparently never diminished.

"Sweetie, why don't you try to rest? Chase will be back shortly and Jenny was going to stop back in after work," she says.

When I wake, Jenny and my mom are catching up and Chase is working in the corner on his Mac. He looks up, and our eyes are drawn together. There is so much left unsaid between us. He has changed clothes and my travel bag is lying next to his chair. I attempt to sit up in bed and catch my breath at the excruciating pain that jolts through my shoulder. Chase is by my side instantly.

"Easy there, Baby. Let me raise the bed for you," he says, adjusting it into a sitting position for me and repositioning the pillows underneath my arm.

"I thought I might not get to see you again tonight," Jenny says, coming over to take my hand. "We were all so worried about you. I should have insisted on going with you to Matt's apartment," she says.

"It's not your fault, Jenny. Mark is clearly troubled and it wasn't the first time he attempted to hurt me. We just didn't know it was him. I had no idea he was in a relationship with Matt, or we might have made the connection," I say, trying to ease the worry from my best friend's face.

"Well, Mark certainly won't be coming after you now. He'll be lucky if he ever gets out of prison for what he's done. Chase said the guy that tried to poison you confessed everything to the Aruban police, so with that and the attempted murder of both you and Matt, I would imagine he'll get a life sentence," Jenny says. She spends a little more time chatting and then leaves when the nurse comes in to let everyone know visiting hours are up. "I'll stop by and see you tomorrow once you get home and settled, as long as that's all right with you, Chase," she says.

"Of course, it is, Jenny. You're always welcome in our home," he says.

She gives me and my mom a hug and is out the door just as the nurse returns to let her know once again that visiting hours are up. She grins at me and waves as she scoots behind the motherly nurse.

The next morning is filled with a flurry of medical staff moving in and out of the room, checking my temp and blood pressure, taking care of my dressing, giving me instructions and scheduling appointments. Chase helps me get dressed being careful to avoid as much movement to my shoulder as possible while we have the room to ourselves. Soon, Jay and a couple security guards come into the room to help us with our stuff and escort us to the car when it is time to leave. "Jay, I heard what you did for me. I don't know how I will ever be able to repay you for saving my life, again," I say.

"Kate, you don't have to thank me. I'm just glad that we figured it all out in time. We need to talk about getting your security schedule in place, though. We haven't taken our eyes off of you, but now that things have settled down I'd like you to have your own team. You'll get to know the guys and begin feeling comfortable with them over time," he says.

"I'll try not to cause you too much grief over it, Jay. If I do, just tell me to quit being such a pain in the ass," I say. I start to laugh, but it hurts my shoulder and Chase narrows his eyes at me as he helps me out of bed.

I crinkle my nose at the wheelchair that has been brought in, preferring to walk out of the hospital on my own, but end up succumbing to the nurse's reiteration of hospital policy. My mom continues to fuss over me as they get me situated until the driver arrives to take her back to the airport. She bends down to hug me before she leaves and Jay, Matt, and Sheldon accompany Chase and I down the hall. "Let's get you home, Baby," Chase says.

As we exit the hospital, the paparazzi are in an absolute frenzy and have canvassed all the entrances to the hospital. Matt and Jay clear a path as Chase wheels me toward the awaiting limousine. The reporters bombard us with questions and cameras flash around us. "Is it true that Kate Meilers was shot in a lover's quarrel? Is it true you were charged with drug trafficking last year? Is it true Mark Powers from Martel Design was having an affair with Kate Meilers' boyfriend, Matt Lenton?" Chase helps me into the limo and Jay pulls away from the crowd. I sag into the leather seat, overwhelmed, trying to keep my emotions in check.

Chase pulls me close, kissing the top of my head. "We're going to stay at the condo in town until after your follow-up. I made an appointment for you in three days. After that, we can decide where you want to stay while you're recovering. I saw Nate in the crowd. I don't think he could get through, but I'll ask him to contact me sometime this week. When he does, I'll give him an exclusive with a detailed account to release to the public and put this to rest," he says.

"Chase, we have more paparazzi camped out at Prestian condo, I'm going to call for backup," Jay says.

We arrive at the sky-rise and true to his word three men assist Matt and Sheldon in clearing a path as we enter the building. Chase guides me into the condo, his hand on the small of my back. The paparazzi have brought all the uncertainty, doubt and questions in my mind to the forefront. I'm exhausted, feeling emotional, and my shoulder is starting to hurt.

"I'm going to lie down for a little while," I say as we enter the condo.

"Do you want lunch first? You didn't eat much for breakfast."

"I'm really not hungry right now, Chase."

"At least take your medicine," he says, opening the medication bottle and pouring me a glass of water.

"I'm too tired to stay awake any longer," I say, swallowing the pill as I head toward the bedroom. I let my skirt fall to the floor and crawl into bed with my shirt still on. I can't get the paparazzi's questions out of my head. *Do I want to know the truth? Can I give him up if it's true?* I can't get my mom's confession about my dad and the fact she never stopped loving him out of my head. The pain medication and emotions of the day are too much, and I feel the tears trickle down my face as I think about Chase. The depth of my feelings for him scares me and I can't help but think of him as I fall into a medicinal and exhaustive sleep.

When I wake, it is dark, and I try to make out the time on the clock. It's almost midnight. Chase is sleeping next to me, and I try not to wake him as I get out of bed. I make my way into the kitchen to take my medicine. I am starving and find turkey and Havarti cheese in the refrigerator and make myself a sandwich. I spy my Mac and decide to eat at his desk, enjoying the view of bright city lights overlooking the magnificent sky-rises as I catch up on email and ponder all that has happened, that my mother shared and already sensing that my life will somehow change. How can it not? I'm the daughter of the eldest son of the East Coast crime syndicate. A real-life mafia princess who's never known her dad, or that side of the family. I sign onto my work account and sigh at the amount in my inbox and start replying to some of it in an attempt to keep my mind busy. As soon as I hit the send button, I receive a response.

BABY, it's after midnight... Why are you working?

I FEEL him before I see him. He is comfortable with his nakedness. The sinewy muscles in his body are mesmerizing, and the city lights provide just enough light to discern the cuts on his thighs, arms and rippled abdomen muscles. He is hard and erect and I feel myself moisten as he approaches. He moves the laptop and my plate to the other side of the desk.

"I think you're in my seat," he says, lifting me by the waist from his chair onto the desk, as he takes his seat and gently pushes my legs apart. "I love the lace against the softness of your skin and the way you smell," he says, rubbing his nose against my clit through my panties, deeply inhaling.

He opens the drawer to his desk and pulls out a pair of scissors. "Trust me, Baby?" he asks, watching me intently, lifting the sides of my panties from my skin before sliding the scissors along the silk, cutting the delicate material on each side.

HE PULLS the material downward leaving me completely exposed to him, blowing gently on my heated skin. His breath is intoxicating. "This is a much better view," he says, running his fingers through the soft hair, exploring, easily finding my clit and circling it with his thumb. I moan. "Still, Baby," he says, grasping my hips and pulling me closer.

DOWNLOAD a free copy of my exclusive story, "A Promise" to receive updates, sneak peeks and fun and games through my newsletter.

WILL CHASE BE able to keep his mafia princess protected and their newfound love alive? Read Degrees of Acceptance to find out what happens next!

THANK YOU

Thank you for reading Degrees of Innocence. Reviews help other readers connect to books they may love. Would you be willing to help your fellow readers learn what you loved about Chase and Katarina? If so, please leave a review.

ACKNOWLEDGMENTS

Wayne, my husband, thank you for always believing in me, supporting my passions, and helping me make my impossible dream come true.

My parents and family have been a steady reminder that you can achieve your goals with determination, hard work, and commitment. Thank you!

Karla, my dear friend, who read the first book first and encouraged me to keep going, and who recommended getting other beta readers, because "You can only read a book for the first time once." Thank you for your unconditional support through all the insanity!

A special thank you to all the people who diligently bring all the aspects of these novels together. It takes an army, and I may be a bit biased, but this team is fantastic!

Debbie, my amazing street team, and all the groups, bloggers, and book lovers who spread the word about these stories, thank you!

Via's House of Vixens, is a "private" Facebook group for readers and fans to connect. If you would like to be part of this group, request to join for loads of fun!

I hope you continue reading Degrees of Acceptance to find out what happens next with Chase and Katarina!

ABOUT VIA MARI

Contemporary romantic suspense author Via Mari likes to keep her readers on the edge, fanning themselves as the action unfolds and the heat rises. Her books, featuring the most handsome, intense males, exemplify extreme romance, with powerful men who will stop at nothing to protect the women they love.

Via was raised in both the United States and United Kingdom. Since childhood, she has enjoyed reading books that carry you away. In fact, you can still find her in the early hours of the morning, curled up in an overstuffed chair by a crackling wood fire, reading a page-turning novel, especially during the harsh winters of the Midwestern United States.

When not writing, Via spends her days with her husband. She enjoys gardening, shopping at the local farmers market, and walking in town or around a big city. And she loves traveling to research her next novel.

She also loves interacting with her readers, so feel free to connect with her on the following social media sites! If you want to stay updated on the latest releases and claim a copy of an exclusive story, **sign up for her newsletter.**